I0651566

Horace Finn Tucker

The New Arcadia

a story of æsthetic London

Horace Finn Tucker

The New Arcadia
a story of æsthetic London

ISBN/EAN: 9783337311599

Printed in Europe, USA, Canada, Australia, Japan

Cover: Foto ©Andreas Hilbeck / pixelio.de

More available books at **www.hansebooks.com**

THE NEW ARCADIA

AN AUSTRALIAN STORY

BY

HORACE TUCKER

" The old order changeth, yielding place to new . . .
Lest one good custom should corrupt the world."

LONDON
SWAN SONNENSCHEIN & CO.
PATERNOSTER SQUARE
1894

RICHARD CLAY AND SONS, LIMITED,
LONDON AND BUNGAY.

CONTENTS.

CHAP.		PAGE
I.	STILLING THE TEMPEST	I
II.	FIVE POUNDS FOR FLESH AND BLOOD ...	7
III.	DICK SHOWN THE BACK-DOOR	12
IV.	A TRIANGULAR DUEL	19
V.	ARCADIA	26
VI.	THE DYING SQUATTER'S DREAM	32
VII.	KEEPING UP APPEARANCES	41
VIII.	THE SCREEN OF DEATH	52
IX.	THE GUEST THAT HAD NOT ON A WEDDING GARMENT	56
X.	PEOPLING THE WILDERNESS ...	64
XI.	TRANSFORMATION SCENE	71
XII.	WHEELS WITHIN WHEELS	79
XIII.	DROWNING THEM LIKE RATS ...	87
XIV.	ALEC'S WHISKY STOPPED	101
XV.	'IT'S LOVE THAT MAKES THE WORLD GO ROUND.'	111
XVI.	HYGEIA	119
XVII.	CUTTING-OUT EXPEDITION AT THE GROTTO	129
XVIII.	THE MILKMAID ALL FORLORN	135

CHAP.		PAGE
XIX.	TOM LORD BECOMES SOPHISTICATED ...	140
XX.	MALDUKE SETS HIS TRAP	146
XXI.	WOUNDED BUT NOT CAUGHT	151
XXII.	HOW TOM WON A RACE	159
XXIII.	AN OASIS IN THE DESERT	171
XXIV.	HELPING LAME DOGS OVER STILES ...	178
XXV.	CHANGES AND CHANCES	185
XXVI.	GREEK MEETS GREEK	192
XXVII.	THE DOCTOR'S DEPARTURE	201
XXVIII.	BROKEN TRAPS AND BREAKING HEARTS	206
XXIX.	BETWEEN DEVIL AND DEEP SEA	215.
XXX.	FIGHTING THE FLAMES	228
XXXI.	THE FLAG HALF-MAST HIGH	242
XXXII.	AMAZONA—THE FLIGHT OF THE MAIDENS	251
XXXIII.	THE WHITE MAN OF THE WOODS ...	266
XXXIV.	THE LIVING DEAD	279
XXXV.	THE LILY-MAID OF ASTOLAT	294
XXXVI.	THE FAIRY ISLAND	305

THE NEW ARCADIA.

CHAPTER I.

STILLING THE TEMPEST.

"We sit on a cloud and sing . . .
And say the world runs smooth—while right below,
Welters the black fermenting heap of life,
On which our State is built."—*The Saint's Tragedy.*

."Some Lancashire lads I know would have made short and cursory
work of waiting for Government. 'Hang the Government!
Why wait for them? Let us co-op. and do the work ourselves!'"—CRAIG.

"PULL him down!" "Knock him off the seat!" "An
aristocrat riding us down like dogs!" A smart fusillade
of such epithets, portending hand-to-hand conflict, broke
from the foremost of a straggling band of workmen ;
some reckless and uncanny in appearance, others listless
and half-interested, but animated, for the moment, as
dullest street crowds are, by occurrence of "an accident."

The dog-cart, apparently of a professional man, had
run over a city waif hanging on the outskirts of a detach-
ment of "the unemployed" on their course to the noon-
tide rendezvous.

The leaders, welcoming a victim, were venting curses
on the head of the luckless Jehu.

"A bright specimen of his class!" cried one.

"Blowed if it ain't Dr. Courtney of St. Clair. He'd ought to know better," chimed in another.

Curbing with difficulty his plunging steed, the individual referred to flung reins to his groom and leaped into the surging sea of scowling countenances about him. He made for the curb-stone, where, supported by a policeman and closed around by a gaping crowd—effectually excluding the air—the little sufferer lay.

As usual, it occurred to no one to render assistance, only to ask questions and pass comments. With a strong arm thrusting the loiterers aside to right and left, the unwitting cause of the disturbance bent anxiously over the little unfortunate. Passing a skilful hand about body and limbs, he said to himself, "A broken leg," and to the lad, "All right, my boy, we'll soon set you right again."

Not far off, of course, was a cabby, eager to bear. away the child, glad to secure a "fare," though suffering or death placed it in his hands.

"They're all the same," remarked one in the crowd. "'It's an ill wind blows no one any good.' Doctor, parson, cabby, undertaker. Death of one's godsend t'others. All living one on another."

"What's the sense of standing and prating there, you big fool!" exclaimed the doctor.

Raising the child in his arms, he hustled the men with his elbow and made with his charge towards the cab. Laying the manly urchin, who had uttered no cry, and was contracting his face to restrain the tears, on the floor of the vehicle, "To the hospital," he cried, "as gently as you like," and was stepping in himself.

"You'll just stay here and answer to us," hissed a coarse voice in his ear as the cab moved forward. The doctor was dragged backward and fell on his knees. The crowd closed round. Cabby, ignorant that he was minus his full load, drove on.

In a second the doctor was on his feet again—the blood mantling his cheeks. "Who dare lay hand on me?" he demanded, defiantly, glaring round on the excited throng.

"Make way, or I'll find it. I'm in no mood to be trifled with." This to a well-bred, shabby-genteel leader who confronted him.

"Curses on you!" the man exclaimed, thrusting himself forward. "What do you mean by running over the little chap? You did it on purpose. You know you did." The speaker delivered no further harangue that day. Incensed at the indignity to which he was subjected, the doctor struck his man a blow that lifted him from his feet and hurled him into the arms of his comrades.

"None of that," a dozen voices cried. "Two can play at that game, you know."

"Move on," suggested a valiant constable in the background.

The men were hustled and urged towards a vacant piece of ground beside a half-finished edifice. Their stricken leader had disappeared.

They were impressed by the bearing of the doctor. His was a powerful face, a high intellectual brow, an eye that flashed as his fist clenched. Sorrow and anger contended in his breast; resentment on account of the treatment to which he was being subjected, coupled with evident sympathy for the men against whom he found himself by accident arrayed. If not actually in want, they were, he knew, anxious concerning a livelihood. Misguided on one hand, maligned on the other.

Finding a footing on some piles of lumber, he shook off the hand that was laid on his shoulder—swept his eye round the grizzled, not unkindly, faces about him, and said—

"Look here, my men, I am going to see that lad whom, unfortunately, I ran over. It was no fault of mine, as you know. The horse shied at that banner of yours the fellow was carrying, who is not here to speak for himself."

A smile rippled across the sea of good-natured faces.

" He's got a headache," suggested one.

" The little fellow," continued the doctor, " ran in front of the trap. I will see to him. Now as to you. That, I am more anxious about. Do not be fools. Do not be led astray by men who put a false construction on everything some of us may do, and who try to make you believe that every fellow who wears a black coat has a black heart. I'll take my jacket off to-morrow to work beside any honest man, as I have done before, if I can serve society better so, or to try to thrash the man who persists that I deliberately ran that youngster down, or want to over-ride any. Is that clear? Now, before I go, let me ask, why are you all hanging about the city, imploring Government and every one else to help you? Why not, for instance, seek the country, where a fair field and means of livelihood awaits you?"

" How can a man go and squat, what's got no tin?" growls one. " My children's had nothing to eat this blessed day." The speaker, who did not himself appear starved, was, like many of his companions, puffing clouds of smoke from an oft-replenished pipe.

" For my part," was the reply, " if my children were hungering I should deny myself a pipe. I'd like to see less incense and more sacrifice.'

" All very well for you to say, governor. Why should a poor beggar lose the one comfort he's got ? "

" Right, my man," was the reply, " in this country, you should command luxuries as well as necessaries. But you will not find them in town. Here you have swarmed to manufacture for a population that does not exist. Go on to the lands and become producers, masters of your own destiny. With a prosperous people settled on the deserted plains and half-ringed forests, your workshops might furnish occupation ; your warehouses cease to be clogged with unsalable goods, while folk are shivering. Your railways, extended by compliant politicians into every hungry corner of the land, might groan with freight, and the cry be for more labourers to harvest the golden store."

" All very well, old man, but how are we to get on the land ? " asked one. " We haven't the price of an axe atween us."

" You want money, you rightly think. What, however, is capital, but pound placed beside pound, one day's labour upon another? Can't you put that together ? Instead of this senseless parading about overgrown cities, might you not ascertain by practical experiment, whether a mode of settlement that has in other countries success-fully identified millions with the soil might not be adopted ? The occupation of our lands has been so far of a tem-porary nature. The squatter is the sojourner merely, that his name implies. God intended other use to be made of our richest lands than to be pastures for count-less sheep. The selector, after destroying valuable timber, building a hut in an inaccessible corner of a ring-barked allotment, scratching a hundred acres of wheat into the sour soil and sitting down the rest of the year to see it grow,—the selector, I say, is not a permanent settler.

From the Murray to the sea you may purchase the lands the Government virtually gave away. Is it not possible, in a social, national sort of way, to establish thousands of you on our virtually vacant lands ? I think it is, and I know how. You'll have to learn another trade—most of you. Exchange plane for plough, house-decorating for vine-dressing. You'll have to work hard—not praying heaven in the morning not to send the job you seek all day; not flinging down your tools at five o'clock. You must be associated together too. Small holdings—all you can get as yet—are unprofitable without co-operation. That is the direction in which relief is coming to these countries, I believe. Now put that into your pipe and smoke it." So saying the speaker disappeared midst ringing cheers from the motley assemblage.

CHAPTER II.

FIVE POUNDS FOR FLESH AND BLOOD.

"A most acute juvenal, voluble, and free of grace."
Love's Labour's Lost.

"So justice while she winks at crimes,
  Stumbles on innocence sometimes."—HUDIBRAS.

"There is now in England a mass, an ever-increasing mass, of
  unemployed labour, supplying victims for unprincipled and
  short-sighted capitalists, or filling our gaols and workhouses;
  try whether association will not gradually assimilate this mass,
  and render it the strength and not the poison, the blessing and
  not the curse of our country."—*Letter of* CHARLES KINGSLEY.

"IT weren't none on your fault, master," the little man
was saying. Dr. Courtenay was expressing regret for the
mishap.

"I'm mighty glad to be here, I can tell you," the
child ran on. "It's so clean and quiet, and them young
ladies," pointing to a group of nurses, "is so kind.
Don't let them take me away again."

"Why do you not want to go home?" inquired the
doctor.

"Home?" the child exclaimed. "It's what they call
hell at the Mission House. Mother she drinks, and
grannie drinks, and they beat me if I doesn't bring
enough home at night. I often sleeps out under the
railway near the wharfs for fear of them. Then they
whacks me more when I gets home for stopping away."

"And where's your father, my little man?" inquired the doctor.

"Ah, that's it!" the child replied with animation.

"Why does not he look after you?"

"He went away, long time ago, last year. He couldn't get no work, and used to come home to find mother and grannie drunk—when mother had had a bit of washing to do. One day I comed home, and father was sitting over the fire-place with no fire in it, and his head in his hands. 'Dad,' says I, 'what's up now?' and he turns his head away, but draws me to him and nigh squeezed me up, and I seed he was crying. I don't often blubber; I didn't to-day, sir, did I? But I howled when I seed father cry. I'll never forget him shakin' and rockin' hisself. Then he knocks away the tears as if he hated them and bit his lip hard. Did you ever see a man cry, sir? Children does, and women, but it's terrible, I thinks, to see a man blub."

"Was your father ill?" interjected the medical man.

"Tough as a tram-cable, sir, and brave as a bulldog. I seed him punch Fitzroy Tom's head when he'd made game of mother for being drunk. All the people in the lane said he was a brick and ought to set up a boxin' saloon."

"What did he cry for then?"

"'Cause of mother"—here the little one broke down and sobbed. "She used to be so good onst—and 'cause of no work. He used to say he wouldn't care what he done, if he could get a job. Then he kisses me and squeezes me up, like a crowd at the theatre door, and goes away.

"'Never you mind, sonny,' he calls out, 'I'll come back some day and make a man of you.'

"We never heard on him since, and mother's been worse nor ever. One day Tim Smith told me father was making a railway. I thought I'd go too. Perhaps I could sell papers to the chaps there. I saved up seven brownies and went to Spencer Street. I told the cove bobbing inside the window, like a jail-bird, to give me a ticket to where the railway was doing. He said they was making railways everywhere, and I might soon have one to the moon, if they got a member 'lected for there, or got the blind side of the commissioners.

"'None of your cheek,' says I, coz I knew he couldn't get through the window at me. 'Give us a ticket, a "holiday excursion" workman's ticket as far as your train will take me for them'—clapping down the brownies. He laughed and gave me one to Donnybrook. When I got there I could see no trains a-making. I just walked and walked. There was fine trees and birds singing in them, and flowers in the grass. But I could not see father. I asked a lot of chaps and they only said, 'Who 're you? What are you a'ter here?' I'd never seen the country before. I didn't wonder father ran away there, only I thought he might'er taken me.

"'I'll stop here always,' says I, 'till I finds dad.'

"But I only found the bobby. He's everywhere! I hanged out in a stable, and a fat man comed in the morning and says I'd been stealing. I'd like to have punched his head. Then he got a bobby, with tights and boots on, looking mighty mashery as though he done no work, and he asked and asked like everybody else. When I told him about my father and mother, he said, 'You're a little runaway, you beggar. I'll send you back to town.' Then he shook me till I seed double. 'We want none of you larrikins here,' he calls out, very brave-like.

"'Surely there's room for me and mother and all in our lane out here, 'stead of starvin' in town.'

"'Don't you be cheeky, young man,' he says, and hits me on the head. 'We don't want no town varmin out here.'

"'But there's plenty o' room,' says I, 'and I does like the birds and the flowers so, and I could help the fat man dig.'

"'Dig! you little fool,' says he; 'he grows sheep, and has miles of this 'ere country, and two or three on 'em has all the rest of it.'

"'And isn't there no corner for me?' I puts in, and begins to cry when I thinks of the dirty streets and men with nothing to do but fight."

"What was the end of it?" suggested the doctor, looking at his watch.

"He sends me back next day with a bobby who were takin' a cove to town who'd been copped, and they fetched me to mother and grannie, and didn't I get it."

At that moment there was a disturbance at the entrance to the ward; a shrill voice was declaiming to a nurse who stopped the way.

"Let me go to my darling; I heard he was run over. He's the only joy of my heart."

"Don't let her come, she'll take me away," cried the child, covering his head with the bedclothes.

The doctor went to the woman. For half-an-hour he talked to her.

"Then you'll give me five pounds for him, my little cherrub?"

"Yes, if you sign this document giving him over entirely to my charge. I'll do the best I can for him. From your own showing and his, you have cared little for him. I shall pay the money to the clergyman whose name you mention, and get him to give you five shillings a week for your rent for three months."

"So I'm to sell my own flesh and blood for a five-pound note?" the woman replied.

" Not unless you like. Come to my house this evening. I will get the clergyman to be there, and we'll settle it up at nine o'clock."

That night a woman emerged from the doctor's dispensary exclaiming, as she hurried along—

" Five pounds for my own flesh and blood ! That's what Melbourne and drink's brought me to ! And we was happy enough before we came to town."

CHAPTER III.

DICK SHOWN THE BACK-DOOR.

"But far more numerous was the herd of such
Who think too little and who talk too much."—DRYDEN.

"Of all the causes which conspire to blind
Man's erring judgment, and misguide the mind,
What the weak head with strongest bias rules,
Is pride, the never-failing vice of fools."—POPE.

"So you have another scheme for reforming the world, father? What a pity you are not the Premier, or rather President of the Trades' Hall! We could all live without working then."

"You're just like your mother, Gwyneth. Never appreciating me and my plans, and you're too plain spoke too! I'll not be treated like this no longer!" laying down his knife and fork.

"Dear father, do not become excited," rejoined the girl, slipping from her seat and imprinting a soft kiss on the knitted brows. "Now tell me all about it. There! I'll sit and sew, and say nothing."

The speaker was a tall girl, with bright hazel eyes and wavy brown hair, straight Grecian nose, firm mouth and chin—one of Nature's queens of common sense and good looks.

Her father, a widower, whose only child she was, had been a soldier in his time, and now lived on the shilling a day his country allowed him—plus another shilling or two his daughter's deft needle won.

"Too clever by half." "Talks more nor he thinks." "Showy, but won't wash!" were the epithets with which his comrades summed up valiant John Elms. He knew something of everything—building, farming, and scheming — was a "bush lawyer," spoke much of "Political Economy," and the "Rights of Man." The anarchists he denounced, and claimed himself to be a Christian Socialist. A son of Erin, he could talk by the hour, like most of his countrymen, with that facility that comes of iteration of the same truths, with varied thumpings of table or tub to drive each platitude home.

The little house in Richmond, thanks to Gwyneth's skill and care, was a model poor man's home. The Sergeant, as Elms liked to be called, was apt at domestic carpentery, as his daughter was with respect to plain upholstery. The parlour, where the Sergeant's meal was laid—he came in at all hours from "meetings"—boasted a small cabinet-organ, a sewing-machine, and a faded drawing-room suite, rendered ever fresh and clean by immaculate holland coverings with red pipings. Rural and military pictures, from the illustrated papers, framed in wood or leather work by father and daughter, decked the walls.

"If there was a prize for the cosiest little home," Dick Malduke, Gwyneth's secret admirer, used to say, "you'd get it, and 'honorary' mention into the bargain."

"I'm full of a new scheme," remarked the father as he drank his tea.

"That's nothing wonderful," responded the undemonstrative daughter, "since you propound (isn't that what you call it?) a fresh theory every day."

"Oh, but I have some one behind me, I feel, now.

Some one I can work upon, to put some of my glorious principles into practice."

"And who may be your latest tool, father?" inquired the girl.

"No tool, by Jove!" was the rejoinder. "A reg'lar big-wig of pluck and spirit, I can tell you. You should have seen him send your Dick sprawling," he added, chuckling.

"He's more to you than to me," replied the girl with emphasis on the pronouns. "I admire him as I do the rest of the talkers who don't work! But what happened to your friend, father? This is really quite interesting."

"It was this way," the Sergeant continued; "we were going with about two hundred of the poor fellows, for whom my heart bleeds, to our place of meeting. Dick was carrying the colours, when a smartish trap came dashing up. The horse shied at the red flag, and ran over a little boy that was following. We surrounded the dog-cart, and the chaps began to hoot at the gent, though it was no fault of his. He didn't care a straw. Just went and looked after the little man and put him into a cab. As he was getting up, Dick and some of the others pulled him down, and the cab went on. My man—he's a real game 'un—glared at them like a lion with his tail trod on. Dick—who's always too much to say and must be first, excuse my remarking it——"

"You can say anything, dear father," interjected his daughter, with an arch smile, "to show what a set of simpletons your followers are, and that Dick's the greatest."

"Dick," continued the Sergeant, with a smile, "told the gentleman he ran over the child on purpose. He said nothing more. The doctor clean lifted him from his feet with one from the shoulder.   And we saw no more of Mr. Malduke."

" Valiant Dick !" exclaimed the maiden.

At that moment there was a knock at the door that opened directly on the street.

"Good-evening, Miss Elms," said a round, thick-set young man as he entered.

" Why, it's Dick himself," exclaimed the girl.   " We were just speaking of you, Mr. Malduke.   Talk of the angels and you see their wings."

The visitor seemed in no mood for badinage.

" What have you that bandage across your eye for ? " asked the girl, not very sympathetically.   " You've been fighting, I do declare."

" Blowed if I have," replied the man moodily ; "it's only a cowardly blow that I'll be avenged for yet."

" Why didn't you up and give it him back then and there ? " suggested the Sergeant, with a laugh.   " Never mind, old boy, he was too big for you.   ' He that fights and runs away '—you know the rest.   You have to fight another day, you know.   Come and have some supper any way, now."

Midst light banter, that the young man only half appreciated, another plate was set, and the events of the day discussed.

" I walked with the doctor towards the hospital," said the elder man, "and he told me—seeing, I suppose, that I knew a thing or two—that he and his friends had a scheme for mending matters.   Strange we should have set upon him !   He's had a practice up country, and seems to know all about the life, and a lot about the social question, too, though of course I could teach him a lot."

The daughter looked up amused, but said nothing.

"I'm to see him again, and promised to co-operate with him, much to his delight."

"It's all rubbish!" commented Dick, tilting back his chair, "this jabber of co-operation and profit-sharing and their 'new systems.' All a device of the capitalist to make men slaves under another name. I see a lot of 'sweatin'' in it, Mr. Elms. Of course he'll own the land and get all the profit in the end. You see!"

"There you're wrong," replied the Sergeant, "as you raving anarchists always are. You know your game would be up if capital and labour joined hands."

"Don't hit him too hard, father," interjected the maiden, who was stitching on, amused. "He has been punished once already."

Dick looked daggers at the girl, whose head was bent over her work, then he continued—

"I don't believe in half-measures. You'll do no good till every blessed thing's burst up and the State takes control, and all's divided fair."

"Every Saturday night?" naïvely suggested the girl; "it'll be necessary I fear."

"Now look here, Dick," said the Sergeant, "don't be a fool; we have the brains. Let us use these fellows. You just fall into line with us. We'll soon get the concern, if it's started, into our own hands and twist things round as we like."

To much sentiment of this character expression was given. At length the girl, who had kept silence for some time, rose from her seat, and with mingled shame and scorn drawing herself to her full height, her dark eyes flashing, said—

"I'm not going to sit here and listen to such unmanly utterances. God knows, I sorrow for those who are hungry and homeless, but they, for the most part, are honest. They will not lend themselves to stinging the hand that would help them. You throughout are thinking of yourselves, not of them." So saying, she swept with dignity into the little kitchen adjoining, shutting the door with something very like a bang.

Dick looked abashed. The father, with a thump on the table, and a somewhat proud though subdued expression on his face, exclaimed—

"Just her mother all over. She was a lady, you know. Ran away with me. I was good-looking in those days, and could always make an impression.

"What Gwyneth thinks, she must say. And she *will* always think for herself, as no woman should, to my thinking. I used to try to tame her. Now I give her head, for her mother's sake, and a bit for my own."

"She's a thund'rin' fine girl all the same," added Dick. "Didn't her eyes flash! I'm sorry we vexed her. I'll go and apologize," and the rash youth entered the kitchen and closed the door.

"Always too much talk, Master Dick," soliloquized the father; "you are putting your head into the lioness's mouth. You'll get more than you bargained for, I'm thinking, and you'll never win my daughter."

Gwyneth, her dress tucked about her, was vigorously "washing up" the supper things. She did not raise her head as the young man entered.

"Miss Elms," he began, "I'm really sorry I vexed you, but you know I must be thorough-going."

"In your own interest," she remarked quietly. "What do you care about the poor you talk so much about? I hate shams."

"I am devoted, you must admit, Miss Elms, to the cause of Labour."

"Then why do you not undertake more of it?" she remarked shortly.

"I work with my brains, Miss Elms, with tongue and heart, for the Great Cause of the People."

"All with capital letters," she sneered. "Why do you not sometimes go and do an honest day's work instead of indulging in tall talk?" she added with contempt.

"I would for you, Miss Elms. I'd break stones if only you would encourage me. Gwyneth," the young man proceeded, laying his hand on the dish-cloth, which she relinquished to him, "why do you always spurn me? Do you not know that I adore the ground you walk on?"

"You should not do that," was the quick reply, "the kitchen's not been scrubbed this week. Now, Dick, don't talk rubbish," the girl continued in her quiet, matter-of-fact manner. "Go home like a good man and take care of your eye. And remember this, if you want to come here any more, don't you dare urge my father, who means well, to play the hypocrite and sneak. Now, good-night. I can let you out at this door. Oh, I'll bid farewell to father for you, you need not go back for that." And the dignified maiden bowed the abashed Agitator out at the back entrance into the narrow right-of-way.

CHAPTER IV.

A TRIANGULAR DUEL.

"For why? Because the good old rule
Sufficeth them, the simple plan,
That they should take who have the power,
And they should keep who can."—WORDSWORTH.

"To knit in loving knowledge rich and poor."
The Saint's Tragedy.

"A huge aggregate of little systems, each of which again is a
small anarchy, the members of which do not work together,
but scramble against each other."—THOS. CARLYLE.

"The simplest and clearest definition of economy, whether public
or private, means the *wise management of labour;* and it means
this mainly in three senses: first, in *applying* your labour
rationally; secondly, in *preserving* its produce carefully; lastly,
in *distributing* its produce seasonably."—RUSKIN.

"EXCUSE me, old fellow, but with all your socialistic
tendencies you manage to make yourself deuced comfortable. This is the jolliest den of a smoking-room I
know."

The speaker was a bright, plump little man, satisfied,
to judge by the smile that always lurked about his mouth,
with himself and his condition; one who, in a good-
natured sort of way, took life easy, and supposed that all
others might do the same if they would. Why should he
bother? He possessed ample means to live upon; not
enough to cause him anxiety. He was influenced by no
desire to add to his belongings or to enlarge his life.

The world was made for him to walk about in, with his hands in his pockets, and he liked his part well !

A school-fellow of Dr. Courtenay, he, to escape the English winter, had come on a few months' visit to his friend.

"I see no objection to a man enjoying the due reward of his toil," replied the doctor. "I've earned all I have, and most I possess is contained within the walls of this abode."

It certainly was a room to add relish to a good cigar. The dado was of leather-work, the walls above covered with a fine Indian matting. Upon the ledge that ran round the walls stood photographs, articles of vertu, and bric-à-brac, that told of European and Eastern travel. On the walls, between dark oak cabinets and brackets, were hung whips, pipes, fencing-sticks, with a few good studies in oils.

The doctor was stretched at length in a lounge that having done duty on shipboard was now lined with red cushions. His companion was coiled up "like a happy little dog," as the doctor termed it, on another lounge, pulling at a cherry-wood pipe almost as long as himself.

Seated opposite these, straddle-legs on a chair, with elbows resting on the back, his dark eyes watching the pair in an amused, half-attentive manner, was a young cleric in short undress coat. His high forehead was surmounted by thick black hair, the close-shaven face revealing a decided mouth, and the set, solid features of a *Manning*.

Frank Brown was vicar of the suburban parish. In his time he had rowed in "the 'Varsity" boat, played in the College Eleven, and been one of the men who were listened to at "The Union." By birth and earlier pre-dilections a Conservative, he had, under the influence of parochial experience in the East of London, and now in his new but poor parish, developed into what he termed an " Eclectic " or a " Philosophical Radical."

" No one objects to your being comfortable, doctor," he interjected. " You do not try to eat two dinners at the same time, and to waste three men's shares of the good things of this life ; but why may not all be better off? Why must these poor fellows of mine experience such a struggle just to live? Surely God has made this world capable of supporting millions more than now cumber it."

" Partly of their own fault," began the doctor.

" Entirely, say I," put in the little man. " Divide your pipes and tobacco of all kinds to-morrow—and you'll need another distribution next week."

" We have heard that before, Tom," continued the doctor. " It is partly men's own fault that the wolf is always at some doors, that you can never drive him far from certain portals, but it is chiefly the result of our social system."

" We've heard *that* before," suggested the little man.

" The principle of competition, that dominates our commercial and social life, involves that the weaker go to the wall. The labourers are the weaker. The strongest among them compete with each other until they drag each other down to a common condition of helplessness."

" But their Labour Unions and Standards of Wages," suggested Tom, " are supposed to keep up prices and check the effects of competition."

" And you know full well that those are not only extreme measures, disastrous in their consequences, but that they are artificial devices opposed to the nature of things."

"Just what I say," retorted Tom; "you cannot check the free and healthful play of competition."

"Yes, you can," replied the doctor; "give men a share in the results of their labour, and their work will be doubly effective, whilst the reward of all parties will be augmented. 'Is it not better,' said the founder of the 'Maison La Claire,' 'to make 500 francs a day and give 300 to the workmen, than to earn 200 francs and keep it all yourself?'"

"But the trouble is," persisted the little man, "your workmen say, 'Share the profits with us, bear the losses yourself!'"

"Not necessarily. Labour will take its fair risk if you put it in a position to do so. Pay the men in cash a quarter of what you give them now. Let the remainder of their interest be invested in the concern."

"But how can they live on a quarter of what they *starve* on now? You'll be called a sweater, and have the agitators down on you again."

"Men can exist comfortably, if accepted principles of co-operation and economy be adopted, on the fourth of what is now expended. For instance, a man now earns £2 a week. Most of it is expended in the cost of living; nothing remains at the end of the year."

"Owing to your Protection run mad," remarked Tom.

"No doubt the cost of living is ruinous to the working-man, but unavoidably so under existing circumstances. Everything now tends to draw men to the city. Lead back some of them to the country. Let them, through their managers, be their own provisioners and salesmen, and they can live on a fourth of that they now spend."

"The squatter can feed a family well on ten shillings a week," suggested the clergyman.

"But what are you going to do with them in the country? The squatter and farmer don't want them."

"I'd bind them together, maintaining them for the cost of their house-rent in town. Then put them in the way of cultivating the soil and supporting themselves otherwise."

"But these men, who are 'on strike' wherever they get a chance, are not going to work for their 'tucker,'" objected Tom.

"Yes, they will," observed Frank Brown, "if they see a prospect of ultimately winning by their industry a home and independence for themselves and their children."

"What do they care for that?" growled the little man.

"Everything," continued the clergyman. "Scratch the Englishman, wherever he lives, and you find the farmer beneath the surface, and the earth-hunger in his breast."

"And a lot of good it does him!"

"It makes him the colonizing creature of the world. Leads him to cross seas, subdue wildernesses, make gardens of howling deserts, and ports for the commerce of England on every shore," said the cleric.

"But you have not stuff to deal with like that. The race is degenerate. Your men are loafers."

"You should have seen them at the doctor's meeting the other day. You should have noted the eager, intelligent manner in which they received his suggestions," continued the clergyman, warmly.

"Where were the idlers I see gathering on waste lands beside your streets and lounging in your parks?" asked Tom.

"Not there," replied Frank. "Our scheme has no attraction for them. They like relief works, so much a week, and soup-kitchens, and all the means adopted for pauperizing them. Our better fellows would starve rather than avail themselves of such methods."

"Was our friend the agitator with the broken nose present?" inquired the little man, poking the doctor playfully with the end of his pipe. "I did not think, Courtenay, that you were coming to that, when I knew and respected you in the old country!"

"He was there, sure enough, looking blacker than ever," replied Frank, "but kept in check by an older man who talked like a book, and brandished his arms."

"My right-hand man," added the doctor, "a fellow named Elms, who knows something of everything."

"A dangerous kind of character," remarked Tom. "But what's coming of all this talk?—we've heard the like before, you know."

"Yes, and you are going to see something of it put into practice at length."

"But where's your money? You must have capital, abuse it as you may."

"I do not underrate it, I assure you," said the doctor; "but I want labour to rely more on itself, to learn its true strength, the vast fund of resource it has in reserve, if it will combine for production rather than for destruction."

"But where's your money to begin with?" persisted the little man. "You know I'm a man of business."

"Excuse me, old fellow, I never knew that before!" said the doctor, slapping the thigh of his neighbour. "I observe that if ever there is a thick-skulled, narrow-minded, short-sighted machine of a dotard knocking around, he claims to be a *business man* above everything. None of your schemes for him!"

" Because the present order suits him well enough,"
suggested Tom.

" While he does not see that it is shaken to its very
foundations—that he and all he has may be swept away
by some tidal wave of social devastation unless a better
way be found."

" But what of the money?" persisted Tom.

" That is the difficulty so far, I admit. I have nothing
to invest. A few hundreds have been promised by some
friends, but what are they?"

" Never mind," said the clergyman; "it will come, I
am sure. You will be able to work out your schemes by
some means yet."

The doctor lay back on his lounge looking doubtful
and troubled.

" It's *faith* you are depending upon then, Rev. Sir,"
said Tom. " What'll *faith* do for you, if you have not
the cash?"

" Faith!" exclaimed the young man, jumping up—
" faith with power that comes of enthusiasm and high
aim, of sympathy for sorrow and suffering, with impatience
of wrongs; faith such as animates our good friend—
incentive rare enough in these cold, calculating days—
will overcome everything. Mark my words, the doctor
will do it!"

" On the strength of capital, not of faith," persisted
the incorrigible Tom.

CHAPTER V.

ARCADIA.

'O gaily sings the bird ! and the wattle-boughs are stirred,
   And rustled by the scented breath of spring.
Oh the weary, wistful longing ! Oh the faces that are thronging !
   Oh the voices that are vaguely whispering."—A. L. GORDON.

  "There's a strange something, which without a brain
  Fools feel, and which e'en wise men can't explain,
  Planted in man, to bind him to that earth,
  In dearest ties, from whence he drew his birth."
            CHURCHILL, *The Farewell.*

"IF ever there was an earthly paradise, it is here, my child."

"You're very fond of the place, father," remarked a girl whose sixteen summers had dyed her rounded cheeks olive and red; her large eyes were hazel, hair golden-brown; a picture of beautiful youth she looked, as she sat at the old man's feet plying her needle.

The cottage stood on a slight eminence. Far away to the right stretched a smiling valley, on either side of it sloped pine-dotted hills, with here and there a huge granite boulder indicating rich soil beneath. A sinuous line of wattle, golden with blossom, marked the winding of the creek, seeming to convert the plain into a series of gigantic primrose-beds. Two miles away, the streak of gold lost itself in a sheet of silver and red, as the creek flowed into a lake, some three miles below. The rays of the setting sun were illuminating its glittering surface.

The hills, that there rose sharper from the lake than further up the valley, presented a dark line of smooth sward broken by boulders, pines, and oaks, against the glowing sunset sky.

"That valley," cried the old man, stretching his clay pipe towards it, "might sustain its thousands. Look at the depth of the soil, fourteen feet there on that bank of the creek."

"It's very sticky after rain, I know," objected the maiden. "I'd rather drive Peter over a dozen miles of the clean iron-stone in the ranges, than two miles on the plain. Yesterday after that sudden shower it stuck to the wheels of the old buggy till it creaked again. I had to stop at length and try to poke the black soil off with a stick. In a hundred yards it was as bad as ever again. I often wish your black soil further, dad."

"You should not say that, my girl; God is good to give us a country like this."

"But what's the use of it? just to fatten so many more sheep for old Mr. Leicester."

Thirty years before, Mr. Leicester, the adjoining squatter, had camped beside the creek with the few sheep he had brought out into the wilderness. He had climbed to the top of this very knoll and claimed, as he told his black shepherd, "all he could see between the hills." It was a fairly "large order"—some thirty thousand acres—but in a few months, in consideration of some imaginary services rendered to the Government, a land grant made it his. A reserve along the stream had been retained by the State. Ten years before the date of this story, this had been put up to auction.

Mr. Dowling was the purchaser. Leicester was absent in England. Dick Dowling was one of an ill-fated party of English gentlefolk who "migrated" to Adelaide in its

earliest days.   Their patrimony they invested in frame·
houses, outfit of an elaborate nature, land and stock
purchased in the colony.   Dowling was a lawyer; his
wife was connected with some of the best county families.
Their eldest daughter, the belle of Fenshire, was delicate
as she was beautiful.   The move broke Grace Dowling's
heart.   She pined for the conditions and companionship
of earlier days, and could see no beauties in eucalyptus
and mimosa.

A tree beside the first homestead marks the spot where
Grace was laid to rest at last.   The grief-stricken parents
with their remaining daughter moved on, with sadly
shrunken means, to the neighbouring colony.

Dowling arrived in Melbourne just in time to purchase
the reserve, to which a·friend at the club had directed
his attention.   The frame-house was again set up, the
hundred and twenty acres fenced, some stock procured;
then the unfortunate lawyer's last· penny was expended.
None knew how the trio existed.

Did he never regret relinquishing the little country
practice, as he ploughed his own lands, laid out his
garden, killed his sheep, took his produce in the spring-
cart to Gumford railway-station?   Did he not repent
his folly, as his daughter swept the dust from ornaments
and furniture that had known better days, from portraits
of ancestors who seemed to be ever wondering how they
came amongst their present surroundings, from the old
clock that had stood centuries " on the stairs " at home
and seemed never quite reconciled to the house that was
all ground-floor?

As the old man saw his daughter milking, even driving
the reaping-machine, while he sat and rattled his bones
over the clods ; as he saw his beautiful old wife making
up the butter with her snowy, tapering fingers, trimming

the lamps, and bearing the week's produce into Gumford in the rattling American wagon, did he not repent his folly?

No, he never regretted it. He revelled in the life of the country. "Health we have, if not wealth," he used to say. "Peace, if not prosperity. We live our own life, and like it."

Mrs. Dowling was happy in her husband's satisfaction. It seemed to her strange that such as he, refined, intellectual, admired, should have voluntarily exiled himself for a struggle for existence such as this.

"What would the old country and its influence be, good wife," he used to say, "if her sons had not been possessed, so often, of a desire to seek a fuller life abroad, to escape from the deadly conventionalities of an effete society, and to extend all that is best in the national life beyond every sea? What would England be save for her soldiers and sailors and settlers, who could not rest and rust at home?

"I know I have failed," he would sometimes admit, with momentary bitterness. "The greater fortune I dreamed of has never come. The little one I brought has vanished. But cheer up, wife, we'll never give in. None shall call us poor. Have I not my books and a little sphere in which, as Carlyle says, 'to create and to rule and be free'? You are happy, my darling. Perhaps we are of more use here in this uncouth, uncultivated land, where we may leave some fragrance of English fields and tastes behind us, than in dear, but dreamy, Fenshire."

The old man, in his shirt-sleeves, with slouched hat and rough buckskin gaiters, looked still as much the true gentleman as when with shining velveteen he followed the hounds at home, or received the Queen when her Majesty visited the provincial town to open the park presented by his elder brother.

"She's as much a lady as ever," he would muse with pride as the good wife with skirts tucked around, her husband's brown cabbage-tree hat on her comely, well-set head, goloshes on her dainty feet, went the round of her fowl-yard, fed the butting calf and leggy lamb, and appeared shortly in the parlour as neat and trim as ever.

"Why should life's plainest, simplest duties be considered menial," he would say, "and the best of its work be delegated to menials?"

"You had better come in," said Mrs. Dowling, appearing at the open French window. "You cannot see any more of your beloved valley to-night, Richard."

"But I can scent its fragrance. Isn't the perfume of the wattle and acacia, borne on the moist airs of night, sweet? And I can hear the music of the vale. Hark to that wailing crescendo of the curlew! The one thing here that evidently has a history—and a pathetic one too. Or does it mourn that the land should lie desolate? Now that 'More Pork,' or cuckoo as we ought to call him, is lonely too, but he is jolly as a sand-boy about it."

"The laughing jackass is my favourite," suggested Eva. "The last one has just giggled itself to sleep. Always so delighted with himself and the day's doings, as it chuckles over the thought of how vainly the six-foot snake tried to bite as he whisked it hundreds of feet in the air, and how green the centipede got in the face when he ferreted it out from our fire-wood stack and gobbled it, and so he croons himself to sleep to dream of children not bitten owing to its protecting care."

"The magpie I claim," said the mother; "all day long as we work it whistles so gleefully, as if to cheer us on our way, while the locust tribe keep up the running accompaniment."

"And the frogs in the lagoon——" began Eva.

"Now that will do, come in at once," insisted Mrs. Dowling; "sit down and sing to us, my child."

Ere long the old settler, oblivious of the labours of the day, was absorbed in Lyell's *Geology;* the maiden was singing sweet ballads of England; the old lady sitting erect, with spotless cap on her silvery hair, was busy with her patch-work quilt, thinking of the by-gone scenes associated with each remnant of "better days."

"I hope I am not superstitious," she remarked, as her husband laid down his book to fill his pipe, "but do you know, Richard, as I arrange these patches I collected before we came out, I often see my sisters who wore the dresses, and the old housekeeper who assorted the remnants —you remember her—the rooms in which the curtains were hung, and the couches from which the covers were cut. I could describe the old house not from memory, but actually as it is now. My patches, when I am weary, not only reanimate the past, but reveal the present."

"Perhaps you are clairvoyant, Mary," suggested her husband with a laugh. "You have heard of the principles of 'trace.'"

"No; what is that?"

"It is claimed that an impress left on certain articles by former associations enables some persons to trace back the history of the object, and, far away, to view their present surroundings."

"Very fanciful; but I really do believe there are times when these bits of remnants make me dream until I see the present condition of those who wore them. I do not like the idea. Of course it is a silly one. I shall do no more to-night."

At this juncture a loud knocking was heard at the back-door. A shrill female voice was calling, "For heaven's sake let me in; he's dying!"

CHAPTER VI.

THE DYING SQUATTER'S DREAM.

"You tell me you have improved the land, but what have you done with the labourers?"—SISMONDI.

> "You have nothing else to do
> But make others work for you.;
> And you never need to know
> How the workers' children grow;
> You need only shut your eyes
> And be selfish, cold, and wise."—HOLYOAKE.

BETWEEN the Dowlings on their little reserve, and the proprietor of the estates extending in all directions around them, a deadly feud existed. The latter owned more than he could ride round in a day, yet he coveted the little farm the decayed gentleman had set by the roadside. The atmosphere of content that surrounded it contrasted with his own feelings of unrest and dissatisfaction. Leicester impounded the poor man's cattle if they strayed, was suspected of setting his dogs on the daughter's "one ewe lamb" when it wandered, summoned the "genteel Cockey," as he termed him, to the Court at Gumford on the charge of "creating a nuisance," when the experimenting lawyer-farmer excavated a silo near the great man's fence. Leicester took his seat on the bench on that occasion and adjudicated on the case; the township Boniface and storekeeper deeming it politic to consent to the order for removal of the nuisance. Poor Dowling's cows yielded no milk that winter.

Leicester, with all his wealth, was the poorest man in all the country-side. The few hands he engaged hated him, and, when they could, neglected his interests. Neighbours' dogs were ever scattering his sheep, selectors persisted in travelling over his huge paddocks, though he had fenced the road across with six-rail wall of wood. Bulls would break his fences, his paddocks be burnt oftener than any one's else, and none have the grace to come to his assistance.

At nightfall the lonely man would return to the huge mansion he had built, no one knew for what purpose. The great drawing-room was filled with furniture evidently purchased to one large order, the library stocked with books procured from England by the ton. In the chiffonier of the long dining-room was his solace. Again and again through the evening the recluse rose from his pile of "weeklies" to refresh his spirit with whisky. He would doze, then rise and pace the dismal corridors and empty rooms like one possessed.

" Is life worth the living ? " he would muse as he toyed with the revolver that ever reposed in the chiffonier drawer. " Had he not given employment to hundreds ? " He would proceed to reckon up the scores of miles of fencing, and thousands of yards of excavation for tanks, the building and clearing he had effected—the thousands of pounds' worth of wool and stock, of which the Messrs. Goldbags and Co. had had the selling for him. Had he not been a benefactor to his race? And lo! the world cared not a straw for him, despised him, would not heed if he died, alone, to-morrow.

Alas for the ingratitude of man !

Now, he was actually compelled by the shire to open some of his closed roads ! The price of wool had fallen —more than a penny—which involved a loss to him of

thousands of pounds a year! He must certainly stop all
his donations of a guinea a year to churches and hospitals!
Added to all his troubles, the married couple, who had
supplied his personal wants for ten years past, could
tolerate his vagaries no longer, and were leaving him.

Alone in the world the millionaire stood in his ghostly
mansion, under his far-reaching hills and valleys of
richest pasture—deserted, despised! He would stand it
no longer! One evening when the whisky was firing
his brain, he had roved from room to room! . . . .
There was a sudden explosion that no one heard! A
heavy fall! Then a silence as of death reigned in the
great house.

"I can't find the master nowheres, Jim," said the
housekeeper, after taking in the last "hot toddy" before
retiring. "I'm afeared for him. He looked so wild
again this evening. Come and have a look; hold the dip."

In the vast, dim drawing-room the faithful couple
almost stumbled over the form of the unfortunate millionaire. The woman screamed and started back with
horror. Her husband knelt and sought the pulse of the
unhappy man.

"Not dead," he reported; "quick, get some water and
some whisky."

Weeping, chattering like two children, the simple pair
bathed the wound above the temple from which blood
was oozing, poured the whisky that had caused the deed
down the throat of the dying man. He was heavy; they
hesitated to try to carry him.

"Jane, old girl, run and call some one," said the man
hoarsely.

"There's no one to fetch."

"Go and ask Mr. Dowling to run across. He'll know
what to do."

" He won't come, Jim ; he can't.   He's never set foot
in the house all these years, and the poor master did
hate him so."

The woman was supporting the dying man's head and
looking with tenderness into the face that had never
smiled on her once.

Why is it that the dog loves most the hand that
commands and never caresses; that the devotion of
woman is most signally displayed for the husband who
acts the brute; that honest Jim and his wife felt as if all
the world was darkening for them as they bent, in the
great dim room, over the man who had never given them
ought but wages, food, and curses?

On their first and last visit in Mr. Leicester's time to
the great White House, Mrs. Dowling insisted upon
accompanying her husband.   The moon bathed the
avenue and orange grove, now neglected, with a ghostly
light.   The unused lounges set around the spacious high
verandah seemed as seats for the dead.   The great front-
door creaked dolefully as, for the first time for many a
month, Jane threw it open.   In the wide hall were hung
brass breastplates inscribed with the names of " Kings "
" Billy " and " Bob," and other chieftains of a vanished
race, whose spears, " waddys," and " nullahs " were disposed around a Walhalla from which all the heroes
and the glory had departed !

As Jane, with trembling hand, flung open the drawing-
room door a weird scene presented itself.   The dim light
of the rude " dip " which Jim had placed on the grand
piano, that never sounded, threw a gruesome light on the
long mirrors and curtains, high cornices and stencilled
walls, the oleographs with gilt frames of immense proportions—a dim light before an unused shrine !   Beside
it a grizzled man lay dying, and another, with soiled

Crimean shirt and moleskin trousers, knelt before the crimson settee in the midst of the velvet-pile carpet.

"Poverty in the midst of riches," whispered Dowling to his wife.

"Yes, that boundary rider is richer than he, poor man !"

"And always has been," the husband replied.

The worthy couples placed the wounded man on a mattress and bore him to his bedroom. All night long the Dowlings sat and watched, while Jane stood at the foot of the bed gazing wistfully at the troubled sleeper, or wandered about the empty rooms of the lonely house, bewailing her impending loss. Her husband had ridden to Gumford for the Doctor.

Towards morning the sick man's breathing became more regular. He opened his eyes and looked long at the two watchers. He averted his gaze, then scanned the anxious faces as the sick are wont to do. The sufferer tried to extend his hand towards the watchers.

"You are better now," said Dowling, taking the hot, moist hand in both of his, while his wife smoothed the pillow and tenderly moistened with a damp cloth the fevered brow.

"Why do you come?" the sick man with difficulty whispered. "Why not, like everybody else, leave me to my fate?"

Quietly they assured him that the world was much what people made it. That sometimes God left men alone that they might discover how empty it was without the love of their kind and of Him.

"And you forgive me?" he said, stretching out his hand again, and looking into the face of the man he had wronged.

"As God forgives. I have angered you unintentionally, and perhaps given you cause for resentment."

"No, you have not," was the reply. "You shall not say that. Is there a Bible about?" he asked, after a pause. "You will find one at the top of the book-case. I used it for the men to take their oaths and declarations upon."

Mrs. Dowling brought the volume.

"Now read to me, slowly, Nathan's parable to King David. You'll find it, you know, about the end of the second book of Samuel. I knew the old Book once," the penitent murmured, half to himself; "my mother taught it me." A tear, that he vainly tried to brush away, rolled down the old man's face. "It was the lust for land and gold," he continued, "that ruined me. I thought the whole country-side was mine, and not the Lord's and His people's. Of what good has it been to me?—Ah! you cannot know the remorse I have experienced of late," he continued; "the terrible conflict that has raged in my breast—between love and hatred, strength and weakness. I have prayed and cursed with the same breath. I could not unbend. I could not change in my demeanour. I could not confess. Yet I knew that I was wrong. In a mad moment I sought to end all. I am dying, but I have not ended all! Now read."

"Let me select something else," Dowling persisted.

"No, I will not. I am going to hear *that*—from you."

As the memorable parable sounded again in the ears of the sinking man, Mrs. Dowling bowed her head and wept, but the dying squatter listened with set countenance as though hearing his doom.

"Read it all," he insisted, as Dowling hesitated. "I know that last verse. Do not shirk it. 'Give it tongue,' as we used to say to the old collie dog. Poor old

Laddie! I wonder will he miss me! Round up the tale, 'Thou art the man!' God gave me miles, or I took it, and I coveted your few feet of land."

"Stay!" interjected the lady—"there is yet another verse you should hear: 'And David said, I have sinned against the Lord. And Nathan said, The Lord hath *put away* thy sin.'"

Thereupon the woman's gentle voice, with tender tact, poured into the closing ear oil of comfort for the broken heart.

"I hate death-bed repentances," the sufferer declared, with a spark of the vehemence that had marked him; "but I *do repent*—I do. . . . I can't do more. I must leave the rest. Stay, quick, yes—I can. I can exercise restitution. Fetch me pen and paper. I will bestow all my goods as best I can. I had resolved to leave all for the State to divide. Another shall perhaps do what I failed to attempt. A Solomon shall apply the hoard of a sorry David to a noble end."

Mr. Dowling was able, in a few words, to pen the preamble to the Will.

"'To my faithful servants, whom I spurned in life '— put that in word for word—' I bequeath the manager's house, garden, and the three paddocks adjoining. To the objects of my mad and bitter animosity, Richard Dowling and his wife Mary '—put down those very words, mind. No trimming the fleece! This is my dying will and confession, remember—' I bequeath the one thousand acres adjoining their homestead——'"

"We cannot accept it," interposed Mrs. Dowling, her native sense of independence and pride gaining the ascendant over feelings of pity and sympathy.

"Will you not let me offer restitution, madam?" said the dying man, with a spice of his old imperiousness.

"May I not unburden my soul? I will do to the last what I will with my own!" Then, after a painful pause, more softly, "Let me leave it to your daughter. It is not much, but you'll think less harshly of me when, in your industrious fashion, you turn up that black soil, Dowling." The sick man tried to smile. "You have slogged away like a brick. I admire your pluck! Give me your hand again. It is harder than once it was. You commend the gentleman to the world. I—and such as I—defame that 'grand old name.' 'All else of which I die possessed I leave to my nephew'—you know the name—'in the hope that he will make a worthy use of the lands I greedily held for myself.' Tell him," he added, "I repent my treatment of him. To come so far," he wandered on, almost to himself, "and then to be driven away. He was proud and wrong-headed. Ah, but my sister's son, with a big heart of his own, that angered because it condemned me."

With difficulty the Will was signed and witnessed. Two men who had come for "killing sheep" were dragged into the room in the early morning to write their names and vanish.

"I wish the sun would rise," Leicester faintly whispered. "Push aside the curtains; right back, please. Often I've lain here and waited for old Sol to appear over the ridge just behind that pine, this time of year. Even now I can see the links of gold, the wattles beside the creek. Jupiter is the morning star just now; there he shines, 'like a diamond in the sky.' Poor old mother. Venus is the evening star, I shall never see it more. Not here at least. Ah, there it is. God's blessed sun!"

And, as they helped him, with a last effort the dying man raised himself, stretched forth his arm towards the distant hills, and cried—

"See ! They are coming. Pouring over the hills ! Troops of happy people." And his eyes shone with a novel lustre. "Women and children. All across the lovely valley, where the sheep feed alone." With trembling hand he shaded his eyes as if to observe more clearly, and continued, " Vines and fig-trees, and pomegranates around their dwellings. Pure rivers of water flowing between. Hark ! hark ! to the children calling. And to the music at their feast." A pause . . . a long breath . . . " A—new—day—has—dawned ! " he whispered slowly, word by word. Then a last gasp.

Sinking back gently, the millionaire left his fields behind. A smile settled on the set face. The eyes fixed for ever. Closing them, the three weeping, kneeled in the silent room into which the first beams of the rising sun were shining.

.

CHAPTER VII.

KEEPING UP APPEARANCES.

" And even while Fashion's brightest arts decoy,
   The heart distrusting asks, if this be joy? "—GOLDSMITH.

" Rapine, avarice, expense,
   This is idolatry ; and these we adore :
   Plain living and high thinking are no more :
   The homely beauty of the good old cause
   Is gone ; our peace, our fearful innocence
   And pure religion, breaking household laws."
                                    WORDSWORTH.

"KEEPING up appearances" when the substance is
wanting, to be prompted by a generous disposition without the power of giving effect to it, moving in a plane of
life above the pecuniary standard of those who occupy
it, is one of the most painful experiences the professional
man—or any—can know.

Such was now Dr. Courtenay's position. His wife, a
clever, stylish woman, was ambitious—for the girls' sake,
as she said. Their elder daughter, Hilda, was a dashing,
thoughtless girl, intent upon pleasure and admiration.
Well-dressed and duly appointed, as, like her mother,
she always managed to be, she was capable of making a
decided impression in any drawing-room to which she
was announced. Art and effect may have contributed
more than nature and grace, vivacity of manner more
than native power, yet so it was that Miss Courtenay

more than held her own in the world of taste and fashion.

Her sister, fair and retiring, with the gentlest of trusting blue eyes, rather large mouth, straight soft hair, regular but not striking features, impressed only those who knew her. She thought herself plain and stupid— neither of which she was. Her sister did not contribute to undeceive her: neither did her mother. Thanks to the latter's tact and devotion to desirable personages, the Courtenays were asked and appeared everywhere—at tennis parties, afternoon teas, dances, and At Homes. Mornings were spent in recovering from the effects of the previous evening's engagements—with a little *soupçon* of watering and arranging of flowers, to give a sense of having been "quite busy this morning."

Afternoons were devoted to ceremonial visitings when no engagements to salons, *matinées*, and other fashionable fixtures intervened. The evening seemed blank and tiresome if no festivity or out-going marked it. A miserable failure the entire round of feverish existence actually was. No time or opportunity was afforded for forming real friendships, for rational converse, for the joys of intellectual or domestic life.

There are some things that cannot go on. Dr. Courtenay found himself sinking deeper and deeper into debt. "Calls" were made by financial institutions that hitherto had paid him handsome dividends. The liabilities his generous nature had led him to incur in the interest of distressed friends or poor patients were accumulating. Something must be done. The carriage and coachman were "put down." The house, not a pretentious one, must be kept up, or the practice would suffer.

"If we do not go out people will cease to ask us,"

pleaded the wife, when her attention was directed to long outstanding accounts at Buckland & Joshua's and Senior the jewellers.

Wearied with a long day's round of professional visiting, and attendance at meetings, the long-suffering doctor must needs dress and take his wife and daughters to some cloying scene of festivity, with a suppressed yawn thanking his gracious hostess for "a most enjoyable evening," when at length Hilda and her mother had been induced to depart.

"The whole thing is so false and hollow," he would say. "I despise myself for uttering these conventional lies, and for participating in this make-believe existence. You do not enjoy it," he would protest, "you are always tired. And what is there to show for all your labours? If it were natural, were we in a position to entertain, if you went out as, and where, you really wished to go, I could understand it. But your fashionable life as now lived is, in my opinion, artificial, unintellectual, and a sham throughout."

"I fear, Charles, you lost at whist to-night," his spouse suggested.

"No, I did not. No such relief to monotony. I only played to pass the time."

"It is your absurd dabbling in every form of charity and in all sorts of social schemes that is dragging us down," the good lady urged, as the conversation was continued at a later hour. "What about those men you have sent away? Who, but you, is responsible for their maintenance?"

"I'm not," the husband replied; "I shall do my best. If others will not help, they must return and starve here in town."

The doctor and some friends had indeed despatched

Elms and a few of his people to a "Selection" that Courtenay had "taken up" years before, when practising near a squatter uncle's in the country. The venture was only an experiment, which for lack of funds and scope did not promise much success.

The doctor had prevailed upon his wife to accompany him to his study. He had been looking into accounts. The good lady protested that "no good came of brooding over what could not be altered."

"Times will change soon," she remarked, toying with an invitation that had just come to Lady Woolenough's " At Home."

"They will change—for the worse," was the man's reply. "We are getting deeper and deeper into the mire, all to keep up these false appearances, and to maintain a position amongst people who possess thousands for our hundreds."

"But you must have regard to your practice and to the girls' prospects."

"What would become of both if anything happened to me ?" he replied bitterly. "My very policies are encumbered. If I died to-morrow, you would be beggars. And people would say, truly, that I had lived a lie."

"But every one else is in the same position ! What squatter or merchant but is in the hands of his bank? Who are there pay cash for what they eat and use and wear? You might ticket every coat, or dress, or house you see as belonging, if all had their own, to some wretched tradesman."

"The fact that others are dishonest, or are content to live in a 'fool's paradise,' is no consolation to me."

At this juncture Hilda with evident excitement entered the room, followed by her sister, looking guilty but resolute.

"Maud says she will not accept Lady Woolenough's invitation. She is not going out any more," explained the elder, flinging herself on the settee with a tennis-racquet in her lap. "She wants to play the heroine."

Poor Maud, looking very guilty, stood beside her parents.

"We have not dresses to go in, and I do not want a new one."

"Why not, pray?" asked the mother.

"Because we cannot afford it."

"For that very reason we cannot afford to drop out of everything," remarked Hilda.

"What makes you think that we are not in a position to go out, Maud?" inquired her mother.

"I am very stupid, I dare say," replied the girl, "but I know that father is worn with care and anxiety. I am not going to add to his embarrassment."

"My dear," remarked her mother, severely, "this is really not your business. This is too bad! It appears to me that even the girls are becoming mercenary in these days. When I was young we never talked of 'ways and means.' Do you not think that your father and I can manage our own financial affairs?"

"She says she is going as a governess," interposed Hilda. "I pity the poor children. An awful lot Maud will teach them!"

"Perhaps so," was the reply. "We girls really learn nothing, now-a-days. All that we have known is forgotten twelve months after we 'come out.' At any rate I shall try to improve matters for myself."

"Very likely we shall let you leave home in that way!" said her father, kindly, drawing the accused towards him. "It would break my heart to think of girls brought up as you have been, becoming drudges of a modern house-

hold, owing, too, to our insane attempt to maintain a
false appearance."

"A governess, of all things!" interposed her mother, ·
warmly. "I had rather you were a housemaid or cook.
Then at least you would receive good wages, and
command employment and fair treatment. The desire
of so many, when they want to earn their own living, to
be governesses and clerks, is prompted by the very same
false pride you think you discern elsewhere in society."

."So I believe," admitted the girl, "but you see I could
not well be a cook while my father practised as a
fashionable doctor. I do not know.why, however. It
would be more honest than our present mode of living
and that of many of our friends. Still I recognize that
we must 'keep up appearances' to a certain extent—
though I do loathe it all."

"My dear," remarked her father, taking the girl's hand
in his, "you shall not go as a cook just yet. Things are
not as bad as that; but," he added, "there is no doubt
that we must economize, and, moreover, we might, I
think, compensate ourselves for less excitement by a
little more rational home life and some social occupa-
tions."

"Practising on the piano, reading dry books, and
carrying soup round to poor people," suggested Hilda,
with a toss of the head.

"We can try to be happy and useful," replied the
father, "without making fools of ourselves."

"Or nuisances either," suggested Mrs. Courtenay,
naïvely. "I consider your ordinary 'charitably-disposed
persons' the greatest bores you ever meet. Such dowdies
as they are! And there is just as much fuss and sham
about them, only of another sort, as with those who do
move in decent society. They all hate and envy one

another. They will pillory you yet. You should hear what Miss Loveless says already."

" I suppose we must expect to meet with human nature everywhere," remarked the doctor. " We can avoid eccentricities and extremes in each direction."

"Then you side with Maud," said the mother, with an air of scorn. " We are to refuse this invitation, sell our dresses to those charming persons who advertise, ' Don't throw away your spoons and old clothes,' and sit and work a sewing-machine all day long."

The doctor was roused.

"You might do worse than that," he remarked. " Be plain, be honest, that's all I ask." And he sat and smoked his cigar in silence.

Poor man !—he had struggled hard to make his practice and position. Visions had been his of honourable, unconventional usefulness. Lately, however, he had drifted into a false position. His daughter standing there, more like culprit than victim, had already dragooned herself into the thought of becoming some scorned, uncared-for drudge of society. He knew that that might come ! He had stretched out his hand to help those that were falling—his own anxieties making him solicitous for those of others. Now his arm was paralyzed by lack of money.

"How I hate it !" he thought. " Those who have, misuse it, those have it not who might put it to good account."

At this moment Elms was announced. He had written stating that he needed a few hundred pounds for the undertaking in which he was engaged.

" You need not go," said the doctor, as the ladies moved to depart. While the two conversed, Mrs. Courtenay said, speaking in a low tone, to her daughters—

"I do not know how it is, but I no more trust that man than I would a burglar. He has designs on your father. Well, there is not much to get out of him, that's one comfort! Women may be fools, but they read facts and hearts better than do these poor men."

"There's no help for it, Elms," the doctor was saying. "The thing must be given up. I have no means myself, and can procure none from those who have."

"It is a great shame, sir," replied the man with evident feeling; "the poor fellows are doing well. They'll be mad if I tell them they'll have to go. They'll blame you, sir."

"Perhaps they will. Let them! Who will be the greater sufferer? I, who have laid out the little money I had, who have spent my time and drawn obloquy upon myself for their sakes, to be denounced by them and jeered at by my friends—or they who have had everything to gain and nothing to lose?"

And the strong man, from whom all upon which he had set his heart seemed slipping, groaned within himself, though his face was set as if he were undergoing an operation. As he was! Slowly his life's hopes were being torn from him, but he would not wince.

"Only why," he was thinking, "so strongly as we desire to live honestly and to some purpose, do we find the means wanting?" Tom Lord and Frank Brown appearing at the door were about to withdraw.

"Do not go," said the doctor; "you are in at the death."

"What death?"

"Only that of my little pet scheme. It has collapsed for want of funds."

"Indeed, I'm sorry," remarked Tom, not looking

particularly grieved either; adding aside to the young clergyman—

"What about your faith, Brown—that was to pull you through?"

The latter did not respond.

"You'll join our party to the theatre to-night?" continued Tom. "'The way the world goes round' is a grand take-off, they say, of fashionable society of to-day. Very clever, I believe. Mrs. Courtenay is taking us all."

That lady looked guilty. Maud remarked—

"I am sorry I cannot go, Mr. Lord, thank you."

"No more shall I," said Hilda, with the air of a martyr.

"But you will not give up the theatre because that set of derelicts has to return to town?" said Lord. "Where's your faith?"—to Brown.

The doctor seemed to be in no mood for pleasantries. A heavy weight lay on his heart—a dark path stretched before him. Maud was looking out of the window, far away into the future—wondering whether filling the minds or the mouths of children were preferable. Hilda was pulling a rose viciously to pieces as it lay on her lap. Brown talked eagerly to Elms, upon whose face a dark, ominous shadow lay. Mrs. Courtenay was reading and re-reading her invitation—wondering what life would be worth without the excitement of balls to be prepared for, and daughters to be danced out.

A knock was heard at the door. The maid delivered a telegram to the doctor, who seized it as a welcome diversion from troubled thought. All eyes turned towards him as he tore open the envelope.

A telegram is a talisman. It turns darkness to light, converts rejoicing into mourning, casts a lightning flash upon distant worlds, revealing achievement won or calamity befallen upon the anxious, waiting heart. It descends as a thunderclap, or instils comfort like the dew. Whose pulse does not throb one beat quicker per minute, when, at critical moments, the red-winged Mercury of modern days appears in the midst!

The doctor read, and leaped from his lounge ; thrusting his fingers through his hair, he read again.

The wife looked over his shoulder, saying, "May I see ? "

The daughters peered over the other and timidly asked, " May we look ? "

The men stood by inquiringly. "Wondering what the deuce it all meant," as Tom explained afterwards.

Like cloud-shadows and sunshine across an April landscape, variations of expression swept over the faces of the readers. Visions of sorrow and of joy; of wonder-ment and anticipation were cast upon each eager countenance. All this in a second.

" I never expected *that*," cried the doctor at length. " Poor old fellow ! Right at last ! Not as bad as we thought him. Who is ? "

The women were looking one to another, then out of the window—to weep and to smile, seeing through a thin veil of tears a long vista of promise and of opportunity ; peopled by each with the objects nearest their hearts. Under the trees of her vision, Maud saw children playing, strong men working as they smiled, women spinning as they sang. Beneath their leafy shades mother and elder daughter beheld processions and pageants, as of cloth-of-gold, fairy trains, the Festival of all the Fashions, themselves set at the vista end, receiving the adulations of gorgeous throngs !

" May we see ? " asked little Tom, recognizing that the telegram was of general interest.

He read aloud—

" Gumford Railway Station.

" Your uncle died last night, bequeathing his estates to you.   Peaceful end.

"RICHARD DOWLING."

" Very wealthy, was he not?" remarked the little man.

" Worth about £200,000," was his friend's reply.

" Courtenay, I congratulate you.   You are worthy of this."

" Not too fast, old fellow, there may be some mistake. ' There's many a slip 'twixt the cup and the lip.' "

" No fear of that.   I always thought you'd come out right."

" No, you did not, excuse me," remarked the clergy-man, wringing the doctor's hand; " you said faith would not do it—and it has."

" Then the work can go on, sir?" inquired Elms.

" Yes, I hope so, on a somewhat larger scale, perhaps. I can see daylight now, I think," said the doctor, " though I am somewhat dazed."

CHAPTER VIII.

THE SCREEN OF DEATH.

"Cheer the weak ones who are bending
'Neath this weary burden now ;
Lift the pallid faces upward,
Smooth the careworn troubled brow ;
Send a bright and hopeful message
To each tried and tempted heart,
That the thick and gloomy shadows
At that sunshine may depart."

ADA CAMBRIDGE.

FOR a moment the doctor stood on the threshold of
the ward surveying the rows of white beds ranging on
the polished floors. A few patients were sitting about
talking quietly or reading, some lay in the beds asleep
or suffering in silence—seeming to read their destinies
on the high, white-washed ceiling. The neatest of nurses
moved with softest tread as about a sanctuary conse-
crated by sorrow and death to resurrection and recovery.

"A good large cheque," the doctor mused, "drawn
by the rich on account of their heavy indebtedness to
the poor. Amongst the fairest fruits of our faith and
civilization. What, in the place of temples such as
these, would a wild commune set up? How would the
poor and suffering fare if leaders of the mob were
ministers of charity?" He shuddered at the thought.

"Well, Willie, and how's the leg?" inquired the

doctor, approaching the bed on which the street-arab had lain many weeks.

"I'm all right now, sir, thank ye. The blooming splinter-boards is off now, and my leg's gettin' strong as a cab-horse's. They say I may leave next week. God knows where I'm a-going."

"Would you like to come with me," said the doctor, "if I never run over you again?"

"If I never get under your horse's feet again, sir. But may I go with you, sir? The only thing is——"

He paused.

"Well, what's the difficulty?"

"I would like to go into the country. The flowers they brought me here—I never seed such a lot before— makes me think of them I picked that one day I was there. They've been readin' to me about gardens and horses and cows and the green grass and the sweet hay. I'm allus thinking of them."

"But there's rain and cold, hard work and dry seasons in the country, lad. Life there is not all flower-picking and rollicking in hay-fields."

"I know that, sir, and I could work. They allus said I slaved like a brick in town; sure there I could, and I might——"

"Might what?"

The little man whispered, while he brushed away a tear—

"I might find father. He's somewhere there."

The doctor was moved.

"You shall go into the country next week," he pro- mised.

"But I should like to be with you, sir. You've been so good to me—all the times you've been here these two months."

"You shall have both your desires. You shall go with me, and live in the country too."

The lad could not speak, but burst into tears.

"Poor little man, he's weak still," said the doctor.

"May I ask one thing more?" said Willie, after a time. "They've read to me 'bout Abr'um. He asked and asked, and God wern't angry; and you're almost as good as he were."

"Don't say that, boy, we are none of us much to talk about."

"Well, sir, could you take *she* with we?" nodding his head towards the end of the ward. "The young lady over there, Nurse Maggie, what's reading to the old man that's dying there, with the screen round his bed. The screen's the last thing they sees here. They'd oughter put jolly fine pictures on 't! I allus thinks how small the world's got for he when I sees the screen put round a poor cove's bed. But they sees into another world, a mighty big and good 'un, all flowers in a blessed country, so th' old parson with the long grey beard says."

"Why do you want Nurse Maggie to go? To take care of you?"

"I can look after myself, never fear. She's got a cough; I heard th' doctor say she'd ought get into the country. T'other nurse said she couldn't 'ford."

"I fear we cannot take the nurses and the hospitals with us."

"Leastways will you think on it, sir? You can do what you has a mind for, I believes."

Next day Dr. Courtenay returned and said—

"Willie, you can have your third wish too. I did think of what you said, and have arranged that Nurse Maggie and ten of the patients who are getting better——"

"Conv'lescents, they calls 'em."

"Yes, that ten convalescents shall stop for a while where we are going, and do a little gardening and looking after the fowls, and so on."

"Oh, my, that will be fine! You can't take the old man, sir, 'cos God's took'd him. The screen's gone round 'nother chap now. But there's many says they don't know where they'll go when they gets better, and it will be fun to have 'em in the flowers and the hay."

CHAPTER IX.

THE GUEST THAT HAD NOT ON A WEDDING GARMENT.

> " I live for those who love me,
>   For those who know me true ;
>   For the heaven that shines above me,
>   And waits my spirit too ;
>   For the cause that lacks assistance,
>   For the wrong that needs resistance,
>   For the future in the distance,
>   For the good that I can do ! "

THE Town-hall was converted for the time being into an enormous bower—suggestive of the leafy glades in which our forefathers held their earliest Witenagemots, or chieftains their marriage festivals.

High above the balcony, at either side, rose tree-ferns, and boughs of pine, native cherry and apple tree, eucalypts of wondrous leaf, and heather of every variety. On the enlarged stage an Arcadian scene had been depicted by some who were exchanging paint-brush for axe and spade. On the vast floor were set tables spread with the best of plain fare, and decked with fern and wild-flowers from distant plains and ranges.

About the building were scattered a thousand smiling, expectant guests, clad in white and red. Men with Crimean shirts and brand-new moleskin trousers—each with a shining tomahawk stuck in his belt, a blue badge on the arm, embroidered with a spade and axe cross-wise, a device of hand clasped in hand above. The men wore a red sash across the shoulder, a harvester's Panama hat on head, with band and streamers of "turkey-red."

Each woman and child was clad in white, with red sash and blue badge.

"Home sweet Home" resounding from the great organ was signal for all to take their places at the feast. They sat by families, children in order of size, father and mother in centre—boys and girls together on either hand. All stood as the first verse of the "Old Hundredth" was sung to the accompaniment of the organ. Then they sat and looked bashfully at the viands arranged before them.

Ladies and gentlemen bustled round and bade the guests eat. They needed little persuasion. Often had they been hungry of late, but one who had himself known care, had resolved they should "hunger no more," if they would work. This was the Inaugural Festival. They started for new scenes to-morrow.

The doctor had decided to put his uncle's lands, which he had inherited, to better use than they had formerly served. His intentions he had communicated by circular to every clergyman and mayor in the metropolis, requesting nominations of suitable persons. Hundreds had been laboriously interviewed, their credentials examined, medical reports procured, and some two hundred and fifty families—a thousand souls—ultimately selected.

The rules and agreements had been signed, a suit of uniform given to each person, and provision made for transfer of families and furniture to Gumford Railway Station.

In the course of his opening remarks the host introduced his son, Travers Courtenay, returned the week before from a prolonged absence in the old country.

He had taken a fair degree at Cambridge, spent two or three years studying engineering in Germany, another twelve months in a leisurely tour through the United States, returning in time to take part in the contemplated social movement.

The young man regarded the undertaking with interest, mingled with misgivings. He was not free from the somewhat indolent, supercilious spirit with which young men of means are prone to regard social questions. He had no great admiration for the working-classes, deemed them dissatisfied without cause, given to intrigue and agitation—not over fond of work. He did not consider that, though existing social conditions suited him, they might be nevertheless imposing intolerable burdens on others less favoured ; that the class to which he belonged was not, by nature, any more in love with labour, for its own sake, than the so-called "labouring classes." They, he thought, should be content to toil twelve hours a day, and be thankful for the privilege of doing so. Travers' disposition was, at the same time, generous as his father's, and the thought of the " desolate and oppressed " ever touched a vibrating chord in his heart.

In the course of the repast, the doctor, with pardonable pride, escorted his intelligent-looking if not actually handsome son, from table to table, and introduced him to some of the company.

"I must take you to an interesting group," said he. " The man talking and eating so energetically at the head of that table is my right-hand man—an important personage in his own estimation, but useful to me. On the right is his daughter."

" I thought her one of the ladies," remarked the son. "Not a bad-looking girl. Observe the grace with which she is addressing that greasy-looking personage."

"That's the fellow I had to thrash. Beside them is Willie, the lad I unfortunately ran over. Come, you must make their acquaintance."

The party rose as the doctor approached. After a few words of introduction, Gwyneth asked, with the ease of a daughter of the best-born—

"May I offer you a cup of tea, sir?"

"Thanks, Miss Elms, I must move amongst our friends."

"Perhaps *you* will stay and have a cup of tea with us?" suggested Elms to the younger man.

"Thanks, very much." Gwyneth made room for the young man at the end of her form.

"I fear you'll find it rather dull in the country," remarked Travers, with a patronizing air. "No theatres, football-matches, or assembly dances, eh?"

"I dare say we can manage to exist, sir, without such dissipation," answered Gwyneth, quietly pouring out the tea. "I fear you imagine we think of nothing save our 'day out.'"

"I am sure you are a cut above that, Miss Elms; but what will you do with yourself in your spare hours?"

"I suppose we can take our books with us, and that my sewing-machine may go; even my piano, I hope, may not be too bulky for transit."

"You play then?" asked Travers.

"You should hear her sing too, sir," suggested the proud father between his munchings of a big bun.

"Some thinks we don't know nothing," growled Dick Malduke, applying with both hands the drum-stick of a chicken to his mouth. Travers looked at the shock-haired young man as though he would not mind shaking him as his father had done.

"Dick calls himself a 'root and branch' man," ex-

E

plained Elms apologetically; "but he's not as ferocious as he talks."

"Nor as he looks," interjected the daughter, eyeing the mangled chicken with a smile.

"And what do you read?" inquired the young man, turning to Gwyneth with growing interest.

"Oh, I suppose penny-dreadfuls, *Scraps* and *Answers*," she replied with a laugh, not caring to parade her literary tastes.

"Nothing of the kind, sir," interjected her father. "She's been all through my books on Political Economy. She's great on history, and is now reading aloud to us of evenings the *Greater Britain.* Her mother was a great reader before her."

"Then you'll be interested in the agricultural communities of America—'Riverside,' 'Oneida,' 'Utah,' and the others. I have been visiting them lately." The young man proceeded to describe phases of social life, as he had observed them in America. "If you do as well as those settlers, you'll be all bloated capitalists in a few years."

"Won't it be fun to see Dick living on the interest of his interest!" said the girl, mischievously.

"Not if I knows it," said Dick, savagely; "I'll be a Knight of Labour to the end of the chapter."

"You'd be the most overbearing and selfish capitalist ever demagogue denounced," continued Gwyneth. "You know you would, Dick, if you ever possessed the opportunity. It is bourgeois bloomed into millionaire that makes the hardest-shelled capitalist. We'll see Dick in the Upper House yet, with a knighthood."

The young man looked as if he could devour the girl, with love or hate, as he replied, with feeling—

"At least, I'll not make slaves of the people, to be

robbed, or, at best, fed like paupers in soup-kitchens and town-halls—just to show off." This with a savage glance at Travers, for whom the agreeable young man seemed already to cherish no special love. "Society will be no better," he added, "till you sweep it away, root and branch, lock, stock, and barrel," and wildly waving his hands as though on the stump, he inadvertently tilted the épergne opposite him into little Will's face, and the cup of coffee into his own lap.

Gwyneth so far forgot herself as to hide her face in her handkerchief to smother her laughter. The elder Elms, roused and vexed, bid his friend "not make a fool of himself," while Travers thought that it took "many people to make a world." He wondered that his father tolerated this destructive young man among his guests.

"Coffee usen't make father drunk," remarked Willie laconically, as he picked up the flowers.

"You shut up," said the angered youth, "or I'll make it hot for you outside."

"Did I not say that democracy is ever tyrannical," remarked Gwyneth, "when it gets the chance?"

"I've spoilt my best trousers any way," said Dick, beginning to recognize the absurdity of the position. "I beg your pardon, Miss Elms, that righteous indignation should get the better of me."

"I've no patience with you," rejoined the girl. "You're not fit to be here. You're always acting, and the fool is your *rôle*."

"Why did you not wear the uniform?" demanded the old soldier. "Then you wouldn't have spoiled your own clothes, at least. Moles will wash, which slops won't."

"I never wore moles in my life, and I'm not going to begin now," was the reply.

"Well, I don't like a fellow as is ashamed of his comrades and his colours," said the Sergeant, decisively.

"I'll wear none of their uniform, if I stop in town for it," swaggered Dick.

Just then his host passed. Hearing the remark he replied—

"Then you can stay in town, Malduke"—adding to Elms—"I won't have your friend at any price, Sergeant."

"Then I'm off," returned the agitator; "I'll wear no capitalist's bloomin' colours, blowed if I does."

"I'd better show the way out," remarked Travers, significantly; "we should make short work of such as you at Cambridge, my fine fellow."

"Oh, I'll denounce you," was the fierce reply. "I'll write to the *Leveller*, and expose your money-making, sweating scheme. I know your little ways." And to the astonishment of the company, the "guest that had not on the wedding garment" swaggered out of the hall.

When well outside, Dick paused a moment, then banging one fist into the palm of the other hand, declared with an oath—

"See if I don't go. And smash it all up too—sure's my name's Dick Malduke."

No one, unless it were Elms, quite understood, later, how it was that, despite his unmanliness and some demur on the doctor's part, Dick was permitted to accompany the emigrants.

The repast ended and tables cleared away, the doctor appeared on the embowered platform, and explained the nature of the undertaking. He was greeted with rounds of applause. Picturesque harvest hats waved in the air, women holding up their children to gesticulate, in

imitation of their fathers. A thousand faces beamed
their thanks on their benefactor.

"And to-morrow they'd howl him down," remarked
Tom Lord, cynically.

"Don't you believe it," replied Frank Brown, also on
the platform. "These people are of the right sort.
They'll be treated well and behave well, I'll guarantee."

"They! They have no generous feelings. The mob
never yet had."

"As true hearts beat under flannel shirts, believe me,
as beneath the whitest starched fronts. The characters
of the wearers of both are much mixed. You'll find
good and bad everywhere."

"And a mighty lot more of bad than good in some
quarters, I am thinking," persisted Tom. But we shall
see.

CHAPTER X.

PEOPLING THE WILDERNESS.

" God the first garden made, and the first city, Cain."

" Without attempting to predict the exact phases through which
co-operation will pass, it can scarcely be doubted that the
principle is so well adapted to agriculture, that it is certain
some day to be applied to that particular branch of industry
with the most beneficial results. . . . The progress towards
co-operative agriculture will no doubt be slow and gradual."
—HENRY FAWCETT.

"THE old place, I fear, is spoiled for me," Mr. Dowling
was saying to his daughter. " My solitude is about to
be invaded. All my life I have fled from the town, and
now, in my old age, the city is spreading out its arms towards me. Its surplus population is to be spread over
the plains I have loved."

"I believe the new-comers are a very respectable sort
of people, father," the daughter replied. " They have
been carefully selected. Dr. Courtenay is hopeful they
will make good neighbours."

" But I don't want neighbours, my child ; I desire to
be left alone. Courtenay is a good fellow, and deserves
to succeed in this wild venture of his. But I wish he
had chosen some other field on which to launch his
experiment."

"Is not that the very crime poor Mr. Leicester committed, father? He wanted to keep all the country-side
to himself. Is not that the sin of half the landowners to-
day?"

"True, my girl; we are all a selfish lot. We, on the one hand, seek to hold the lands; the working-classes, for their part, will not permit needy cousins in the old country to share with them the bounties of this. If a man possess a trade or profession, he will keep all he can of it. 'Protection,' 'monopolies,' 'favoured classes,' 'locked-up' lands, and streams, and forests, all are barbarisms—un-English, un-Christian. In theory I am in favour of freedom, and fairer divisions of the good things of this life, but in practice—well, I'd like to be left alone."

"I'm so eager to see the people, father. Won't they be delighted with this charming valley, and the neat-looking tents, with everything prepared for them?"

"They ought to be," observed Mr. Dowling, doubtfully, "The pangs of hunger they have felt, and been oppressed by loads of care; they have had no interest in the country they have assisted to develop, nor in the undertakings in which they have been employed. Now they will have but to work; I hope they'll do it. Poor Courtenay! His work's cut out for him."

"Come and see the tents, father, before the settlers arrive. There are the Courtenays, and Jim and his wife, putting the finishing touch on everything."

The wide expanse of valley that spread beneath Heatherside—the Dowlings' abode—was strangely altered in appearance. The wattles and pine-ridges still dotted its undulating surface with clumps of trees midst sweeps of verdure; the creek, its waters still unpolluted, chattered in its willow-shaded channel. Magpies hopped and piped from the gaunt ringed timber; the grass was knee-deep, since the dead squatter's sheep had been sold or removed to the outer paddocks. Orchids and buttercups reared their heads above the meadow-like pastures, as if wondering how much higher their slender stalks must

rise to surmount the unwonted growth.   In the distance
the lake, a mirror of silver, reflected the day's declining
rays.   All was silent, expectant—an earthly paradise
awaiting the new race of Seth.   Across the valley from
side to side stretched a chain of tents, in squares and
crescents.   Each little tabernacle, labelled with the name
of the intended occupant, stood open in a plot of five
acres, duly pegged off.   The belongings of each family,
sent forward the day before, had been neatly bestowed
in the allotted tent.   The night previous, the balloting
had taken place at the White House ; Jim and Elms
drawing, one the number of the allotment, the other
the name of the future settler, from the doctor's hat
on the one hand, from Mrs. Courtenay's reticule on the
other.   The good lady had protested.

"I want you to have a hand in it, my dear," the
doctor had urged.

"I suppose because I do not approve."

"Oh, yes, you do ; you are deeply interested already."

"Only for your sake."

"No wonder the lady demurs," remarked the incorrigible Tom, who had come to have a peep at the
place.   "Naturally she objects to have one man's hand
in her reticule and another's in her husband's pocket.
Typical and significant."

"Well, they'll soon be empty again," remarked the
good lady.   "My husband has not calculated what it
will cost to feed a thousand mouths for two or three
years, and to run all his factories."

"The labourers will feed themselves, my dear, if I
give them the chance."

"But will they ? "

"That is just the problem we are going to solve."

Now the doctor and his followers were putting the last
rickety chair on its faulty legs in one tent, propping up

a derelict chest of drawers in another, tidying articles of vertu in a third.

"Well, what do you think of the camp?" asked the doctor of Dowling as he approached. "My back's broken with stooping about in these cramped little cribs all day," and the strong man threw back his shoulders and expanded his great chest as though to get his form into shape again.

"Your men are fortunate fellows," replied Dowling. "The valley is picturesque indeed, with its lines of white amongst the green and gold. You could not have selected a better site. The land will grow anything, if it's only scratched."

"We will do more than that," said the doctor. "We shall deepen the lagoons and have a splendid natural reservoir. We can shape the creek into a canal; get our craft from the centre of the settlement on to the lake, into the Silverbourne, to the Murray, and the world."

"Have you fully considered the cost of all these works?"

"Every penny. We shall accomplish all with our own labour, which we shall merely have to feed. After six months, provisioning will cost next to nothing."

"But men will not work for their food only."

"They will for homes and lands and share in the profits."

"You have launched upon an enormous undertaking."

"Not at all. In the ordinary course I must have invested scores of thousands of pounds in the enterprise. As it is, the settlers share the risk."

"How so?"

"They advance their labour. I put my land at their disposal. If the worst comes to the worst, I have drawn no profit from land, which at the same time has been improved; they, on the other hand, have toiled to little purpose. But they have lived in comfort meanwhile, and are better off than when they started. I have no fear, however, of failure, if they only rise to the occasion, and work like free men."

"That's the rub," said Dowling; "can you ever teach them to do that?"

"If making them interested principals—partners, in fact—will not do it, nothing will."

"How can you compel those to work who do not like it? You will have some such."

"No doubt; all, however, have entered into a contract. If any will not work, neither shall they eat; they can go."

"Which a mighty lot will do."

"Not after the first few months. They will have given 'hostages to fortune.' Every month's labour will forge a chain of vested interest about them. Men will think twice before they abandon, in a tiff, their embryo farms and homes."

"But these people have always been of a roving disposition."

" Because you have never tried to interest them in their undertakings. Each week you give them a wage that virtually pays them off, buys out that healthful interest that should, by every means, be fostered. If these men worked for my uncle, or a contractor, they could depart any Saturday and leave him in the lurch, taking all their belongings with them. In this case they would have to abandon two-thirds of the result of their labour."

"Then you have the idea of dragooning and coercing them?"

"Certainly not, save for their own good. I desire to make labour more effective, more directly interested, and so more content. It is to the men's own interest that they should postpone receipt of the fullest revenue of their toil, not grab what they can every Saturday night. We can feed them for half what it cost them to cater for themselves. *That* they have to the good. Undertakings that yield no profit under the wages system you will find we can prosecute to advantage, accepting lowest prices, reaping fullest profits."

" Well, we shall see."

" What is that music sounding over the hill?" asked Eva Dowling, running towards the speakers.

" You ought to know the sighing of the wind in the she-oaks on the hills," replied her father.

" Listen!" insisted the girl. " It is music, martial music—'The Campbells are coming.'"

" By Jove, it is some band. I can hear it, Courtenay. What does it mean?"

" My army, coming in peace and joy," replied the doctor, "to win its victories. Here they are!" he shouted to his wife further down the hill.

" Why have they a band?" inquired Dowling.

" To cheer them, of course, as music ever does," answered the doctor. " Why should not our regiment be enlivened through all its hard campaign by inspiriting strains? Why may not life here be brightened by the healthful accessories that render the city so attractive? We are going to set up 'counter attractions' on these plains, I assure you."

" Barmaids and dice," suggested Tom, coming up with the others. " I thought yours was to be a temperance settlement, Courtenay?"

" Not of your milk-and-water sort. A vigorous, manly life our people shall lead here. All that can properly delight eye and ear, and improve heart and mind, shall they know, if I can secure it."

"I see them—here they come!" cried Eva with excitement.

Forthwith over the very ridges that the dying eye of the squatter had looked upon last, a troop bearing banners appeared. Instruments of brass shone in the sunlight—horse-teams, bullock-wagons, spring-carts, and drays, laden with singing, laughing, gesticulating women and children; men astride fowl-coops, youths waving their caps from the top of swaying loads, children running alongside, plucking the heather as the caravan descended into the valley—a long, animated line, winding through the solitary pine-trees, round the granite rocks, pilgrims from the dreary city, escaping to the paradise God had prepared for them.

In the midst of Settlement Square—as it was to be called—on "the village green" they met, the benefactors and the beneficiaries.

"Home, sweet Home," the band struck up as the players, all settlers, took their stand under a wide-spreading gum. There were wringing of hands, shouts of delight, capering of children, with some shedding of tears, as all speeded to see on which tent their names were inscribed, and what plot was to be the scene of their future labour.

As, an hour later, the doctor took his wife's arm and led her slowly homeward his hand trembled.

"It was almost too much for me," he confessed, "to see the pale-faced creatures, brave with hope, sweeping into the lovely valley. God help them—and us. The responsibility is great, and so is the joy." . . . .

"Do you remember the old squatter's last vision?" said Dowling to his wife as they walked home. "It was fulfilled, surely, this very evening."

CHAPTER XI.

TRANSFORMATION SCENE.

" Seek to delight that they may mend mankind,
    And while they captivate, inform the mind."—COWPER

" So flows beneath our good and ill
    A viewless stream of common will,
    A gathering force, a present might,
    That from its silent depths of gloom
    At Wisdom's voice shall leap to light,
    And tide our barren fields in bloom,
    Till, all our sundering lines of love o'ergrown,
    Our bounds shall be the girdling seas alone."
        Australian Poets, J. BRUNTON STEPHENS.

COULD the walls of the homestead at Mimosa Vale have spoken, striking contrasts might they have described between the selfish life they had witnessed of old, and the generous one they looked down upon to-day. The costly furniture of the late squatter was the skeleton about which a hundred nameless nicknacks and niceties of refined female taste were disposed. The great halls were real " living-rooms " now, suggestive of culture, comfort, and use. The wide verandah that surrounded the building presented at every turn vistas of ferny bowers. The avenue was well kept, the plantation and orangery clipped and cleaned.

With a pony carriage, tandem-team, and riding-horses at their disposal, Hilda and her mother found to their surprise the country life not intolerable, while Maud discovered a hundred objects of interest. Her father and Travers had few spare moments.

Every Saturday a score or two of the families were invited to tea. Later the girls sang to them in the drawing-room, round games were indulged in, and finally a few dances.

In the course of the clear frosty nights the doctor would interest the men with the microscope in his study, or the telescope on the verandah. No talk of "shop" was permitted—that was reserved for meetings when papers were read and discussed in the wool-shed, improvised for the present into a hall.

"We have something other to do," the doctor would say, "than to make money. The bane of Englishmen has been that they are engrossed in business. We must have play of fancy here, contact of mind with mind, heart with heart, and soul with its Maker, if we are not to become more mechanical than the slaves of the city. 'Work while you work,' and then, betimes, talk, converse like rational men, or sport for a while as children."

Every alternate evening the band played on the village green, while children and their elders enjoyed "rounders" close by; great babies of men playing "hide and seek" with the little ones about the tents, as for an hour jollity prevailed.

"Ours is an Italian climate," the doctor remarked sometimes; "while we cling to our sturdy English sense of decency and duty, let us sun ourselves betimes, and acquire some of the tastes and graces of a southern life."

*   *   *   *   *   *

Among the neighbouring squatter folk who took more or less interest in the presence and projects of the Courtenays was one Larry O'Lochlan, a red-haired, good-looking young Celt, dare-devil yet tender, rollicking or serious by turns, as circumstances determined ; a typical Irish gentleman, with the most distinct though refined of brogues; who rode across country on the best bred of steeds, as though his wire fences were no more treacherous than the stone walls of Galloway. His boundary rider he would knock down " soon as look at him " if he were impudent, ride scores of miles for the doctor for a sick " hand," whom he would nurse and care for with the tenderness of a woman. Every one knew and loved Larry O'Lochlan, as all the country-side styled him. Though proud of his birth, he ever had a cheery greeting or a word of banter for all he met. He could pick off with rifle his wallaby or dingo at a thousand yards, as others with shot at a hundred. Larry was much interested in Courtenay's venture. He thought it a prime joke. Moreover, he declared his daughter Hilda " the one girl he had met out here who knew how to sit a horse without giving him a bad back." " A deuced fine-looking girl too. Knows how to talk. None of your Matriculation-Miss about her."

Larry had come to lunch, leading a young mare " that Miss Courtenay must ride. The creature had a mouth of velvet, action like a fighting cock, pace of a greyhound. She'd take you across one of those tents like a kitten over a cucumber."

" What a remarkable horse, Mr. O'Lochlan ! " suggested Mrs. Courtenay ; " she must be Irish, surely."

" Now, you are laughing at me, Mrs. Courtenay. You come too, Miss Maud, with your tandem-team, and see if she isn't an angel."

" Which—the lady or the pony ? " asked Tom.

" Oh, you English are so matter-of-fact. I don't hesitate to say that Miss Hilda rides like an angel."

"Angels don't ride," replied Hilda. "You'll have none of your horses in heaven."

"Then I'm not on to go there, if I do get the chance. Excuse me, Mrs. Courtenay, I mean nothing naughty. But there will be ponies in heaven, and dogs too," continued Larry; "I've seen them going that way."

"What *do* you mean?" inquired the ladies, laughing.

"I've seen them lie down and die for me, and I've watched their last look of love, saying as distinctly as they ever spoke in life, 'We'll meet again, master.' And I believe we shall."

"I did not know," said Tom, "that we were in the fabled fields where the creatures conversed like Christians."

"No man yet ever got work and devotion from beast or man that did not talk to it, and it to him. Why, my chestnut turns round and speaks to me—I'm not so barbarous as to drive with winkers—every mile we go. Every horse has a soul, if you only try to find it.

"Well, doctor, how are those poor creatures of yours getting on?" Larry asked of his host as he joined the party. "You'll do more than I ever could with that sort if you get anything reasonable out of them."

"We will ride round after lunch, and you can judge for yourself."

"Excuse me," remarked O'Lochlan, at the conclusion of the well-appointed repast, "but you have less trouble than I experience with servants. You seem to have a most superior set."

"All 'my children,' as I call them," said Mrs. Courtenay. "I receive the daughters of our people for two or three months, teach them what I can, and then secure engagements for them amongst my friends in town."

"You must·have trouble in breaking in the young fillies—I beg your pardon—the maids, I mean."

" I take no credit to myself; my daughter Maud takes them in hand."

" That accounts for their ' grace and goodness,' " remarked the Irishman ; "merely to come in contact with some people is to be the better for it."

"It is," said the doctor, "the affection my daughter lavishes on them that wins. If you take interest in human beings, you know, you can get even better results than from horses and dogs."

" I think it very rude of you, Mr. O'Lochlan," remarked Maud playfully, but not without a blush, " to discuss our servants. I shall criticize the appointments of your house when we visit Bullaroo."

" Mine's a wild barracks sort of place, I fear, but we will get the ' married couple ' to tidy up and give you a welcome, such as it is, when you do come."

"We shall have to send some of our people across," suggested the doctor, " to show your folk how to work."

" Excuse me, I would not have one at any price. I do not believe in co-operative slaveys. Menials are all very well in their place."

" Do not our men and maids ' know their place '? " inquired Hilda.

"None dare presume in Miss Hilda's presence—or that of her mother."

" I think I know one who has done so, nevertheless," was the quick rejoinder, "just a little."

" It's all in a good cause, so forgive me. You see I am trying to learn all I can of your emigrants."

"You certainly have altered the appearance of this prime piece of country," remarked O'Lochlan, as the doctor and he rode across the valley.

The pair halted in the midst of the settlement. Two miles down the valley, and athwart it, ran the lines of

F

cottages, some already finished. All were of the same style of architecture, with high gables, projecting eaves, and trellised verandahs. Before each house a couple of acres had been ploughed. In many instances vegetables, vines, or fruit-trees had already been planted. At the corner of each garden a poplar had been placed, while a mere path separated each allotment from the adjoining one. Already the water had been laid on ; in some parts a clear stream was flowing along the top of each garden farm. Along two great avenues, that ran cross-wise, trees were planted, and a little tram-line was being constructed.

" What is the tramway for ? " inquired Larry.

" To bring once a week supplies of wood and provisions to each cottage, and to bear produce, etc. into the stores."

" What is your motive power? Do the youngsters shove the trucks along ? "

" Our methods are not quite so primitive, as we shall see later on."

" But you have no fences."

" Are they so beautiful ? Our people, unlike the 'Cockies' of whom you complain, have something other to do than spend their first year in fencing themselves off from their kind. Their Aryan forefathers knew better than that."

" What are those low brick-walls you are running one above the other, on the hill-side ? "

" That is our open-air 'hot-house.' "

" A rather big one. What on earth do you mean ? "

" Those bricks that our men have made, will catch and store the heat of the sun's rays. The vines on the top of each wall, the strawberries at foot, with currants

clambering about, will bear fruit a month before any are
ripe elsewhere. We shall be able to put the choicest
fruits on the earliest market. This oval we call our
village green. This is the cricketing-pitch, these again
the football-goals."

"The children, evidently, appreciate the swings and
merry-go-rounds."

"We like them to be happy while they can. Work
enough lies before them. We run our school on our
own lines."

"How so?"

"No home-lessons. All learn a little Latin, some
Greek, to exercise their minds. History and geography
we teach them together, and Christianity with morality."

"I suppose you impart the rudiments of science,
agriculture, cooking, and the like in these model schools
of yours?"

"No, that follows in due course. First, we open the
minds and hearts of the children, teach them how and
why to work. Technical instruction is, then, easily
imparte.1 later on. The youths and young women come,
for two hours every evening, to receive instruction in the
more practical or in the higher arts. What do you think
of our church, just finished?" continued the doctor,
"with its little peal of bells, sanctuary, and parson's
house complete?"

"I should have thought they could have done without
that luxury for a while. You must have quite enough to
do to change the conditions of life as you are doing,
without troubling about faiths and feelings."

"I do not know about that. I am strongly convinced
that only by improving the moral standing of men,
striking the highest chords in their nature, can we hope
to ameliorate their social condition. I want them to act

as brothers. To do that, they must first realize that they are sons."

"Then you make the poor beggars go to church, whether they like it or no?"

"Not in the least. There is no compulsion in the matter. As a fact, nearly all *do* attend the Sunday service; some the one before breakfast, some the short daily prayer at seven; but of course not many do *that*."

"And who's your parson?"

"Yonder he is, the Rev. Frank Brown—hoeing up his potatoes. That little boy helping is the youngster I ran over last year."

"Is that broad-shouldered fellow in mole-skin trousers, with his coat off and that huge hat on, the parson? Not a very conventional one."

"No, but a really fine fellow. He'll box with you, ride with you, or farm; but he is devoted to these people and their work. You must meet him another time. Now we must be getting back if you are to have your ride with the ladies. That building in course of erection is to be our hall and theatre. Adjoining it you see the stores, which we keep well supplied, though no money passes over the counter. It's only open two hours a day; we spend the maximum of time producing, the minimum in doling out. Next you see the butchery, bakery, blacksmiths' and wheelwrights' shops. Pretty busy, are they not?"

"By St. Patrick they are. I confess you have done wonders. Now tell me how you accomplish it?"

"Simply by believing in these people, as you draw devotion from your very horses and dogs. Sympathy is the talisman that opens the barred treasure-house of the heart, and helps a man to rise to the best that is in him."

CHAPTER XII.

WHEELS WITHIN WHEELS.

" Loveliness
Needs not the foreign aid of ornament,
But is when unadorned, adorned the most."
THOMSON.

"Mechanism is not always to be our hard taskmaster, but one
day to be our pliant, all-ministering servant."
THOMAS CARLYLE.

"Co-operation rightly understood is but the endeavour to realize
in economic life the social ideal of Christianity."
C. W. STUBBS.

So, with alternating success and failure, two years sped
away. The Courtenays, father and son, were, in different
ways, admirably adapted to educe its highest product from
labour. The doctor was powerfully charged with that
human magnetism that instinctively unites man to man,
and gives some the leadership. His was a touch, we
call tact, that could turn dust into gold, and strike the
best chords in human hearts. It enabled him to select
his agents, as by instinct, and to apply the labour of
each man's hands and brains to its most appropriate
occupation.

His very confidence in man, his belief in the better
nature lying somewhere, as he supposed, in the breasts
of all, rendered him liable to deception, and subjected
him to bitter disappointment. The atmosphere, how-

ever, of trust and hopefulness in which he moved caused many with whom he was brought in contact to surpass themselves, and surprise their friends.

His son, of a somewhat similar disposition, impulsive, warm-hearted, brimful of the cheerfulness and frankness of youth, played his part easily and naturally. Seemingly on terms of perfect equality, he mingled with those amongst whom his lot was cast without spice of patronage or condescension, invested merely with that native dignity education and worth impart, hedging round true nobility from encroachments familiarity might encourage.

One thing young Travers did think and puzzle much about. Not so much the social as the mechanical question. Years of practical apprenticeship in the workshops of Germany, together with observation in America, had constituted him a resourceful engineer of the modern school. So much—little as yet—that could be acquired of electrical science and its practical application, he was conversant with. Machinery, he recognized, had served to augment the social inequalities that he with his father deplored. His aim was to cause science and machinery to serve for once the people's good.

"You band the men together, see that their hearts beat right," he would say to his father; "I will put a subtle power into their hands that shall yet again redouble their strength."

At the head of the valley the stream from the mountains passed through two or three reed-covered lagoons—the banks converging towards a narrow inlet. There the waters leapt and dashed over the huge boulders that spanned the gorge.

"Bubble on, pretty brook," the young engineer had said, "you, like all else here, must henceforth work,

turning all the wheels—and they shall be many—of
Mimosa Vale."

A breastwork of masonry was thrown across the
gorge by merely filling up, as it were, the gaps between
the boulders through which the waters had swept for
centuries.

The central aperture was raised and built into a race.
The lagoons were expanded into one great lake by the
addition of six feet of water. A huge wheel was set
across the stream at the falls, and eventually the needed
power secured.

"'There's not more nor enough to turn one mill, and
how he's a-goin' to work a dozen, I doesn't know," was
the criticism of the villager who acted as head-mason.

Turbine and dynamo were, however, duly set up, and
the mystic wires that should convey the electric power
run from gum-tree to gum-tree down the busy vale.

There in due course, without steam, smoke, or noise,
the factories were at work. Here the saw- and flour-
mills, there the butter factory and creamery. Alongside,
spaces were set apart for the projected fruitery plant,
woollen factory, canning, evaporating, and other works.
Far down the valley, between avenues and cottages, ran
mystic wire carrying light and power to every house,
and propelling the cars or trucks that glided as needed
to the wharf on the main lake.

A connection was now in course of construction
between the lower lake, "Grassmere," and the Silverbourne river, five miles distant. The wide, high-banked
creek presented few engineering difficulties. One lock,
where the creek debouched into the river, would throw
back along the creek, whose fall was very slight, sufficient water to float the steamers of light draught
proposed to be used. To preserve the banks it was

proposed to haul the steamers through the canals by electric power supplied by an overhead line in course of erection.

After lunch one Saturday afternoon Travers set forth in his dog-cart to inspect the works while operations were suspended owing to the weekly half-holiday. As he passed down the main avenue the scene that presented itself was an animated one. All hands were busy at home before the football match of the day began. Some forming paths, others setting up rustic sheds and bowers, turning the generous waters to the roots of melons and "Turk's-heads," that spread like vegetable octopi over every available space, between giant rows of Pandrosa tomatoes, clumps of arrowroot, and lines of many-hued herbs. Another man was extending the shelter that protected a valuable and flourishing crop of mushrooms. Everything betokened special culture and scientific treatment that spoke volumes for the lectures delivered each night by the resident experts.

Potatoes, fodder, wheat, &c., were grown by the hundred acres on the common land, while the individual settlers were encouraged to apply their long spare hours at home to the raising of the products that experts indicated as most profitable.

About verandahs, over rustic archways, bowers of dolichos and impomœa had already found footing, to be swept away, like other vigorous make-shifts, when more worthy growths were ready to take their place.

Valuable prizes, to be competed for each year, had been offered for the best appointed home, most neatly kept garden, for wisest application of land, greatest progress and quickest returns. The agricultural, horticultural, and poultry show of the settlement, to be held in a few months, offered liberal inducement for all to produce the best returns from choicest seeds and plants, supplied upon application at the store.

Travers, passing a gay word with here a dame and there a busy settler, reined in his steed before one of the farmeries that promised well for more than one of the coveted prizes.

At the wicket was a little archway covered with quick-growing creepers—a seat on either side—like some ancient minster's lych-gate built up anew in a southern field. Within were paths of whitest gravel, borders of yellow-green native pine, festoons of blue sarsaparilla and golden clematis stretching from bower to bower. An acacia hedge was in full bloom. Behind the cottage lay the trimmest of vegetable gardens, with beds of flowers for the market. Beside the house was a fernery of wattles, half covered with creepers, while round the four acres ran a hedge of walnuts, almonds, and cherry plums.

"Good-morning, Miss Elms," said the young man, as, leaving his horse with Willie, he sauntered along the pathway. The girl stepped from the bed in which she had been lashing a tall dahlia to its stake. Hurriedly, by magic—as is a woman's way—she let fall the skirt pinned round her slender waist.

"I must not shake hands, Mr. Travers, mine are too dirty. You should not pop in upon us on 'arbour day' without notice," the maid complained.

"You ought not then to train your creepers and plant those pepper-trees to shut out all view of the roadway, if you do not desire visitors to come unannounced. 'Pon my word, your garden is becoming like Fair Rosamond's Bower. Lord Tennyson's retreat at Freshwater is such a one as yours will ere long be."

"You are always welcome," said the girl, with a pretty

blush, as she stood with her white dress and broad-brimmed hat, suggestive of Tennyson's "Gardener's Daughter." So Travers thought, but then he was becoming unduly interested in the pretty young villager.

"May I pick some of this heliotrope, my favourite flower?"

"Certainly; let me make you a little buttonhole, of my best," and as they talked she proceeded to set together rosebud, mignonette and violet, daphne and maidenhair. Tying them with cotton from her rustic work-table near at hand, she presented the miniature bouquet to the young man.

"Why does this suggest the Tribuna of the Uffizzi?" he asked.

"I thought the gallery was called the 'Pitti,'" said the girl.

"No; that is further on—but have you ever been there?"

"Unfortunately not, only I was lately reading Ruskin's *Makers of Florence*, and Mrs. Oliphant's and Trollope's charming descriptions of the city. But why is my humble gift like the Tribuna? That is the little salon at Florence, is it not, in which the choicest masterpieces are gathered?"

"Yes; and this little nosegay contains, in the same way, the fairest flowers of your mimosa garden. Can you tell me where your father is? I called to ascertain."

"I thought you came to see me," the maiden was about to reply, but refrained. She remembered that in the world his position was other than hers.

"We have nothing to do with the 'outer world,'" he would urge, when the Sergeant's daughter gave expression to such thoughts.

"My father has not returned," said the girl with

some anxiety. " He should have been here an hour ago."

" I am going to the works. Let me have the pleasure of taking you. You have never properly seen the lake yet, from the hillside, which we are going to call Fiesole."

" No ; I should be delighted to do so, but——"

" But what, Miss Elms ? "

" I don't know."

" Well, I do. You think people will talk. Why should I not take whom I like for a drive ? Such nonsense ! We have come here to escape Mrs. Grundy. We refused her a block, and left her lamenting in town."

" But discretion is not nonsense."

" Look here, Gwyneth—I beg pardon—Miss Elms—you know I hate ' mistering ' and ' missing ' every one, as we are everlastingly doing. May I call you Gwyneth ? "

The girl hesitated.

" Perhaps you might, when we are by ourselves."

" Gwyneth, what you and I do deliberately is right ; that makes it so for us. Now, please, come at once like a good girl. I ought to be on my way."

" Just let me run and put on my bonnet."

" Pray do not. I want you to come just as you are—the ' Gardener's Daughter.' You cannot improve upon Tennyson. Shall you leave the front door open ? " he asked.

" Of course. Our doors and windows have no bolts. Happily we have left such insignia of modern life behind us. None here have need to steal—nor the inclination.—You said Willie might come," exclaimed Gwyneth as she passed out. She desired that some one should play propriety.

In a moment they were speeding down the avenue ;

she in front, Willie behind, looking particularly proud of himself.

"Manager's daughter's getting up in the world," remarked Mrs. Smith to Mrs. Robinson, as the trio dashed past the garden in which the housewives were working. "What 'll Dick Malduke say? I believe she keeps company with he."

"Not her. He's made a fool of himself about her long afore we come here."

"Well, he's a nasty-tempered brute. I hope there'll be no mischief over the girl, for she's good-hearted, and clever too."

"Yes, and handsome. See the way she sits in the trap and talks like a lady at her ease. And doesn't that big hat set her off now?"

So Dames Smith, Brown, Jones, and Robinson, with many others, watched the pair as they dashed along the two miles of cottage-lined avenue.

CHAPTER XIII.

DROWNING THEM LIKE RATS.

" Plough of Nature !   Hånd of God !
Fallow deep the hills eternal !
Bless for these the mountain sod
  With full fruit and pasture vernal !
Somewhere in the by-and-by,
  Sounds of distant life are humming ;
They are nearing, though not nigh,
  And the day of homes is coming."
                    Australian Poets, II. H. BLACKHAM.

"High in the far-off glens rose thin blue curls from the homesteads ;
Softly the low of the herds, and the pipe of the outgoing herds-
    man,
Fled to her ear on the water, and melted her heart into weeping."
                    KINGSLEY, *Andromeda.*

As Travers and Gwyneth turned along the hill-side,
who should the unconventional couple meet but Hilda
and Maud, riding with Larry O'Lochlan. Both parties
were moving too rapidly for it to be marked that they
did not pull up. Neither desired to do so. The men
doffed their hats gaily. The women looked at their
horses' heads demurely.

"Who is that young 'Duchess of Devonshire' with
the buttercups round her hat?" asked Larry of Hilda,
when they were well out of ear-shot.

"A young person from the village that my brother
has picked up. Not very considerate of him. I believe
she's respectable enough."

" Do not speak of her in that way," interjected Maud.
" She is really a good clever girl. I often meet her."

" But that is no reason why our brother should demean
himself by driving her out."

"You know he has peculiar notions," said Maud,
"concerning social distinctions. With respect to them
he regards only education and character. After all, we
are by ourselves in this community."

" She makes a pretty picture, at any rate," remarked
Larry.

" Pretty pictures should be hung up at home, in their
proper place," replied Hilda, with undisguised vexation.
" But everything's topsy-turvy here," she continued. " I
wish we were back in the city, and had never seen the
place."

At the top of a ridge, as the dog-cart still ascended,
Travers drew rein to afford his companion an opportunity
of observing the view.

"See what a year or two has effected since you descended this hill the day of the Hegira ! "

" It is beautiful. I thought so that evening, when I
looked on the sleeping valley with its clumps of tents.
It is changed as if by magic. How picturesque the two
long avenues with the crops and vines and pastures
beyond ! The lakes alone are the same."

" They will appear animated before long."

" I do admire those boulders and these light-hued trees
—what do you call them ? "

" That is the native cherry. Has it not a soft yellow-
green leaf? That a pine. Those sombre-looking sentinels,
she-oaks. This again an apple-tree."

In the scattered gum-trees, white with flower, parrots
of rosy hue were chattering, darting from bloom to bloom
like bees about the honeysuckle. Below, as if watching

for the crops to ripen, a cloud of cockatoos were shrieking—now sweeping in a white mass upon the plain, now
swarming again about another clump of trees, like flakes
of snow on a mountain fir. In the pauses between the
shrieks and chatter of the feathery tribe, sounds of children's laughter, the lowing of cattle, shouts of animated
groups watching the football contest on the village green
far below, arose, as if a few hundred yards away, on the
clear air softened and sweet as from another world.
Wreaths of smoke ascended lazily from three hundred
scattered cottages, the perfume of flowers from a hundred
gardens mingled with the stronger odours of eucalypts on
the hill-side.

"Better than the crowded slums and dreary artisans'
quarters of most of our cities," Travers suggested.

His companion was too moved to reply at once.
Feelings of gratitude and joy were filling her breast, in
which the light of a new-born love was kindling.

"I should like to live here," she said at length as if to
herself, "and look always on that scene, watch the trees
we have planted grow, see the first-fruits of our labours
bearing down the boughs, and all the promise of the land
unfolding and fulfilled."

"So you shall," her companion had almost replied;
checking himself he remarked—

"Strange to say, I have selected this very site for
myself. Already I have a lodge erected beyond those
trees. Some day, when our ships literally come home,
and lie, not two or three, in that broad lake, I shall build
a bungalow palace on this hill-side and watch the development of our village of the vale."

"Do you remember," suddenly asked the maiden,
seeking to change the conversation, "Carlyle's 'Everlast-
ing Yea,' in his *Sartor Resartus* ?"

"Aye, well I do, one of the finest chapters the sage ever dreamed."

"You remember," she continued, "the world-sick Teufelsdröckh ascending the mountain-side, breathing disappointment and defiance with every step, and, looking down on a scene such as this, being softened at last by the sights and sounds of a smiling hamlet. Beautiful it was to sit there musing and meditating," repeated the girl. "I think I know the passage by heart. 'In the high table-lands in front of the mountains; over me the roof, the azure dome . . . And then to fancy the fair castles that stood sheltered in these mountain hollows, or, better still, the straw-roofed cottages, wherein stood many a mother baking bread, with her children around her—all hidden and protectingly folded up in the valley folds.' I forget the rest," said the maiden, hesitatingly. "You remember," she continued after a pause, "the homely descriptions, and, further on, that pathetic passage—may I try to quote it?—'With other eyes could I now look upon my fellow-men; with an infinite love; with an infinite pity. Art thou not tried and beaten with stripes, even as I? Art thou not so weary, so heavy-laden, and thy bed of rest is but the grave? Oh, my brother, my brother, why cannot I shelter thee in my bosom, and wipe away all tears from thy eyes? The poor Earth, with her poor joys, was now my needy mother. Man, with his so mad wants and so mean endeavours, had become the dearer to me; and even for his suffering and his sins I now first named him Brother.'"

"Thank you very much," replied Travers, as they drove on. "I shall always associate this familiar scene with that passage. There is much that is soothing and invigorating in the prospect of Nature's peace, especially when evidences of man's domestic joys and husbandry are prominent. The village, nestling at the foot of the mountain, has a thousand more interests hidden away about it, than all the snowy peaks, giddy ravines, and dazzling splendours of lonely mountain heights. Though world on world, in myriad myriad, roll round us . . . What know we greater than the soul ? . . . than man ? Yet no life—is it not strange?—is so stunted and distraught at the present day as the social."

"You are going to alter that here, at any rate," she said, cheerfully. "In this valley, human existence is not to be the only sorrowful failure in creation."

"I hope not," he said, thoughtfully, flicking a fly from his leader's back.

"Whose sheep are those sweeping round the hill beyond the lake ? " asked the girl. "What yellow specks the lambs appear ! How distinctly the bleating of the little truants is carried across the water ! "

"Do you not recognize your own property ? " replied Travers, laughing.

"I ? I have not one lamb to my name."

"No great loss. The sweet pet-lamb is a myth ; the reality has cream-clogged chin, body like a child's toy-horse, stiff legs to fit a hogget. When it matures into something comely, it ungratefully takes itself off to the flocks. But do you not know that those sheep are yours ? "

"The property of the village you mean."

"Yes, and a very valuable one too, I assure you," replied Travers.

"But the profit will be your father's."

"Not at all. He will charge a nominal interest, that is all. By degrees his share will be purchased, and you will own the entire property."

"I wonder where father is," said the girl after a time, with evident anxiety. "We ought to have met him."

G

" I will find him out in two minutes, if you like."

" How can you?   We are, I suppose, five miles from home."

"Hold the reins, please.   We'll soon ring him up."

"Please do not laugh at me, I really am anxious."

"I am not joking, as you will see."

From beneath the seat of the dog-cart the young engineer drew a small machine, which, leaping from the vehicle, he attached to the top rail of the wire fence, and began vigorously turning a handle.

"What are you doing?" cried Gwyneth, laughing, while Willie, forgetting himself, stood up at the back and peered over Gwyneth's shoulder with amazement.

"Why, it's a coffee-grinder, I do believe," the lad whispered.

A little bell began to ring.

" Are you there?" inquired Travers, bending over an almost inaudible disc.

"Who's speaking?"

"Oh, my office, is it?   Ask whether Mr. Elms has returned."

In a few moments the words came—"He has just arrived."

"Tell him we shall be home by six.   Has the mail arrived?"

"No other news?"

" In the Lovibanks Paddock?"

" Send a man to repair it."

" That's all."

Leaping into the trap, disposing the instrument under the seat, the dog-cart was in a moment whirling again on its way.

" Your father has returned," reported Travers; "I have told him we shall be back by six.   Good sales reported from Melbourne. The telephone shows a great gap in the fence—a fire perhaps—and some trees fallen."

"Do you mean to say you can telephone all about the place?"

"As readily as in a city. The top wire of all the fences outside, and of some cross ones, like this, are rendered continuous."

"But there must be many breaks."

"No; a slight connecting wire carries the current round the straining-post—such as that one there; do you see?"

In a few moments the head of the lake was reached. Handing the reins to his companion, Travers began inspecting the dam, while Gwyneth surveyed the scene and chatted with Willie. The lad, restrained hereto by Travers' presence, opened his heart as to the beauties of the place—the new life, and the telephone, that seemed to impress him much. There was only one trouble, he was no nearer finding his father.

"I wish I could go and look for him, miss."

"But you would not leave me and Mimosa Vale?"

"No; but I'd like some one belonging to me, in all the world."

"So I have caught you, have I?" said a voice from behind, as a man, with a gun across his shoulder, stood before them. Gwyneth started involuntarily.

"Oh, it's only Dick," said the girl, recognizing her quondam lover. "You quite startled me. What brings you here?"

"Rabbits!" was the laconic reply; "but I didn't expect to meet lovers."

"I do not know what you mean," replied the girl, reddening.

"Yes you do; and more than that, you know what it is to play fast and loose with two at the same time."

"You cannot think what you are saying."

"Don't I?" was the reply. "Mark you, he shall never have you. Not content with robbing us of the reward of our labour, these capitalists would steal our very flesh and blood."

"You are talking riddles."

"Then this is the solution of them. You shall never be the wife of that man, Gwyneth," he continued, with a faltering voice. "We have known each other since we were children. Are you going to cast me off for this squatter's son? Consider well. I have a lot of good—or a lot of bad—in me."

The girl was moved. She had never given her affections to this strange man. She had despised him. Had she taken enough trouble to convince him that his suit was hopeless? Perhaps not. In truth she had never seriously regarded it.

Willie had wandered away, plucking flowers. The young man put down his gun, took the girl's hand, and said hurriedly—

"Gwyneth, dear Gwyneth, is it to be heaven or hell in my heart? Do you choose poverty or wealth? A plain man who will love you, or a gilded creature who will play with you, and then cast you aside?"

Gwyneth had had time to recover herself. Withdrawing her hand she replied—

"Richard Malduke, you must relinquish these wild fancies. You force me to say that I do not love you; that I never did, that I never can. But let us be friends, Dick, and not make fools of ourselves."

"Then you love that man?"

She was about to deny the allegation, but the lie she would utter refused to pass her lips.

"That is no business of yours," she replied.

"Is it not?" he exclaimed bitterly. "It used to be," he hissed out, "when you were only a plain carpenter's daughter. Now that you are a rich young rogue's plaything——"

Scarcely were the words uttered, when down came the wattle-stick, with which the girl had been toying, across the young man's face, leaving from forehead to cheek its fiery mark.

Malduke started forward. At that moment, Travers, intent on his work, appeared at the end of the dam.

"Blow for blow a man cannot give, not in one way—perhaps he can in another," muttered the socialist, as, catching up the gun, and shaking his fist at the trembling girl, he disappeared down the bank.

Gwyneth sat on a log and mused. Enraged at the insult to which she had been subjected, she did not regret the summary chastisement she had inflicted, but a sense of danger impending for herself and for others crept over her.

"What is the matter, Gwyneth? You seem excited. Your hand is shaking," said Travers, approaching.

"Oh, nothing. A rabbit started up beside me; I suppose I am nervous."

"Is that all? Come for a stroll down the bank."

The girl begged to return home, but seeing Travers intent as a matter of duty upon examining the canal, and not wishing to be left alone, she went with him.

The two were soon at the bottom of the works.

Thirty feet above them the dam towered; on either side the smooth sides rose perpendicularly.

" I suppose the dam could not break away?" the girl remarked.

" I should hope not. The flood would swallow us up in an instant, like rats in a hole. But there is no fear of that," he said with a laugh.

Further on between the sheer walls the pair proceeded. A head, unobserved, appeared above the works.

"Yes, 'like rats in a hole,'" Malduke muttered. " Into 'the valley of death' they are wandering. How easily I could do it—if it was only him! If she were out of the way. Why so?"

He wiped his brow, on which drops of perspiration were hanging; blood appeared on his palm.

"She struck the blow, and walks there, tripping beside him—the smooth-faced fool. It shall be their last lovers' walk. She's brought it on herself!"

Picking up a long iron rod, the man stepped on to a tree that had fallen into the lake, and plunged the bar into the soft side of the dam just below the water-level. Entering a short distance it stuck in the damp loam. Seizing a heavy maul that lay on the bank, he drove the bar through the bank until it protruded on the other side. Working the rod backwards and forwards, Malduke succeeded in withdrawing it a few feet; but further out it would not come. The sound of a footstep on the bank caused him to steal along the dam, and hide himself in the scrub on the hillside.

Willie, who had returned from his flower quest, had caught Travers' remark as the lovers descended into the gorge: "We should be drowned like rats." To the child's horror water was even now spurting from a hole in the narrow embankment. Every instant the stream increased in volume. Willie cooeyed and called, but the distant pair could not hear. Throwing himself into the slush the child literally battled with the waters. Finding at length the mouth of the orifice, he pressed his tiny hands upon the aperture. For an instant they held back the gurgling waters. Looking round, Willie could see the two, unconscious of their danger, walking on further into the canal bed. When would they turn? Hours it seemed, as he struggled with the swelling flood.

Should he not escape while he could? The lake level was feet above him. His hands, his knees were stiff. He was drenched with the oozing waters. What! leave his friends to be drowned like rats! With redoubled energy the child held back the angry, baffled tide.

A watcher on the bank raised a gun to his shoulder.

"The darned little cuss. He'll give them time to get back yet! He *is* game though," he muttered, lowering his gun.

The waters shooting now from the fissure almost washed the child away. Now he was hurled down the bank. Now struggled up again, fighting with the flood for the life of his friends. Nails and knees were torn and bleeding. New fissures, through which the waters were gushing, appeared running upward from the orifice and enclosing a solid triangular mass of embankment.

"Run for your life, lad," rang another voice from the bushes. Unheeding, raising himself on tiptoe, pressing his whole weight against the mass that quivered under his hands, he stood there, staggering, dripping, bleeding; deluged with slush and clay as if holding back the mass that was quivering above him. He was eleven years old. Horace Bellmaine was younger by half, yet the words apply—

"You sob and splutter out your soul; with baby gasps you strive
To play the man as best you can, thou flounderer of five.
D'ye know we ask no harder task, no sterner test of worth,
From those who carve a country's fate—the men who salt the earth."

A few moments more, and with a roar as of the surf breaking through a crevice in the rocks, the body of earth was belched forth. The waters rushed headlong into the chasm below. The child disappeared in the seething waters.

"Great God! the dam has burst," exclaimed Travers, seeing the solid wall of water coming down the cutting towards them like a sudden flood in a northern Bilabong. Seemingly there was no escape. Gwyneth, who had not recovered from her former excitement, seeing the body of water approaching, sank in a swoon.

Seizing the unconscious girl in his arms, leaping on to a bank of clay that had been left obtruding, the young man flung his burden on some bushes that were growing on a ledge a few feet above. Just as he himself clutched a sapling, the waters roaring down the ravine washed the clay from beneath his feet, flooding the works twenty feet deep! For some seconds the young man hung suspended above the water-floods, then with a violent effort flung himself, as only an athlete could do, across the sapling. Lifting Gwyneth on to the top of the bank, he began to chafe her hands and call her by name. In a few moments the girl was sufficiently recovered to walk unaided.

As they returned, and Travers was wondering how the embankment came to give way, thanking heaven meanwhile for their miraculous escape, they came upon a man with a child upon his knees. The stranger was rocking himself, weeping and laughing by turns. The boy was drenched. Face and hands and legs were blood-marked.

"He's coming round! He's coming to! My son! My son!" the man was saying as the pair approached.

"It's Willie! How did he get hurt?" asked Travers, as the child opened his eyes.

"How did he get hurt? How did he ever escape?" the stranger asked. "You should have seen him standing there in the rushing waters pushing back the bank as he seemed to think. I was coming down the track there," he continued, "and called out, 'Run for your life.' It was too late, the dam burst that moment. I stood over the roaring abyss and looked for the lad. That minute he comes up, then goes down again. I hesitated to jump in. 'He's done for, anyhow, I thought,' and a man could not swim in them waters. Then up he comes again. 'He's some one's poor child,' I thought, 'I'll try anyhow,' and in I jumps. I don't know how I got him out. I was nigh done myself, and swallowed gallons. I was dazed with the waters whirling me about. Just then he almost knocked agin me. I grabbed him. Round we goes again; somehow out of the eddy at last. With a last stroke I gets to the shore. Then the rummiest thing of all comes. Makes me think I'm in a dream. I washes his face and looks, and I sees—it's my son."

Again the poor fellow began to rock the lad in his arms and to weep like a child.

"How he got there at all, I don't know; I left him in town."

"You must be mistaken," said Travers, who had not heard the child's story; "but never mind, come and get him into the trap."

Willie was now recovering; he rubbed his eyes.

"Am I awake?" he said, looking round bewildered. "I thought you was drownded, miss. I seed yous two walkin' on and on—you'd not come back nor wait for me—along to the gates of Paradise they singed about at t' hospital. The only thing was, you was going down, down, somehow, 'stead of up above."

Willie rubbed his eyes again, and stared up at the rough head bent over him in wonder.

"I was dreamin' I was dead too, and the angels was turnin' me round and round to see if I was fit to go along wi' they, I suppose." He tried to laugh. "Just as we was crossin' Jordan, and the water was mighty deep, I sees my father. He catches hold on me—and—I—forgets the rest."

Again the child gazed with a distant look into the rugged face above him. He sat up.

"Blowed if it ain't my father, be we live or be we dead."

Recovered at length, the lad leaping up flung his arms about the dripping, dust-stained neck, exclaiming—

"S'help me Bob, I do believe, my dear old dad at last."

"It must be he," whispered Gwyneth to Travers. "You know the child had lost his father, and was always longing to find him."

The pair were much affected when they heard of Willie's strenuous efforts to save their lives. Hurrying him to the dog-cart, and hastily telephoning for a gang to repair the embankment, the party rapidly drove back to the village.

Willie insisted that he had heard hammering behind the dam, and had seen a man slip away into the bushes. Travers was inclined to treat lightly the story, of which the lad had a very hazy idea, owing doubtless to the mental strain and physical shock to which he had been subjected. Gwyneth heard the words, and pondered them in her heart.

That night, however, there was rejoicing in the hospitable abode of Jim and his wife. Chattering and exclaiming, they received father and son who had been " dead and were alive again, lost and were found."

CHAPTER XIV.

ALEC'S WHISKY STOPPED.

> " Man he loved
> As man, and to the mean and the obscure,
> And all the homely in their homely works,
> Transferred a courtesy which had no air
> Of condescension."   WORDSWORTH.

FRANK BROWN was one of an army the nineteenth
century has enrolled, crusaders who, at home, spend
their days fighting " for Christ and Holy Land "—their
England ; knights who walk abroad, in crowded narrow
streets, " redressing human wrong " ; " Hearts of Oak,"
upon whose homely deeds of love no earthly lustre
shines ; work-day philanthropists seeking, in the sphere
of their own life, to work out the social problems others
in words dilate upon.

On the river and cricket-field, on platform, in pulpit,
Frank Brown had distinguished himself. The fire, however, that inflamed his breast and flashed in his eye,
kindled by concern for sinning and sorrowing outcasts of
Church and nation, whose unequal lot he grieved over,
impelled him to a life far removed from the conventional
one in which he had sought to expend his ardour.

The ordinary pastoral work of hunting up parishioners,
to augment congregations, and swell collections ; the
weekly preaching, to order, a discourse to interest or
gratify; for the moment, a small circle of self-centred

patrons; the preferment-seeking, brother-grudging, heresy-hunting proclivities of a prevalent type of Churchmanship, he "could not away with." Lack of sympathy in his brethren drove him back upon himself and his ideals. Upon One especially. There was a Life that had been, had given impulse to his. He would live it again. He would get back to the childhood of Christianity, drink of its fountain-springs, and fired by its enthusiasm for humanity, its broad brotherhood, its spirit of unselfishness and simplicity, he would seek in his own sphere to live the life rather than prate the parrot-cry.

He was young, and he was wrong. Beneath all the unattractive, repellent exterior of much modern Church life and charitable endeavour, their lies a vast substratum of renewing, regenerating influence. With the impetuosity of youth he stayed not to probe beneath the surface. The men who led the multitude, who talked of manhood's rights and human wrongs, who brought forth each their special panacea for relief of the social disorder they magnified—legislator, socialist, philosophical-radical—all seemed to lack earnestness and sincerity. What did they care? Whom did they love? In what did they believe? For himself he would seek a new scene where perchance facility might be afforded for working out his ideal.

The venture of his friend the doctor offered this opportunity. Wedding himself once more to the Church, vowing before the altar abstinence for others' sake, perpetual celibacy that his heart might be single, Frank relinquished his portion of prominence and promise, and cast in his lot with the villagers of the vale.

A "prophet's chamber" at the White House was offered, with provision for a stipend that should not leave him a loser.

None of this he would have. His lot should be with

his people. With them he wrought, with his own hands, to put up the little Hermitage beside the church. Himself, with aid that was pressed upon him, he fenced and sowed and planted the comely little God's-acre that smiled around the Hermitage and village sanctuary. In all things he would share with others. His rations he would draw from the store. For worldly means he would be dependent upon his own cultivation and live stock. As he worked with or moved amongst his flock, he preached unspoken sermons. His unselfishness silently rebuked the spirit of envy and greed that, born of a vicious system of competition, evidenced itself at every turn in the words and bearings of his people.

In his suburban parish the young vicar had taken interest in a simple couple. Old Alec and his wife, like many other humble folk, almost worshipped the ground on which the "young parson" walked.

Alec was a tall, well-set old soldier, for years trusted servant of the colonel whose memory he revered. The old man was honest, strictly religious, good-natured to a fault; without an enemy in all the world, save himself. The Company of whose drill-room he was caretaker spoiled him. The gay, thoughtless militiamen pressed whisky upon the genial attendant, then laughed at his queer muddled talk.

His wife Jinnie, some five feet high, was one of those over-careful, highly-respectable little people who, in excess of zeal for probity, impel so often to recklessness. Jinnie scolded, starved, locked up her six-foot lord, when he returned "the worse for liquor" to the little picture of a garden and model of a home that Jinnie's frugality and Alec's industry had established. Alec smiled when assailed, submitted patiently to "correction," but persevered in his evil course.

"He went on Sunday to the church, and sat among the boys," and, on Monday, to the drill-room, to forget his heart-felt contrition, and to accept, to his ruin, the "oft proffered" whisky. He went from bad to worse. The choice plants nurtured with such care were sold to pay the rent. The prize fowls followed, leaving the back-yard and ingeniously constructed outhouses, once so animated, desolate and silent as the grave. The old clock that had stood "ninety years" and more, in humble homes on the Border, vanished; dark, curious-wrought furniture, once so oiled and cared for, followed suit.

Friends who loved the old couple exerted their utmost to save them. Well-meaning people dragged the old man to temperance meetings, and compelled him, when he knew not what he did, to "sign the pledge"; others secured his "conversion" in similar mood, and with like result. Alec thanked his friends, went out—and had "a liquor up."

Frank Brown spent many an hour in seeking to make Alec soberer of habit, and Jinnie sweeter in temper.

One sweltering afternoon the young clergyman dropped in as he passed, regarding with sorrow the desolation that reigned around. Jinnie sat repairing a pair of the old soldier's pants.

"Never too late to mend," remarked the visitor brightly, as he observed that already the garments consisted more of patch than of pristine propriety.

"It is 'too late' at least for my old man to mend," replied Jinnie with a deep sigh. "Look at him there—the beast!"

Stretched on the sofa, last remaining joy of the once good stock of furniture, the warrior lay. Only a shirt covered his still muscular frame. He had found the "inner chamber" unduly close, and had crept forth to complete his "sleeping it off" in a cooler quarter.

"Get up there, you drunken loafer!" cried Jinnie. Seizing a broom the indignant little woman, as if to give vent to her feelings, rushed to the couch of the sleeping giant, and began to belabour his almost nude nether limbs. Slowly Alec opened his eyes, and smiled as was his wont. Putting forth his arm, he sought languidly to parry the furious blows of his irate spouse.

"Not so hard, lassie—not so hard!" he protested: that was all.

Frank Brown seized the opportunity of making a last appeal before he left the parish. He reasoned with, scolded, implored the erring weakling. He pointed out the ruin to which the home had been reduced, the wreck Jinnie was becoming. The old man, sobered now, hid his face in his hands, and sobbed like a child. For the first time in his life the soldier faltered—and yielded.

"You give me a chance, sir," he asked at length, with streaming eyes, "and I'll never touch a drop again. The old place is ruined, I can never mend here; but let me go with you, sir. I can plough and sow, and plant and farm, with the best of them. Take me out of this, and God will take me out of myself, and my sin."

Jinnie, quieter now, shook her head and rocked herself hopelessly.

"It's been coming on him forty year," she moaned. "He'll never give it up now."

"'Never too late to mend,' we were saying of the pants," the cleric suggested.

The old soldier seized the young man's hands.

"Did I ever tell a lie, sir, though I often made a beast o' mysel'?" He looked unflinchingly to his wife, to his priest. Even Jinnie could not lay untruthfulness to

his charge. "Have I ever, with all my foolishness,
blasphemed my God?" Again a pause and a look of
challenge. "Now, sir, you take us two. Jinnie 'll care
for you, and I'll be no hindrance. Take me and I'll swear
—I, Alec McDowl, who never broke his word to man
or God, when he know'd what he was doing, as I do
now—I'll swear never to touch a drop again till my dying
day."

And he never did!

The Book was fetched : the vow taken. Even Jinnie
was impressed and hopeful for once. The curly grey
head of the veteran was bowed on the table, as the
young clergyman sealed the oath with a prayer.

Till, again, he prayed, and himself wept, long years
after, beside the lifeless form of his faithful servant, old
Alec kept his vow.

Another lie given to that libel oft aimed against our
human nature and God's goodness, to the effect that the
inveterate drunkard cannot, midst new and helpful surroundings, by exerting his will, and drawing on another
source of strength, overcome his deadly habit, shake off
his fetters, and walk forth fearless and free.

The spirit of homeliness and comfort that had vanished
from Alec's abode, was transferred to the Hermitage
at Mimosa Vale. There Jinnie held gentle sway. She
cared for the creature comforts of "the young master"
with more effect than a host of hirelings would have done.
The parson's home was a model for his people, of clean-
liness and grace, and his garden, under Alec's care, of
order and beauty—as his life, of quietude and strength.
Alec got his potatoes in earlier, his crops off sooner,
than any one else ; his vines the right depth ; the
tender root of young fruit-trees he trailed gently over the

central mound of mould closing in the earth around, as though he were burying living treasures. As indeed he was. He generally contrived to make his plants grow and flowers bloom when neighbours lamented over failure. Years of soldiering had not impaired that mystic intimacy with Nature and her ways that the Northern farmer displays. Far and wide across the settlement old Alec's advice and aid were sought when there was a suspicion of vine or rose-cuttings being planted up-side down, when cows were contumacious, chickens caught the measles, or swine the mumps.

Nothing the old couple enjoyed more than, when supper, which they ate with their master, was cleared away, to stroll to the village green and " listen to the music."

Bantering youths and maidens sat about in groups, parents talking between the pieces of the day's doings in field and home, while children scampered in an outer circle of their own, or lay wearied at their parents' feet. The doctor, with pipe and smoking-cap, sauntering familiarly amongst the company, chatting here with a "boss" concerning some new fixing for the mill; there with head-gardener, or chief farm-hand, about the new Reaper-and-binder, or price of the early crop of tomatoes.

Alec and Jinnie seated themselves, one balmy evening, on a bench, beside Jim and his wife. The two "old hands," deeming themselves superior to the tyros at country work, looked curiously and critically upon the achievements of the villagers.

" How's the 'Jummies' looking, Jim?" asked Alec.

" All the world like the pictur' in the drawin'-room afore which t'old master died. They'll shear fine; but atween you and me and the post, that's a playthin' bit of a fence

H

they've put up t'other side the lake. The lambs is allus
in the corn; the postes be all rammed at t' top of t'
hole, 'stead of bottom." The old stockman chuckled
merrily as though echoing the last notes of the jackass in
the tree above.

" *You* didn't learn it all in a day, Jim," remonstrated
his wife. " It seems to me, you and Mr. McDowl thinks
you knows everythink. What do you say to that toon
now? You couldn't play the likes of that if you was
paid."

"They plays all right, but they won't make their
fortunes fiddlin'."

"Who said they would?" sharply demanded Jinnie.

The two cronies spake more low, since their wives
seemed not in sympathy with the drift of their conversation.

"It'll be a mighty busy time soon," continued Jim,
"harvesting and shearing at same time—and we've got
to do it all oursel's. There'll be some tar wantin', I'm
thinkin'."

" Lots of the young fellows *says* they can shear."

" I know their style. ' Rouseabouts ' and ' Pickers-up '
—and bad at that. They'll find it hot work this
season."

"They've done wonders all the same," claimed Alec.

" It's all along of the management. That's what's pulled
it through."

" There's one thing I'm afeared on."

"What's that?" asked Jim.

" It's the discipline. They don't like it. Leastways
some don't. They ben't used to it. It's ' go as you
please,' mostly, in town."

" Most on them means well and works well. But
they're easy led. They ben't soldiers ready to stand by

their guns and swear by their officers, and put up with a bit of bullying sometimes."

" I'm afeared they're feather-bed soldiers, a lot of them."

" They'd oughter pull it out," remarked Jim. " They've got a mighty good start."

" Their mill and machines work stunnin'; they're good at that. Them houses is fit for squatters."

" Eh, and mark you, it's a fine thing to be able to take it all away by canal and river to the sea. They do say the Store in town's well-nigh finished; that'll open people's eyes ! And two ships they've bought. Going to work everythink theyselves, and pocket all the profits."

" Couldna be no better idee," replied Alec. " It's bound to come." And the old man sang—

> " ' For a' that, an' a' that,
> It's comin' yet for a' that,
> When man to man, the warld o'er,
> Shall brithers be for a' that.'

" T' only thing is," continued Alec, " will these high-cock-a-doodle coves playing like children go through with the campaign ? They won't mutiny, will they ? "

" That's the danger," nodded Jim, significantly.

" See that fellow there they calls Malduke ? He means no good."

" I don't think as he do."

" See him gassin' with them simpletons who fancies theysel's. They're goin' to have a meetin' to-night ' to consider matters.' "

" That was a rummy business, that burstin' of the dam t'other night. There's somethin' behind that."

" See Mr. Travers talking and laughing with Elms's daughter. There'll be trouble over that. What do they want to bring love-affairs into a concern like this for ?

Love and foolishness is at the bottom of all smashes-up and breaks-down."

"Well, I do like that!" exclaimed Jinnie, who had caught the concluding sentence. Digging her elbow into her patient husband's side, she ejaculated—

"You was young once, and cared for some one too. For shame to talk like that, you hard-hearted old wretch!"

•   .

CHAPTER XV.

"IT'S LOVE THAT MAKES THE WORLD GO ROUND."

> "In peace, love tunes the shepherd's reed ;
> In war, he mounts the warrior's steed ;
> In halls, in gay attire is seen ;
> In hamlets, dances on the green.
> Love rules the court, the camp, the grove,
> And men below, and saints above ;
> For love is heaven, and heaven is love."—SCOTT.

" IT's perfectly disgraceful," remarked Hilda, vigorously thrusting a dahlia into the épergne of flowers she was arranging. "Travers ought to be ashamed of himself to be carrying on as he is doing with that village hussy." ·

" What has the poor boy been doing now ? " asked Maud, who stood at the other end of the dining-room table, "cutting out" some children's garments preparatory to the sewing-meeting at the Grotto.

" Doing ! " replied her sister, flinging aside disdainfully a huge "flag" bloom that had found its way amongst the flowers. " I might as well set this coarse thing into my specimen vase, as he seek to bring this brazen creature into our family."

" Hilda, you should not speak so strongly," interposed her sister. "It is unworthy of you. Miss Elms is a quiet, unassuming girl—as modest as she is beautiful."

"Then why," asked her sister, "does she encourage him so shamefully?"

"I have noted nothing very marked," replied her sister.

"You were not on the lake yesterday afternoon. I was, sailing with Larry——"

"And you object to Travers riding out with *his* friends?"

"But Larry is a gentleman. He will bring no disgrace on our name. Now that we are engaged, I suppose I may sometimes venture with him; even amongst all these prying eyes that I am getting to hate."

"For my part," replied Maud, "I rejoice in the life and movement that presents itself everywhere here."

"But you're a saint, Maud. You like common people. I confess I do not. But to return to the wretched rencontre. As we were gliding amongst the dingeys and skiffs, in which these spoilt people were disporting themselves as though all the lake belonged to them——"

"So it does."

"Maud, dear, do not interrupt me. Just as I was thinking how beautiful the scene was—here a boat-load of crowing children and smiling parents—there some lads learning to row—here a party of girls and young men bobbing under a jibboom——"

"I am sure they were all behaving themselves."

"Simply because they had to do so. They knew that if there was any shrieking or rudeness they would be ordered to shore by the ubiquitous Master of Ceremonies who was cruising round. It's no credit for them to behave themselves here; they have to do so."

"They like to," said Maud. "Public opinion is opposed to coarseness and vulgarity. I am sure the lake looked lovely."

"It did. Apart from the animated life on its surface——

the miles of golden harvest stretching up the valley amongst the creeper-covered cottages, with patches of cultivation about them; the mills in the distance; the terraced vines putting forth their first rich growth on the hill-sides—the scene was fair enough."

" Then why could you not enjoy it ? "

" Just as we hove-to, to watch the scratch eight, who should dash round the steam-launch, on which father and mother and the Dowlings with some Gumford people were standing, but a boat with that girl with a wide-brimmed hat—I'll confess rather becoming—at the tiller-ropes, and Travers pulling ! He passed close beside us, shipped oars, and began to wipe his brow and smile and nod at us in his provoking manner, as though nothing ever could disconcert or shame him."

" Why should it ? " interjected Maud.

" It spoiled the afternoon for me—the gold-and-green terraces became black—the sounds of merriment grated on my ears. I wished I was anywhere, and that Travers would take himself and his gardener's daughter out of my sight for ever." Hilda's eyes filled with tears as she spoke. Sitting down she began worrying to death a hyacinth.

" Sister dear," reasoned Maud, " he is a good old boy. Mr. Dowling says that the perfection to which he has brought the mechanical appliances on every hand has never been equalled."

" And a pretty pass he's bringing the *social* life to. You do not know who's who, here. Jack's as good as his master ; and his daughter better than her mistress."

" But there is no master-and-servant relationship here. We have left all that behind us."

" Yes, and the good old times, when people knew ·their place, and good breeding went for something."

" Surely native worth and culture are the main considerations."

" Then family standing and social distinctions are
immaterial ? "

" Not in the least.   Those in whose blood virtue and
refinement are so established that the highest qualities
have become hereditary, will always be honoured and
respected by the wise and good."

" But what have you in common with these people for
whom you are always pottering about ? "

" A thousand things," replied Maud, with spirit.
"Their domestic concerns, their maternal solicitude,
their loving and hating—all touch a chord that vibrates
in my heart.   Mother, daughter, and child, all present
points of contact, especially for those of their own sex
and age—that does make 'the whole world kin.' "

" But they are dull and uneducated."

" By no means.   This girl is as well instructed as you.
Far more clever—than I, at least."

" Clever in a way."

" The men, Mr. Dowling, who has observed them
closely, says, are, many of them, really intellectual, only
needing their hearts to be softened, and the better, un-
selfish side of their natures to be touched, to make
splendid citizens.   Mr. Brown thinks the same."

" Of course Mr. Brown agrees with you," said the
elder, significantly.   " You are all tarred with the same
brush, it seems to me.   At least he's a gentleman, so I
shall not forbid those banns, my dear."

" Do not joke about that, Hilda," said the younger,
blushing to the roots of her hair, as on the slightest provocation she was wont to do.   " You know he is under a
vow of perpetual celibacy.   He despises the words-without-
deeds of social reformers, and I, too, mean never to marry."

" And so you go about hand-in-hand."

" My dear, we never do."

" I mean, metaphorically, visiting your precious people, hob-nobbing with them, drinking mild tea, in their gossipy bowers."

"Thank you, we do not gossip. We have always something practical to do."

" Yes, and something very impracticable to perform— to be about, always together, a handsome, over-affectionate pair of enthusiasts. Loving all the world, you are never to lose your hearts to each other. Very probable ! "

"Of course we shall not. I have, as you know, liked Frank since he was a boy. We are as brother and sister —that is all."

" Why, you are all in all to each other already. You think you are living for these people, you are existing for one another."

" Hilda, it is unkind of you to speak so," said Maud, with some feeling, as she began to roll up her score of varied-shaped calico. " I must go now."

" Not with a frown on your sweet face," said her sister, imprinting a kiss on the smooth brow.

Left to herself, Hilda sat down and pondered.

"It is my duty," she murmured to herself, " for his sake, for all our sakes, for Larry's. Yes, I will do it now, before I relent."

Seizing a piece of note-paper, she hurriedly penned the note she had thought upon many a day. It ran thus—

"WHITE HOUSE, MIMOSA VALE,
August 1891.

" DEAR MISS ELMS,

" Our brother's attentions have not escaped us. We know that he is the soul of honour, and that you are as high-spirited and disingenuous as you appear. Before it is too late, allow me to point out that we could never welcome any choice of his from local circles ; and that when he marries it should be, in view of the equivocal social relationship in which we are placed here, to one of his own station in life. Assuring you that I write in kindness, and with feelings of highest respect for you as a neighbour,

" Believe me,
" Yours faithfully,
" HILDA COURTENAY."

Hurriedly closing the cruel little missive, and seeking the gardener, she commissioned him to let one of the lads deliver it by hand.

The men were streaming homeward from labour in field and mill, garden and vineyard. Children hastening forth to meet them, were hiding tiny hands in hard brown palms, or helping to carry empty lunch-bags. On hundreds of joints the basting was being poured, while children were assembling around simple but well-supplied family boards.

" Good-morning, Gwyneth. Is dinner ready ? " was Travers' greeting, as he stood with raised hat at the Sergeant's door.

Hearing a step on the gravel, the girl had hurried to the embowered porch to welcome her father, as she supposed.

" What brings you here ? " she demanded, with surprise not unmixed with evident pleasure. " Where is my father ? "

" At the canal. He telephoned that he could not

return till evening. I thought I would bring word myself. How are you going to repay me."

"With thanks."

"That's not good enough. I must ask myself to your father's dinner. It is a shame it should be wasted. Besides," he added, taking the hesitating girl's arm and leading her into the parlour, where the dinner was laid, "I want to finish our conversation. Come now, you say grace, and I'll carve. The first of many a dinner we will have together, Gwyneth."

. "But, Travers, I've been thinking——"

"No, you have not—no second thoughts. I stand by the vow you gave me yesterday. Allow me to help you to this juicy mutton. I've come for the token you promised. I see you are wearing the ring. What does your father say."

"He had not noticed it. I have not told him."

"But you must. Allow me to pour you out some tea."

"Travers, you are incorrigible. You come to preside at my table."

"Long may I do so!"

"You are too rude. Would you usurp my very tea-things?"

The meal, with much lovers' talk, finished, Travers insisted upon being invested with the promised token. After much parley it was brought forth—a silver pocket-case with portrait of Gwyneth and her mother painted on ivory. The case had been her mother's. After a profitable contract, her father had had the two photographs copied, and presented it to his daughter two years before.

"You look, in the portrait, almost as sweet as you are, my Gwyneth."

" Please be sensible."

" You are very much like your mother. She must have been charming."

" Poor thing! She paid dearly for it," said Gwyneth, with a sigh.

" You shall not suffer for your beauty and spirit, my darling."

" I value this," said the girl, " more than anything I possess."

" Save me," suggested the young man.

" And my father."

" Well ? "

" I give it to you—though you do not deserve it--for your persistency, on the condition that you permit no one to see it. Rather than be the cause of trouble in the valley, I would do anything," said Gwyneth, with warmth.

" Even to giving me up? "

" I do not say that ; but, Travers dear, you must not come to see me so often."

" I shall take the reflection of you here," said the young man, putting the silver case into his breast-pocket ; " and in my heart ; but I must pop in and see you sometimes."

" Once a week," she suggested.

" Once a day only," he replied, as, snatching a kiss, he leapt the hedge and disappeared.

Meanwhile the form of another man was stealing away through the embowered beds in the opposite direction, muttering to himself—

" No one shall see it ! Oh no ! "

CHAPTER XVI.

HYGEIA.

"Our human refuse shall be utilized, like our material refuse, when man as man, down to the weakest and most ignorant, shall be found to be (as he really is), so valuable that it will be worth while to preserve his health to the level of his capabilities, to save him alive, body, intellect, and character, at any cost: because men will see that a man is, after all, the most precious and useful thing on the earth, and that no cost spent on the development of human beings can possibly be thrown away."

C. KINGSLEY.

THE doctor had not forgotten his promise to Willie, that Nurse Maggie and some of the convalescents should accompany him to the country. So beneficial was the change in their case, that Dr. Courtenay resolved upon putting into effect a project he had long contemplated of settling, not only the poor and distressed, but the sick and afflicted on the generous soil.

The conditions of commerce and industry may possibly necessitate the congregation of the busy and strong in the crowded metropolis. He failed, however, to see the wisdom of confining the suffering and afflicted in huge, antiquated edifices reeking with disease; condemning them to breathe, to the last, the polluted air of the city they rendered still more deadly; depriving them of the solace Nature might have afforded, and of occupation with which to relieve their dark days and last years.

The cost of maintaining the unfortunates in town he

knew to be double what it would be in the country, even if they were unable to contribute by their labour towards their own support.

The doctor called a meeting of chairmen of hospitals and benevolent institutions, to which also public officials and charitable workers were invited. His offer to select from various institutions patients suited for his proposed treatment was gladly accepted. He asked a grant for each at the rate of half the present cost of their maintenance, holding out hopes that at no distant time the subsidy would be unnecessary, and his infirmary village become self-supporting. With the aid of a committee of medical men, convalescents were drafted from the various hospitals ; the stronger patients from the benevolent asylums, and even from homes of the incurable.

Eventually the deaf and dumb institution was removed bodily ; a selection was very carefully made from patients of the lunatic asylums, even from criminals of a promising character undergoing their first sentence. Arrangements were completed for transfer of the juvenile reformatories to the new settlement. The female refuges were relieved of their more hopeful cases. Special provision was made for the reception and treatment of the intemperate. The good doctor was too capable an organizer to dream of herding all these together.

Across the lake at Mimosa Vale, beyond the spot where Gwyneth and Travers had nearly met their death, the flats and sloping hill-sides were specially prepared. Lands were cleared and ploughed, cottages and dairies erected, avenues laid out on the plan of Mimosa Vale. Each cottage accommodated two or three patients, or a household. Where possible, family life was reconstituted. The deaf and dumb child restored to its parents, one of whom might be under treatment for intemperance, or suffering from partial paralysis. The grand-parents were rescued from the benevolent asylum and restored to their children's home. So the strong of a family were able to help the weak. Those in rude health cheered the less fortunate. Each household was debited with the value of the weekly rations received, and seed, tools, and other necessaries supplied.

Around each cottage a few acres were ploughed. Provision was made for gardening, fruit-planting, dairying, poultry-keeping, basket-making, broom manufacture, silk-worm culture, and other industries suited to the capacities of the less strong and active. All were expected to render some service.

Many so-called "incurables" recovered, and after being subjected to a careful examination, were allotted a block at Kokiana, when that settlement was formed. Within two years Hygeia was entirely self-supporting. In a short time it maintained its own receiving-hospital, accident wards, and the like in the city.

On the top of the hill overlooking the lake, consumptives in the first stage were afforded a home and opportunity of recovery. A mile further down the stream, the reformatory was stationed.

All who did not abuse it were afforded freedom within their own settlement. The warders' cottages and gardens were disposed along the ridges that shut in the successive bends of the river. All were afforded an opportunity of not only purchasing full freedom with their labour, but of acquiring a homestead-block in an independent community further on. Every means were adopted of sweetening the life and elevating the tastes of those who had fallen under a cloud. Precautions were taken to prevent contagion, physical or moral, between the respective cantonments of Hygeia.

Some few, of course, of the criminal class fled away, were re-arrested, and completed their term in the barrack gaols in town. The operation of the law of heredity was not suspended, but in the majority of cases love and wisdom wrought their work. The youth whose existence had become a menace to society was transformed in the course of years into a prospering yeoman. The prospect of winning land and a home by honest means, of acquiring an assured position among a free community, won the wavering to the ranks of industry. The alternative to a life of vice and crime was no longer one of hopeless, life-long drudgery. " Honesty " was at length "the better policy," and self-interest threw its tremendous weight into the scales that were trembling in the balance.

This spirit of hope, prospect of betterment, and of ownership, wrought a like transforming effect upon those mentally and physically afflicted. Their spirits revived, and in many instances lifted them out of the trammels of disease in which they had long lain.

If any spark of health lingers in the pallid cheek, in the confused mind or vitiated heart, let the free air of the country play on that cheek and gladden, as it must, that heart ; put some implement of industry into the unsteady hand ; let the man work for himself, for a home, and if it be not altogether too late, the sick will revive, and rejoice in the healthful pleasure of making a plot of God's earth fruitful, and their own.

One Saturday afternoon Gwyneth, taking Willie with her for company, sailed across the lake—she was an expert yachtswoman now—to see how Nurse Maggie and her friends fared at Hygeia. A dozen times she paused, after landing, and peeped into happy homes, within or about which, young and old, hale and sick were

resting or labouring. More than one Willie recognized
as erstwhile fellow-inmates of the hospital.

"You did not bring the terrible screen with you,"
he said to a nurse he knew; "you'll never want it
here."

" We have to thank you, young man, for inciting the
doctor to initiate a reform with respect to hospital
methods and management that has long been awaiting
some one to start it."

"When I look around on these scenes," the nurse
added to Gwyneth, " I shudder as I think of those blank
white-washed walls, with the lines of close-packed houses
and dusty, stifling streets on which we used to look.
Nearly all, we find, can do something here—feed fowls,
cut flowers for the market, and see to the silk-worms.
Others garden and farm quite effectively. It is the sense
of home and ownership that prompts them."

"You remember," said Gwyneth, " the saying of
Arthur Young—was it not—somewhat to this effect?
'Set a man to work in the garden of another, and it will
speedily become a wilderness; give him personal interest
in a desert rock, and he will cause it to flourish, and
blossom as the rose.' "

A long visit Gwyneth paid to the consumptives on the
hill. They had a peculiar attraction for her. Their lot
was so hopeless, where all others were renewing their
strength.

" They seem half-way to heaven already," said Willie,
as in the hot afternoon the two panted up the hill. " I
fear they've got the screen here."

" It's a terrible disease," replied the girl, as though
communing with her own thoughts. " Largely bred of
foul air, and unhealthy, unnatural conditions of modern
life. The scourge of God ! My mother fell its victim.

I

And my heart always goes out towards those who pine away on the hill-top."

A few hours later the pair came upon the village green of the deaf mutes. Frank Brown was playing cricket with the lads. Maud, beside a table, beneath an awning, was preparing sandwiches and refreshments.

"Do you two never get tired of your self-imposed tasks?" asked Gwyneth, exchanging an affectionate greeting with her friend.

"I might fairly ask that of you," replied Maud. "There is not much task about it either. We had the most delightful sail across the lake, and a scamper on ponies to the Reformatory Bend."

"Is it true that you are engaged?" whispered Gwyneth, casting a questioning glance on the radiant face of sweet content beside her.

"You all are ever imagining that," said Maud, amused. "We are 'engaged' in a common and a pleasant work."

"And nothing else?"

"Why should there be anything more? Cannot people like each other and work together without love-making? We have eschewed such nonsense."

After a while Gwyneth moved on.

"Nothing more!" Maud repeated to herself as she cut and patted her sandwiches. "I think not. Sometimes I am afraid. I shall be disappointed if we come to grief like other selfish people. It is so nice in theory to be brother and sister, but so hard in practice."

"Now, Maud, have you a grand lunch for these famished urchins?" called Frank, as he came to where she was engaged. "I do not know what I should do without you," he added, looking admiringly at the busy maiden.

"You'd go on just the same in your happy-go-lucky fashion."

" Indeed I should not. I should become dull as ditch-water, and miserable as a bandicoot."

" Do not say that, Frank. I like to think of you as the one single-minded man in the universe—doing good for the love of it."

" Then you do not care to be identified inseparably with my day-dreams ? "

" Do not ask what I want. We try not to be introspective and self-contemplative."

" A high ideal, Maud ! Are we succeeding ? "

The girl looked furtively at her companion and averted her eyes, while the colour deepened on her cheeks.

" Maud, must there never be anything more ? "

The words she had lately heard from another startled her.

" Is my vow, do you think, to be ever binding ? I was young when I made it. We are both older now." He laid his hand on hers. She did not remove it. She hesitated. Then, with the tenacity of a good woman clinging to her ideal, she raised her eyes, after a pause, and answered—

" I could never be party to your breaking it, Frank."

" Then we must leave the question as it is, I suppose," replied the young man, withdrawing his hand with a sigh.

Gulping down the tender feelings arising in his breast, the young man joked and grimaced with his afflicted friends as though all his life were wrapped up in making them happy. But it was not.

" I believe he is quite content in just performing his daily task," thought Maud, as she looked on, vexed with herself because the thought brought her no pleasure.

Amongst the domains of the inebriates, Gwyneth and Willie were moving.

" We have had few cases of desertion and failure," said
the farmer's wife who acted as matron. " One case, however, perplexes me. I wish you would try your persuasive
powers, Miss Elms; the sound of your voice and touch
of your hands are more soothing than whole sermons of
others."

"I would it were so," replied Gwyneth, laughing.
"Where is your patient?"

In a bright room opening from the broad verandah a
woman lay on a snow-white pallet. A wealth of dark
hair contrasted with the pallor of the worn face it
encircled; large hazel eyes almost glared at the intruders.
The woman turned her face towards the wall.

" Poor thing!" said the matron. "She has drunk for
years. Now that, for the first time, she has awakened to
a sense of her position, she is crushed with remorse."

Quietly, Gwyneth took her seat beside the patient.
The woman turned her head for a moment, as though
resenting the advance. Gwyneth's hand lay carelessly,
as it were, on the shrinking shoulder, and the gentle
light in her eyes shed its radiance on the troubled brow.
The woman, with a deep sigh, turned, more quietly, away.

Gwyneth motioned for the matron to leave. Insensibly,
almost without signs or words, by the sheer attraction of
her presence and influence, the visitor drew the woman
out from herself. The hard look slowly disappeared.
Bending forward till the dark tresses covered the hands
that held hers, the pent-up soul poured out its grief in
tears that had not flowed for months.

"The kindness here," she sobbed, "the beauty and
quiet of the place, make me feel my sin and loss the more.
They remind me of the happy home I once had, which,
owing to discontent and longing for excitement, we broke
up to seek our fortune in the city. My husband found no

work. I fell into bad company. He left me. I actually sold my one child for drink! I did not know what I was doing. . . . Now my sin has found me out. . . . No one accuses me. . . . I condemn myself. . . . I am lost and alone."

Gwyneth calmed the conscience-stricken woman with words of which she well knew the comfort herself. Willie's story flashed to her mind as she recognized the unmistakable likeness existing between mother and child.

" If your husband and son were restored to you, could you serve them truly, and retrieve the past ? "

" If they were ! . . . But that is impossible ! Could I see my child again, and work and slave for him ; could I show my husband that the devil has gone out of me at last, that the sweetness of this place has entered into my soul, I should feel that God had not cast me off. But that is impossible. My family, my God, have deserted me."

" If you had the chance of making a new home here, for your husband and son, would you never fail again, from the old cause ? "

The woman clutched the girl's hands, her eyes rolled with excitement.

" Ah, miss," she cried, sinking back on to her pillow, " if I had that chance, I would show I valued it to my dying day ; but I have not. Do not mock me ! "

The woman lay still. The hard expression settled on her face again.

Gwyneth rose and lightly tapped on the window, beckoning to Willie, who was picking flowers in the garden.

" See what I have got for you ! The sick people grew them all themselves," cried the lad, bursting into the room.

He stopped on the threshold, holding the door in his hand. He looked hard and long at the sick woman, who was gazing in wonderment upon him. The boy hesitated, blushed scarlet, and stood toying with the flowers as if doubting whether to flee or to stand his ground.

"Do you not know this person?" inquired Gwyneth.

"Course I do. Her's my mother."

"Are you not glad?"

"That depends."

"Depends upon what?"

"Whether she's gived up the drink."

"Your mother is filled with remorse for all her past doings. She is going to live a new life in this sweet garden, and wants you to help her."

Slowly the lad drew towards the mother's side, and, kneeling down, showered kisses upon the weeping face.

The next day the grandmother joined them, and the next the father.

Removed from all special temptation, the four established themselves permanently and happily beside the lake.

"At the least," said the doctor to himself, after paying the household a visit, "I have set that little man on his feet again, and led one lost woman to value the 'flesh and blood' she so lightly sold for a five-pound note. Undoubtedly the land can do wonders. Some of the most diseased trees of the city merely require careful transplanting."

CHAPTER XVII.

CUTTING-OUT EXPEDITION AT THE GROTTO.

" Our most earnest philanthropists and zealous workers in the fields
of sin and misery in crowded cities, are coming, more and more
every day, to the conviction that an improvement in the
physical conditions of life is the first indispensable condition of
moral and religious progress."—S. LAING.

THE women and girls of Mimosa Vale had assembled
at the Grotto for their bi-weekly meeting, over which
Maud presided.

"Anything to get away from wholesale factory life,"
the doctor often remarked when taking counsel as to
means for clothing his huge family. Power had been
laid on to many of the cottages. Sewing-machine or
mangle, spindle or loom, could be attached and worked
at a moment's notice.

The good people required, however, direction and
assistance. For this purpose "cutting-out" expeditions
had been provided at the Grotto. The clothing of one
thousand souls—or rather bodies—was no small matter.
Two-thirds of their means and energies humble people
ordinarily spend in clothing their offspring. Intent, at
every turn, upon economizing human labour, and
sweetening the conditions of life, the doctor under-
took to clothe, as to feed, his *protégés* with the expendi-

ture of half the time and thought usually involved in the process.

The Grotto consisted of a large hall, decorated with pictures and statuary. The panels of the walls, on either hand, were hung on hinges from the wall-plates. In fine weather these sides, like the front of Eastern bazaars, were opened out and attached to a frame ten feet high. Beyond on either side lay a luxuriant garden of tree-ferns and shrubs. At the upper end was a rockery, about which lichens and maiden-hair, stag-horn and bird-nest were seeking to hide rugged rocks and gnarled roots. Down the centre a stream of water fell from rock to basin and fern-bed, winding through the well-kept grass-plots on either side of the hall. About the buildings and gardens were rustic seats and tables. In a bower at the upper end was, on one hand the "tea-garden," on the other the *café*.

When Maud arrived operations were in full swing. With a smile here and a word there, she glided through the groups of workers, and deposited her bundle on the long table on the daïs. There a score or so were busily engaged "cutting out." A committee were delivering to those who applied, calicoes, flannelettes, woollens, tweeds, and other materials. Two girl-clerks entered the goods against the applicants' names.

"The prettiest scene, I always think this," said Gwyneth to Maud, "in all the village."

"It is interesting," replied the latter, looking round upon the animated scene.

A buzz of animated conversation, ripples of happy laughter, mingled with the sound of the falling waters, and the singing of birds in the aviary. At every little table women sat cutting and arranging various articles of need-ful attire. The gowns the women wore were loose and flowing, gathered with a blue girdle about the waist, reaching somewhat below the knee. There was no corset-factory at Mimosa Vale. Material was not furnished, or aid given, for the manufacture of needless trappings and trammels. The consequence was that the women were as strong as the men. The two doctors of the community spent most of their time at the Perfume farm. For the men were being made red flannel shirts, white trousers, and white military-cut jackets. Waistcoats were discredited as unnecessary.

Some girls were engaged plaiting straw, others shaping and stitching hats—the men's with high crown, the women's with broad brim. Others were affixing red trimmings or bands.

Adjoining the Grotto was "the Bower," consisting of a hall with sides opening on to a garden, similar in arrangement to the Grotto, save that more machinery in the shape of sewing-machines, &c. was disposed about it. Only a partition, now pushed aside, separated the two enclosures. Here in the morning a party of boot-makers had wrought. Girls now occupied the room, sewing "uppers" and other concomitants for boot manufacture. (High heels, tapering toes, and kindred abominations were discarded.) Women wore sensible boots like the men, and walked, worked, and ran as though at length locomotion was not penance.

At one end of this building some girls and boys, with a few old men and women—grandfathers and grandmothers—were engaged in basket, brush, and broom manufacture. The broom-millet was grown most successfully on the estate. The stalk had been cut up and consigned to the silos by the ton. Thousands of bushels of the seed, much like sorghum, had been deposited in the poultry-farm granary. The broom fibres—oft blessed by all who ever possessed a foul pipe—were now being manufactured by old folk and children into an article superior to any " American broom." The fibre was quickly gathered together by hand, and bound round with fine wire worked by a spindle. The broomsticks, of native woods fashioned at the saw-mill, were inserted, and an article that brought each year thousands of pounds to the community was ready for use or sale.

Now from *café* and tea-garden fresh-cheeked waitresses, girls of the settlement, were emerging with tray in hand, serving tea and coffee and slices of brown bread or oat-cake to the busy workers.

A blind father played beneath a fern-tree upon the harp he had made, his grandchildren, boy and girl, accompanying him on violins.

Gwyneth played the piano. Then the blacksmith's daughter poured through the buzz of conversation the swelling tones of the organ.

Maud touched a button—a dozen gongs sounded in Grotto and Bower, garden and hall, a signal for strict silence to be maintained.

The doctor appeared on the platform. He had promised half-an-hour's address. " A Grain of Wheat " was his topic.

Graphically, but lightly, with the aid of diagrams, he explained, for the benefit of the mothers and housekeepers of the present and coming generation, how three elements conduce to the building up of the human frame—Phosphates, Nitrates, and Carbonates, supplying respectively bone and sinew, flesh and fibre, fat and heat. The grain, he pointed out, contained in exact proportions the constituents needed for support of man. " Hence we speak," he said, " of ' the staff of life.' But men, in the outer world, had broken that staff, stripped the good grain of God of its precious outer coating; 'bolted,' refined, and 'silk-dressed' the *product of Providence* until nothing was left in the pasty, consumptive-looking 'refined flour' save fat and heat. God gives you 'whole meal,' satisfying, healthful nourishment. Never again," he concluded, "deprive your children of 'the food of God.'"

Again the buzz of conversation proceeded, with much comment on the doctor's playful sallies; the work never slackening meanwhile. By special request Maud recited, quietly, but very feelingly, Hood's 'Song of the Shirt.' More than one eye was moistened. Dark visions of the old life arose for a moment in many a mind, like spectres of the past, thoughts of "sweating" in crowded alleys, vain bargainings for a halfpenny more a dozen with unfeeling representatives of fashionable firms—a dark background that cast into grateful relief the generous, rational life of the new world of labour.

"Thank you so much," whispered one of the girls, drying her eyes, "not only for the poetry, but for everything. I often think we are not half grateful enough. It was that very 'stitch, stitch, stitch!' that killed my mother. The life of the factory-hand in town—girl, boy, or man—is as different from this as jail must be from Government House. Oh, the crowd, the air, the noise, the tone!" The girl shuddered involuntarily as she recalled painful incidents of the past.

Once more the gongs sounded. "Gwyneth Elms," Maud announced, "will sing." From the Bower some of the girls strayed in, that they might hear better, for Gwyneth was prime favourite.

"'I cannot sing the old songs,' let us have that," suggested one.

"'I cannot sing the old songs,'" echoed a dozen voices.

"It is a little sad," expostulated Gwyneth.

Seating herself, however, at the piano, she struck the first chord, and the workers, peeping round distant pillars and above leafy ferns, stood in attitude of expectancy.

At that moment a child stepped on to the platform and handed a letter to Gwyneth. A boy had left it at the door. "Urgent" was written across the envelope. Gwyneth's voice failed; coughing, she asked for a glass of water. Thought of impending trouble, mishap to her father, or to some one else, instinctively prompted her to peep at the letter, as one handed the water. As she read, a flush of indignation mantled her cheeks, then a sense of cruel wrong and indignity caused her to turn pale and tremble. Remembering in a second that a hundred eyes were riveted upon her, she slipped the missive into her pocket and began her song.

"Cannot people pretend when they sing!" remarked stout Mrs. Strong. "You'd think to hear her that her heart was breaking."

"So it is, I believe," replied lean Mrs. Long; "don't you make no mistake, she feels it all. Didn't you see her get that letter just now?"

"She did have a turn. I thought she'd faint."

"It's all along of that Mr. Courtenay, that she's been carrying on with lately. Only trouble will come out of that, you mark my words."

"I'll never hear that song," replied her companion, threading her needle, "without hearin' that sweet tremblin' voice, and seein' that poor scared-lookin' face. It'll be many a day afore she sings that again, I'll be bound!"

CHAPTER XVIII.

THE MILKMAID ALL FORLORN.

> " Question not, but live and labour
>   Till your goal be won,
> Helping every feeble neighbour,
>   Seeking help from none.
> Life is mostly froth and bubble ;
>   Two things stand like stone :
> Kindness in another's trouble—
>   Courage in your own."—A. L. GORDON.

EARLY that evening Gwyneth, complaining of a headache, retired to her room. Again and again she read
the cruel letter. What did the woman mean? Gwyneth
did not want her brother. She crushed the note in her
hand and flung it from her.

"Yes, I do," she soliloquized with herself. "That
is the terrible part of it. I do love him. Why should
I not?" she argued. "His affection drew forth
mine." Then again her thoughts took another turn.
"Yes; this is the way of society. It cast my mother
off and broke her heart, because she presumed to love
one 'beneath her.' Now I am shamed and insulted,
torn from the object of my affection, because the traditions of society forbid my allying myself with one
'above me.' Does not God teach us to love? Attached
as Travers and I are, having so much in common, can

He intend that, owing to mere accidents of birth and station, we should be separated for ever?"

Long the rival feelings of love and pride wrestled together in her breast. "He would ever be the same. What business was it of any one else?"

But it *was* other persons' concern. Perhaps they had not considered that enough. She did love him, she repeated, and she kissed the ring he had set on her delicate finger. But, for his sake, she would not come between him and his family and prospects. She would never be an object of toleration; she had no wish to slip in amongst those who did not desire her presence. No; for his sake, on that ring, as she kissed it, she swore she would give him up. She would be hard and cold, to turn his thoughts, his heart away from her.

Then as she looked back on the late happy weeks, the drives, the sailings on the lake, the walks about the hills, refined converse of books and work and travel—conversation so different from that to which she was ordinarily wont to lend her ears—as she realized what she was giving up, she wept, as trembling on the brink of some deep abyss. She set her firm lips, however, till the colour vanished, beating the resolve into her very soul—"It shall be as though it had never been." And so, from very weariness and sadness, she slept.

Before the sun was up, Gwyneth, as was her wont, was lighting the fire, putting away her father's pipes and books, letting the sweet perfume of the flowers in at every opened door and casement. But she had no song this morning to mingle with those of the doves and canaries. Her dog followed her with saddened amazement when his morning greeting was unreturned. The very brightness of the early morning jarred upon her feelings. Why should all else be glad?

"Gwyn, my girl, what ails thee?" asked the father, scanning her face curiously as he munched his toast. "You haven't been crying?"

"I'm only a little tired, father," replied Gwyneth, trying to brighten up.

"I never knowed thee tired and miserable-looking before. What's crossed thee, girl?"

"Nothing, father. Please do not tease me." Then relenting, "One cannot always be gay."

"I will not tease thee." Elms often used the singular pronoun as token of endearment. "But if anything goes wrong, you let me know. I could twist this settlement round my finger; those who cheer the doctor and his son to-day would hoot them to-morrow, if I gave the word. But I do not want to—not yet. Let that young man, however, trifle with you— You need not look like that. Though you haven't told your old father, he's seed what was going on. I suppose he's thrown you over?"

"Who? Mr. Travers? He has done nothing of the kind. There is nothing between us. I have given him up for ever."

"Then you are a bigger fool than I thought."

"That's my affair, father. Please let us change the subject. I'll try to do right, for your sake, father, as well as for others. Please, father," she added, "do not talk as you did just now about the people. I cannot think that they would be so fickle and ungrateful as you often suggest. I will not entertain the idea for one moment."

"Then, my dear, you do not know human nature as I do."

"There must, then, be something wrong, radically, in Church, State, and Society, or somewhere, if the great mass of our people are the cold-blooded, calculating, childish set you always depict them as being. But I must be off to my cows. Good-bye, dad." Imprinting a kiss on his brow, the daughter brisked lightly out of the room.

"I'm not going to make others miserable," Gwyneth thought to herself, as she set on her pretty head the wide-brimmed hat, and with milk-bucket in hand and milking-stool over her arm, sallied forth to the cow-yard.

The vale was alive. Strings of people streaming up from the morning bathe at the lake, women and children returning on the trollies, men and boys on foot. Each family had its own space staked out on the shingly shallows of the lake. All bathed together in families. A regulation swimming attire, composed of rough sacking cloth that did not hold the water nor cling to the figure, had to be worn. A Master of Ceremonies checked the slightest infringement of the rules that regulated all proceedings at the bathing-station. Unless exempted by medical certificate, all were expected to bathe regularly. The morning swim and gambol in the waters flowing from the creek out into the deep lake, conduced more than anything to the health and good spirits of the community.

This morning Gwyneth avoided the groups of returning bathers, and sought her cows amongst the two hundred that were lowing about the great milking-shed. It consisted of a long open roof of sawn palings, protecting two rows of bails, thirty on each side. In the centre, rails for the trollies ran, bringing down fodder from the fields and silos a quarter of a mile away, or bearing away the milk in huge vats to the creamery and butter factory attached to the lower end of the long building. To each cow, as it was milked, a stated supply of fodder was given by lads in the centre, while a couple of men received the milk and weighed it, entering in a book the amount to be credited to the person contributing.

Next to Gwyneth, old Alec was milking, and next again, the Rev. F. Brown. He usually milked a cow or two, after the morning swim. In the cow-yard he met many he would not otherwise come in contact with in the course of the day. He could spin the genial liquid forth with two hands, frothing the bucket as it rapidly filled, without once staining his white trousers.

"You have not been singing this morning, Miss Elms," remarked Alec, as he let the maiden's cow out of the bail.

"Do not, please, call me miss," remarked Gwyneth, almost petulantly. "I am only a brown milkmaid. Be so good as to turn that cow away, she's been milked."

"Milkmaid or no," replied Alec, gallantly, "I consider the likes of you as much a lady as any that never was no use but to be looked at."

"But I'm only a working-man's daughter, and have no wish to be a 'miss.' This young cow will not give down her milk this morning."

"Owing to me standing here, maybe," replied Alec, apologetically, while he continued—"It's what you are, not what your father was, I looks to. In life the best goes to the top, like the cream up there in the factory whirligig, and I puts you up top, anyhow," and doffing his hat, the good soul returned to his milking operations.

K

CHAPTER XIX.

TOM LORD BECOMES SOPHISTICATED.

> "We think
> That when, like babes with fingers burned,
> We count one bitter maxim more,
> Our lesson all the world has learned,
> And men are wiser than before.
> That when we sob o'er fancied woes,
> The angels hovering overhead
> Count every pitying drop that flows,
> And love us for the tears we shed."
> OLIVER WENDELL HOLMES.

"HULLO, Brown, old man, who'd have imagined you'd come to this!" It was Tom Lord who spoke. Arrived at the Homestead the night before, he had sauntered out before breakfast to see his friend, the young parson. "I thought to find you saying morning prayers with the milkmaids. Why, that is a pretty clerical get-up of yours!"

"Funny little man!" exclaimed Frank, rising from his stool. "I cannot give you a paw."

"Dripping, as usual, with the milk of human kindness," replied Tom, grinning, as was his wont, from ear to ear, his hands in his pockets, hat on the side of his head.

"We have not come to grief yet, you see," suggested Frank.

"By Jove, no; the place looks stunning. No strikes yet, or lock-outs?"

"Only Good Fortune struck, and Care locked out,"

replied the clergyman, with his head set against the cow's side.

"But I say, Brown, the 'living' cannot be a rich one if you have to milk your own cows before breakfast—they might provide you with a slavey."

"There are no slaveys here. I like to come and mingle with the young people and old folk while the freshness of morning lights on them. I don't care to look on with my hands in my pockets, so I milk a cow or two."

"One for my nob, I suppose ; but I could not milk a cow if I was paid for it."

"No? Just loose that leg-rope, like a good fellow."

"How the deuce do you manage it ? Won't untie," said Tom, who, while Frank was delivering his pailful to the man at the vat in the centre, was fumbling at the creature's leg, trying to untie the running knot on the rope about the cow's leg.

"Look out, man," cried Frank, laughing. "She'll kick your head off; she's a youngster."

"They don't kick, do they ? "

"Only when they're scalded."

"Now, what do you do that for ? To wash them ? I heard that the whole box-and-dice of you have a swim in common every morning. That's jolly ! I shall go to-morrow and see the fun.

"By Jove ! what's that ? My horse in a fit," exclaimed the townsman, "with the boss's best saddle on. Hullo ! —look at his legs in the air. He seems to like it."

Frank looked round and roared with laughter.

"You are a city gossoon. He's only rolling. I'm glad it's not my saddle."

"Will he die ? " asked Tom, anxiously. " Talk of turning up feet to the roses ! I do believe the beggar wants to smash that confounded saddle, the way he goes back and back on to it. 'If at first you don't succeed, try, try, and try again.' There, he's over now on the other side." Putting up his eye-glass, Tom inquired—"Are you sure he's not ill?"

"Which—the saddle or the horse? The former very much so. You old brute," cried Frank, "up you get!" When the creature stood and shook himself, Frank examined the saddle, and put the rein over a fence.

"I rode over," explained Tom, "and thought I'd let him stray about and feed."

"Please remember we don't do that here," remonstrated Frank. "Though fairly prosperous, we are compelled to consider saddlery and other little items."

"He's such a confounded height," growled Tom. "I led him to half-a-dozen fences to scramble up, but the brute *would* walk off just as I got my foot in the stirrup. You see, I'm not used to riding."

"No, I should think not.—What are you doing over there?" continued Frank. "That's the wrong side of the horse, never fool about there. A skittish beast wouldn't stand it. Hullo!—look out, you'll pull the saddle over! What on earth are you at?"

"I'm just practising getting up while you are there. Don't let him lean away from the fence, please, as he always does when I want him to stand as close as he can; and don't, like a good fellow, allow him to go on when I'm half up. It's deuced undignified snatching for reins and pummel and the other stirrup that you can never find, while, like John Brown's soul, your nag will 'go marching on.'"

Frank roared.

"Why, you little fool, you're getting up the wrong side."

"Blow'd if I am," insisted Tom, with the little breath left in his round body, as he balanced on the backbone of the animal, leaving it doubtful whether he would succeed in pulling a captured leg from under him, and as to which side he would roll off on.

"There you're wrong," persisted Tom. "One injunction they gave me at the stables in town was, 'Keep to the right, sir, that's the rule of the road.' I always remember that, and know, at least, on which side to mount my horse."

"Well, get down now. Here, on the right side. Not like that," said Frank. "Grasp the mane and reins in your hand, and come down—so; let me turn you round, beside the shoulder, not at the flank, ready to be kicked."

"Then what'll a fellow do if he runs away? I like to keep my eye on the brute all the while."

"Come on," laughed Frank, "I must be off to my pigs."

Beyond the great cow-yard was the piggery. From the creamery a pipe high in air conveyed the skim-milk to a long trough about which pigs many and sundry were grunting, jostling, thrusting with nose and shoulder, devouring what they could; then, if the young people would let them, trampling the residue with their feet.

"Greedy creatures, these dirty pigs," soliloquized Tom, as the two leaned for a moment upon the fence.

"Irresistibly reminding of your vaunted social life in town—both alike a selfish, dog-in-the-manger scramble," remarked Frank, waggishly.

"That's rough, old man."

"But true to life nevertheless. There's a lot of the hog in our nature, and it comes out very strongly in the city. But these pigs are not dirty. Look at their glossy coats."

"But all pigs are dirty by nature."

"There you are generalizing again, and accepting

traditional misbeliefs, as you do with respect to certain of your fellow-beings. Some working-men are indolent and ill-conditioned—therefore all are. Some poor people live in slums, are dirty and wretched—therefore all must be. Fallacy of the particular to the universal. You ought to know better, Tom."

"But how on earth can you keep pigs clean?"

"You see that race over the stream. Every day all the piggies," exclaimed Frank, "are driven through that trough before they get in here for their breakfast. If such care had ever been taken, Moses would not have condemned swine's flesh."

From the milk-duct, women and girls were drawing off the skim-milk and bearing it to round kiosk kind of sties with triangular-shaped compartments.

"What are those other sets of kiosks?" asked Tom, putting up his eye-glass; "not more pigs, I hope."

"We have a soul above bacon, though there are tons of it in the store—some of my own fattening too. That you are looking at is the poultry-farm."

"You wash your hens in that race as you do your pigs? I am getting quite sophisticated."

"Not unless they have a mania for setting. The geese and ducks revel in that mimic lake."

"You are a soaring sort here. I see your very ducks and geese take their pastime high in air," said Tom, pointing to a flight of birds sweeping above the water.

"By Jove! they settle in the trees too. 'Pon my soul I never saw a duck do that before. Do your fishes fly?"

"My dear fellow, you have everything to learn. Those are wild-fowl."

"They are mighty tame nevertheless, to judge by the way they make themselves at home."

"No one is allowed to disturb them. Our lakes and streams are alive with such. Those are black duck. These, in the tree, shags. These again, wild-geese."

"Ah, yes, standing on one leg, and sententiously surveying the water, now hiding their head so that we shall not see them."

"You muff! Don't you know a crane when you see one?"

"At least I recognize the 'rara avis.' Your black swans, now, *are* dignified."

"These," continued Frank, approaching another series of circular houses, "are our poultry-yards."

"You are death on triangles," remarked Tom, "like the first book of Euclid."

"All have a separate compartment for their fowls, and make what use they choose of this common run."

"That is, they take their chance of their ducks being considerably mixed, or being pecked at like a poor Benedict, or of being set upon by some game bird. I'd keep fighting-cocks if I went in for poultry here."

"'Every care and no responsibility,' is our rule."

"Who is that nice-looking girl fussing about those incubators?" asked Tom, as they looked in at a large shed, in which were artificial "mothers" and hundreds of chickens chirping. "I saw her just now at the milking-sheds."

"That's Miss Elms, the daughter of one of our overseers."

"There's no mistaking that face," replied Tom. "I saw it yesterday under peculiar circumstances. Thereby hangs a tale."

"Well, come home, and let's have it over the chops."

CHAPTER XX.

MALDUKE SETS HIS TRAP.

"Is it your moral of life?
  Such a web simple and subtle,
Weave we on earth here in impotent strife,
  Backward and forward each throwing his shuttle,
Death ending all with a knife ! "—BROWNING.

As the two friends sat at breakfast, Tom related the incident that the sight of Gwyneth's face had recalled.

"Hearing that you were engaged with some meeting or other, and the doctor being over at O'Lochlan's, I strolled down to the Dowlings'. They had a score or two of these precious people in to their 'Monthly Social,' as they called it."

"It's very good of Dowling," said Frank. "He only half likes it all. He has certain old-fashioned notions about the movement."

"So I should think. He talked pretty straight to one or two last night. Mrs. Dowling and her pretty daughter," continued Tom, "gathered the women into the big kitchen, explaining some kind of new-fangled style of sewing. The men were with Dowling smoking on the verandah.

"One of them—named Malduke, I think—was treating the company to some wild rhodomontade of a lightly-flavoured socialistic order. Dowling set the fellow down properly. The man did not take it kindly, and I noted that one or two seemed to sympathize with him.

"Those confounded mosquitoes will always make for me," Tom continued. "As they were particularly aggressive, and I did not desire to be drawn into conversation, in which case I might have spoken my mind too freely, I withdrew to the other end of the verandah, and enjoyed my pipe behind some creepers with less molestation from human and insectile bores. The window of a little room off the parlour," continued Tom, "was open close to me."

"'That is Eva Dowling's apartment," remarked Frank.

"I must have dozed. I was aroused by the sense of some one moving beside me. Lo and behold! our socialistic friend was in the room examining a silver pocket-case. As he held it near a turned-down lamp beside the window, the light fell on two portraits, painted on ivory. One was that of an elderly lady, and the other, that very girl with the striking face, whom, in this place where everything is topsy-turvy, you set to milk cows and feed pigs."

"Gwyneth Elms!" said Frank. "But what on earth was the fellow doing in Eva's room?"

"Wait and you shall hear. The stupid fellow hurriedly kissed the portrait, whipped out his knife, quick as lightning removed the miniatures, and substituted two photographs. Closing the case he deposited it carefully on a shelf containing a lot of girls' books and nicknacks. In a moment he was out of the room.

"Now what did all that mean? Some devilment, I'll be bound, for there was a wicked expression on the scoundrel's face all the while.

"When I rejoined the motley company I was glad to find Travers amongst them. He expressed regret that he had to go to Gumford next day. Dowling said that he, too, ought to pay a visit to the Bank, but the old horse, Peter, was ailing.

"Travers offered to drive him. Dowling remarked, however, that he had another engagement, and suggested that his daughter could do his business, and it was arranged that Travers should give her a lift.

"'Deuced lucky fellow,' I whispered him afterwards."

"You were on the wrong scent there. He's head over ears in love with some one else."

"'Don't be a fool,' he replied, 'she's only a child. If it were some one else whom you do not know, then you might envy me my drive. I'll introduce you to-morrow. But I'm glad to oblige the Dowlings. Eva is a sensible piece of goods, too; does half the business in Gumford and on the farm. Her parents slave in the same way, yet are as refined as they are plucky.'"

Though Frank affected to treat the incident lightly, it set him thinking.

"Come and have a sail on the lake," he suggested. "I am going to take a holiday on your account. We will ask Miss Maud to come too."

"Are you and she still carrying on?" asked Tom.

"None of your nonsense, Lord. We never did and never shall make love. We are devoted to ——"

"Each other. Yes, I know all about it, old fellow. You still make believe. Happy innocents!"

Smiting his friend on the chest, and bidding him not make senseless suggestions, Frank with his companion jumped into a car, pressed a button, and were in an instant gliding swiftly towards the lake.

Gwyneth had promised to spend the morning at Mrs. Dowling's, and to read to the old lady the Laureate's latest poem.   The girl's heart was ill attuned for social intercourse.   As she walked across the fields, the fragrance of the fresh-mown grass had no charm for her.

Catching sight of Malduke at work in the field, she turned aside and, further on, sat for a moment on one of the benches, set at every few hundred yards beside the unfenced roadways.   Scarce had she seated herself than she observed a high dog-cart, with tandem team, that she knew well, rattling along towards the spot where she sat.   It was too late to move.

Could she believe her eyes?   There sat Travers with the laughing, evidently delighted, Eva Dowling beside him.   Since so often Gwyneth had scolded him for noticing her in public, the youth did not draw rein, but, smiling, doffed his hat, while Eva waved her hand towards the girl.   A cloud of dust from the horses' feet circling at that moment into a little whirlwind, enveloped her. The girl's heart beat fast.   Had the horrid sister instructed him to insult her?   Was he subservient?   Already interested in this child of the forest he had picked up.

"Excuse my intrusion, Miss Elms," said Malduke, appearing at this juncture with a hay-fork over his shoulder.

"I do not excuse it.   Be careful."   Then, almost savagely, "You remember what happened last time we met!"

"I have something very important to tell you," he urged, "something you ought to know.   Gwyneth," he continued, with earnestness, "though you rebuff me, I cannot calmly see you scorned by another."

"What do you mean?" said she, her cheeks flushing.

"I mean this," Malduke answered hurriedly.   "Travers Courtenay has long hesitated as to whether to give his affections to you or to Miss Dowling.   His friends, as you may know, have brought pressure to bear. Last night he virtually settled matters with Miss Dowling and her parents. I was there; saw him kiss her in the garden; and, listen,"—for Gwyneth was hurrying away— "I saw her later in her own room—the window was open —imprinting a kiss on the silver case you once owned, which now contains his portrait and hers, side by side. I could not help seeing it."

"It is a lie," replied the girl, passionately. "You have concocted this story to make mischief. I *know*," she continued, "that Eva has not my silver case."

"No," was the reply; "she placed it—I could not avoid observing—on the top of a little book-case hanging on the wall."

"I do not believe one word you say." She stamped her foot petulantly on the ground.

"Were you blind just now?" the man hissed. "Even before the dust from his horses' feet smothered you. Can you not see he despises you—as a poor man's daughter? that they both enjoyed the fun?"

"That again is untrue. But I will not discuss it with you. I will listen no longer to your base suggestions." And Gwyneth hurried along the road towards Heatherside.

"You'll find your property on the little book-case," called he after her.

"The iron is entering into her soul now," he muttered, walking away. "Serve her right. She'll be glad to turn from her gilded lover to the arms of the simple champion of the People, humble though he be. After all," he soliloquized, tossing the hay almost jubilantly, "she might have a better chance of being a fine lady, mistress of all she surveys, with me for her husband, than as the wife of the great Travers. The ground on which he stands is mined."

CHAPTER XXI.

WOUNDED BUT NOT CAUGHT.

"Only a silent grief
  When in her room alone ;
But tears bring no relief
  When every hope is flown.
Only the constant memory
  Of their meeting 'neath the trees,
Yet a girl's fine heart is breaking
  Over trifles such as these."
          Australian Poets, FRANCES S. LEWIN.

"Why, let the stricken deer go weep,
  The hart ungallèd play ;
For some must watch, while some must sleep,
  So runs the world away."—SHAKESPEARE.

MRS. DOWLING was one of those genial, sunny natures who have a warm welcome for all. A specially cordial one she extended to Gwyneth as she met her at the open French window.

"Come in, child," she said. "You look pale, and usually you have such a fresh colour. What is the matter, my dear?"

"Nothing, thank you ; I hurried rather."

"Well, then, sit down, and give me all the news," and the old lady proceeded to retail hers.

"I must tell you about Eva's good fortune," said the garrulous old dame. "She has gone to Gumford, you'll

be glad to hear, with Travers Courtenay. I may tell
you," she added, lowering her voice confidingly, "you
are so sensible. She is really very fond of the dear
young fellow. We all are. She has been cooped up
here all her life. And he's about the first real gentleman,
other than her father, she has ever met. Do you not
think the young man charming, dear? But I suppose
you have not seen much of him. How should you?"

"Not much," was the reply. "You see he is a gentleman, and I——" The old lady was not versed in the
gossip of the place.

"Eva was pleased as a child to go with him," the
dame ran on. "He has often been here of late. I am
not sure whether it is only to consult Mr. Dowling, as he
professes. Certainly they did talk a good deal of 'shop.'
But his taking Eva to Gumford to-day looks as though
he were interested in the child. Does it not?" Mrs.
Dowling was not aware that her husband had, in the
simplicity of his heart, and for his own convenience,
himself proposed the arrangement. "I do despise anything like match-making," continued the old lady, "but,
do you know, if it came about in a natural sort of way,
of course there is no one I would rather have for a
son-in-law than young Mr. Courtenay. You should be
bridesmaid, dear. Would not that be nice? We have
known Travers' parents so long. Then, again, it is not
wrong to remember that he will, of course, be wealthy."

"And you really think she returns his affection?" suggested Gwyneth. She was choking, but felt she must
say something.

"I am sure he has a very warm place in her heart,
but of course she is young and unsophisticated. I should
not let her marry for a couple of years, I think. Would
you?"

".I do not know," replied Gwyneth, with difficulty retaining her calmness. "The sooner the better, I should think "—with some suspicion of bitterness.

The old lady looked up and eyed her in the kind, rude way elderly folk often affect.

"You do not seem quite to like the idea. You are not yourself this morning, dear. You know no ill of the young man, do you? One has to be so careful in these days. Eva is the apple of our eyes," and the proud mother paused and pondered as she wiped the gathering moisture from her spectacles.

"Shall I get the book now, Mrs. Dowling?" asked Gwyneth, as cheerfully as she could, while a burden was pressing upon her heart, and a storm of mingled feelings agitating her. But, despite her sorrow, she would do her duty.

"Yes, dear, please do; you will find the volume in Eva's room, on her little book-case over the bed."

Gwyneth involuntarily started, but in a moment rose calmly and sought Eva's apartment. She seized the book nervously, intending to hurry back with it. Her eye would rove, however. It caught sight of a shining object on the top shelf.

"It could not be!" she exclaimed in anguish. "I will not believe it. I shall not even look." She hesitated. "Yes, I will," she continued, "to settle the matter. Of course it cannot be mine!" Standing on tip-toe the girl reached down the little case. Her heart beat wildly. Behold, in her hand, her poor, dead mother's gift passed on by her child to the man who swore he loved her! With trembling fingers she opened the case, and closed it again, and sat, lest she should fall, on the pallet bed, and gazed far across the creek, through the gum-trees to the fields beyond, where reaping-machines were merrily rattling, and harvest-hands, youths and maidens, mothers with their children, sang as they set up into stooks the golden sheaves. All became as night for Gwyneth. Then a cruel glare; and in the centre was fixed the vision of her mother's gift, with the portraits of Eva and the man she loved side by side!

"It is too cruel! too cruel!" she sobbed. "He might at least have returned my gift." There must be some mistake, she tried to think, but all was so circumstantial! What her father and Malduke had wildly uttered of yore concerning the heartlessness, the viciousness, the cruelty of the "upper classes," flooded her mind. For a moment the stricken thing lay on the bed, her face buried in her hands, as she moaned, and called her mother's name. Had she been at hand to guide, her child would not have yielded herself so freely, to be cast off with scorn by the first monied youth, with attractive face and speech, who pretended to woo her.

"Can you not find it, dear?" the old lady was calling from within.

Quietly, now, the girl replaced the silver case—took up the blithesome *Foresters*, and hurried forth. She smiled as she entered the room.

"I was looking at *Lancelot and Elaine*," she remarked, cheerfully. "I have brought it too. May I read that, instead of the babble of Robin Hood and Maid Marion? It is somewhat weak and wearisome."

"Anything you like, my child. But how your hand is shaking! Are you sure you are not ill?"

"Oh, dear, no"—with a light scornful gesture—"only indignant at the thought of the gay knight's treatment of 'the Lily-maid of Astolat.' I was peeping at a few pages. I suppose it's the way of the world, especially of knights and gentlefolk."

"My dear, I never heard you speak like that before. The true gentleman is the soul of honour. Blood always tells."

"Yes; and sometimes cries to heaven for vengeance!" Gwyneth spoke with vehemence. "What a picture is this!" and she read in tones of mingled pity and indignation—

> "In her right hand the lily, in her left
> The letter—all her bright hair streaming down—
> And all the coverlid was cloth-of-gold,
> Drawn to her waist; and she herself in white,
> All but her face, and that clear-featured face
> Was lovely, for she did not seem as dead,
> But fast asleep, and lay as though she smiled."

"My dear," said Mrs. Dowling, "how your voice trembles! You enter too fully into the feelings of these mere creations of the imagination. Your nerves are too finely strung."

The girl read on, of the last missive of that other broken-hearted maiden—

> "I, sometime called the maid of Astolat,
> Come, for you left me taking no farewell,
> Hither, to take my last farewell of you.
> I loved you, and my love had no return,
> And therefore my true love has been my death."

The old dame wiped her eyes and spectacles, saying, as she curiously scanned the girl's face—

"Gwyneth, darling, I believe you have a history. You have been badly treated some time or other."

"Perhaps I have," replied the girl, shortly; "but what is that? I am only a plain common girl!"

As, after an hour's reading, Gwyneth stepped quickly with beating heart towards her home, glad to be free from the guileless but garrulous old soul, the returning

L

dog-cart flashed past her. True to his sense of propriety, Travers again did not rein his horse. Without raising her head Gwyneth passed on.

"Strange she did not see us," remarked Eva.

"Dear Gwyneth, whither so quickly?" called Travers, a few minutes later, having deposited his charge at the gate and hastily turned to pursue the retreating figure. "You are playing me a trick," exclaimed the young man. Though close beside her, he failed to attract the girl's attention. He slackened speed to the pace of her walk. Jumping out of the trap, though still holding the reins, he laid his hand on her arm. It trembled. The maiden shook as though she would fall. As she turned, Travers, observing the pale face and strange, wild expression on the countenance, ordinarily so serene, drew back.

"Gwyneth, what has happened?" he exclaimed, thinking some dire misfortune had overtaken her—as indeed it had.

"You must not touch me," she almost shrieked, shrinking away. "You must not call me by that name. Leave me. I can be played with no longer." She looked round like a hunted thing.

"Gwyneth, what do you mean? Played with! You know I love you, as no one else in the world. What has come over you? What has risen up between us? Who has been troubling you, my darling?"

Gwyneth faltered. Could this fervour be all assumed? But the sister's letter!—that revealed like a lightning-flash their relative positions. She would give her life to know that all she had lately seen and heard was indeed a dream, as it sometimes appeared. Might she not take his outstretched hand and trust him to answer? She hesitated.

Turning, she looked the young man full in the face—

eyed him as though she, the penniless carpenter's daughter, were princess, and he humble yeoman.

"Show me the keepsake." She would give him one last chance. "Return that to me, and at least we will part in peace."

The young man coloured, became confused, so unusual with him.

"Gwyneth, I hastened after you partly because I was eager to confess to you that I had lost it. Do not look like that. What have I done? I flung off my coat to show that fellow Malduke and some others how to straighten a fence. Half-an-hour after the pocket-case was gone. I cannot trace it."

Ah, had she not seen it herself, amongst the trinkets of the girl he had been driving about all day—the photographs side by side?—had she not heard the old lady talking? Otherwise she would have believed him. But all was against him. His manner was refined, no doubt. Splendidly he lied, finely he acted and braved it out, and yet—she loved him. Her heart was breaking, but her lips did not falter as she said deliberately—

"I am sorry to say I cannot believe you. Unfortunately I know the truth. Choose your gentlewoman, but pray leave me alone. Do not come after me," she said, as the young man stepped towards her, "I cannot bear it." She bounded away. Travers stood as one stunned, holding the horse's reins and gazing after her. Then, as in a dream, he mounted his trap and drove moodily away, feeling that for him all the light had fled from Mimosa Vale.

"Miss Elms, dearest Gwyneth, let me comfort you. The proud upstart has cast you off; let a humble follower lay the tribute of his devotion at your feet."

It was Malduke who thus accosted the pale, scared-looking creature as she entered her garden—calm retreat no longer.

"How dare you speak to me? Step from my path at once," imperiously insisted the long-suffering girl, as she moved towards the porch.

"Because Travers Courtenay is a fraud and a deceiver, a specimen of his class."

"Again you lie," was the reply. "He is not false. I will not believe it. But he is nothing to me," she added, recovering herself; "much less so are you. Begone, Richard Malduke, and dare not dog me or cross my path again." She fairly glared at him. She scarce knew what she said.

Like a whipped hound, the young man retired, muttering to himself—

"Not tamed yet! But she shall be."

Meanwhile Gwyneth flung herself on her bed and sobbed her heart out. Then she sat up, put her hair back from her face, and gazed over the lake, on which they had sailed so happily, and said—

"I cannot, I will not believe it. But there is an end to it all. A foolish fancy! But the trouble is—I love him still."

CHAPTER XXII.

HOW TOM WON A RACE.

"Looking at the moral aspect of the question alone, no one will
deny the advantages which the possession of landed property
must confer upon a man or a body of men—that it imparts a
higher sense of independence and security, greater self-respect,
and supplies stronger motives for industry, frugality, and fore-
thought, than any other kind of property."—COBDEN.

Two or three years had elapsed since the emigrants
trooped over the hills and sought their rest in Mimosa
Vale. Each anniversary of the Hegira was commemor-
ated by two days' high festival.

The sky on the present occasion was cloudless; so
rare and transparent the air, that the vines on the terraced
slopes about the red-brick walls stood out as though a
few hundred yards away. At six o'clock in the morning
a special service was conducted in the church for those
who cared to attend. The entire community was represented, largely out of respect for the settler parson. The
doctor read the lessons; the Bishop of the Campaspe,
who had come the night before to take part in the
festival, preached.

"Two are better than one, and a threefold cord is not
quickly broken," was the text from which the good man
educed lessons as to the benefits arising from "brotherly
union and concord." The transformation that had been
effected in the lonely valley, he said, witnessed to the

ability of human labour to establish itself, under free and fair conditions, without aid of the State, dole of charity, or the Church. They had learned, he pointed out, that by loving their neighbours as themselves, life became, in spiritual as in all temporal things, trebly richer.

In a loft above the wide chancel-screen the band was playing. With the surpliced choir of men and boys, some clergy and singers from town were associated. The chairs, free to all, were every one occupied. As orchestra, choir, and people joined in the *Te Deum*, and all faced, like one army, the figured eastern light, high above the home-carved reredos and glowing altar, the first beams of the dawning shed a soft light about the sacred building. Frank Brown felt that a better day was indeed being ushered in.

Later, all repaired, by tramway and on foot, to the lake. The common daily bathe was enlivened by swimming contests—for families, for men, and for women. The lake rang with laughter, that coursed along its surface, and set the magpies in the few gaunt gums remaining, piping a loud symphony of song.

The morning ablutions over, the prize-winners announced, all assembled in a bower of saplings and gum-boughs specially erected for the purpose. Here about one thousand five hundred persons sat down to the breakfast that a committee of the villagers dispensed. The band played ; the 'Song of the Village Settlers' was sung ; the doctor and the bishop delivered short addresses inseparable from all British social gatherings.

Later, a stream of visitors wound down the hill-side in four-in-hands, wagons, and Cobb & Co.'s coaches ; in every and any kind of vehicle. Half the township of Gumford, miners of Tin-pot Gully, " Cockies " from the selections, "hands" from the stations, were among the visitors. The sham-fight between the yeomanry and their neighbours resulted in victory for the local organized force.

The regatta in the afternoon was the principal event of the first day. The *Mimosa*, of one thousand tons, yachts, barges, rafts, and pontoons were placed in requisition by onlookers, while the wattle-lined shores were crowded with eager partisans.

The "eights" did good rowing, though a crew from the Yarra carried off the prize. That for the "fours" fell to the villagers. Amusement was caused by the awkward attempts of some of these latter to manage their crafts. Cheers and laughter burst from the onlookers as here and there two village-made boots shot upward, a well-rounded back disappeared into the bottom of a boat that discharged its awkward cargo into the smiling lake.

The gig and dingey chase made an exciting finish. Travers happened to be the dingey man ; a crack oarsman from the town the occupant of the gig. Breathless excitement reigned as the champion of the vale careered in his cockle-shell round his antagonist in long razor-back boat. Here dingey just saved himself by backing, there by darting aside. A roar of delight rang across the water as gig, trying to seize his nimble antagonist, almost capsized. In an incautious moment dingey allowed himself to be closed in by the sides of the *Mimosa*.

"Gig has him now !" was the cry.

"Dodge him, dingey !" echoed back others.

Catching a rope suspended from a spar, Travers flung himself clear of his boat just as gig dashed at him, and, missing his man, fell headlong into the water. Now Travers is on the spar, straddling towards the thronged bulwarks. Gig in his turn has the rope, and is raising himself, hand over hand, to the beam, in eager pursuit. Peals of laughter greet his dripping and bedraggled appearance.

"Quick, dingey, he's upon you!" is the cry.

Through the throng on deck Travers pushed his way, dodged round the companion, about the mainmast, disappeared down the forecastle, in a trice dashing up the ladder from the hold. Now gigantic gig presses him sore. For a moment dingey stands on the bulwark on the side opposite his boat. He almost brushes past Gwyneth, who leaned there. Their eyes met. So eagerly was she watching the chase, she forgot the restraint set upon her. She smiled, then recovered herself. In a moment dingey dives into the lake, coming up twenty feet from the vessel's side. Another second, and gig follows.

"Poor dingey, you're done at last!" some murmur.

Gig's head appears a few feet from the object of his pursuit. A few strokes, that evinced the superiority of gig's swimming powers, bring him close alongside.

"It's all up!" shout hundreds of voices. Again dingey disappears. Gig waits for him to come to the surface. Breathless seconds pass! A minute!—two! Gig looks anxious; dives down, down, with open, staring eyes, seeking in the dark depths of the lake the form of him who, he feared, must be unconscious. The stillness of death lay upon the steamer. As she leaned over, with her boat's spar in the water, eagerly all watched the surface from which the face of him so full of life a few moments before had disappeared. The strain became intense. Another and another dived from the vessel's side.

"Will no one save him?" almost shrieked Gwyneth,

as she clutched convulsively at the arm nearest hers. Two ashen faces looked blankly on each other! Despair was written on each—Hilda's and Gwyneth's.

"Oh, my wicked letter!" thought the former.

"How could I mistrust him?" murmured the latter.

All this in two seconds.

Hark! a cheer that rends the air. The report of the gun shakes the little vessel, causing the ladies to stop their ears—after the report is over.

"Time's up! Dingey's won!" a hundred voices are shouting. A rush now to the other side of the vessel. Gig climbs disconsolately on to the spar and regains the *Mimosa*.

"Hang him, I thought he was drowned. I could have caught him otherwise," growled the discomfited one, as he saw the victor on the other side, paddling to his yacht midst the plaudits of the onlookers.

"No, you would not have caught him," said the *Mimosa* skipper. "Not a man on board could dive under the ship as he did."

Somewhat disdainfully Hilda drew her arm away and looked coldly at Gwyneth, as though she would say, "What do you mean by touching me, minion?"

Gwyneth heaved a sigh of relief and looked out across the lake, thinking—

"What business had I to smile at him and he at me! I'll be very careful not to do it again."

The varied entertainments of the evening over, the visitors repaired to tents that had been pitched for their accommodation. Tom insisted upon "camping out" for the first time.

In the dead of night groaning, as of a man dying, awoke him.

"Good God! what's that?" he cried as he clutched the

arm of his sleeping companion, a grumpy old "Cockie" whose team had been beaten in the tug-of-war the day before.

"Hold to it, boys! All together now. Bend your backs," responded the sleeper.

"Wake up, man," cried Tom, "some one's *dying!* Hearken to the terrible moan."

The champion of the team at length leaped up, growling—

"What the deuce do you want?"

"Some one's dying, I say."

The champion listened a moment, cast a pitying, withering glance at the little man shivering in his pyjamas, and flung himself back into his nest of blankets, exclaiming—"Pity you're not dying. Don't yer know a native bear when yer hear it snore?"

"A bear!" cried Tom, seeking his revolver; "black or white? Are they large, or ferocious, hereabouts, sir?"

"By Jove, *arn't* they! Eat you up, soon as look at you!" This was the only information the little man could elicit.

Reconnoitring for himself, expecting to encounter some huge creature intent on a deadly embrace, Tom was disappointed to trace the gruesome sounds to a rounded mass suggestive of an overgrown 'possum.

"Is that their native bear?" exclaimed the Englishman, disdaining to fire. "Everything's disappointing in this country, even its beasts and adventures. Now I thought I'd something to write home about," and he wrapped himself in his rug, and hoped that no snakes had taken possession of it in his absence. While pondering as to the proper mode of procedure, if one discovered itself coiled coquettishly on his breast, he fell asleep.

"Hullo, I say, covey, lend us your 'billy' to chop some wood to boil the 'tommy,'" Tom called to a neighbour next morning.

Novice-like, Tom was intent upon parading technical terms applying to the paraphernalia of the camp.

"What on earth do you mean?" retorted the Gumford bank-clerk, who had occupied the adjoining tent, and was also making preparations for the early morning meal.

"I was inclined to forget which was which—'billy' or 'tommy,'" explained the Englishman; "but I remember that 'billy' is short for 'bill-hook'—the affair the fellows top the shrubs with at home. So 'tommy' must be t'other thing—the can or pot you boil your tea in. This billy's mighty blunt," he added critically, rubbing the rough edge of the weapon.

"Not the only city-tool that's taken that way," replied the rude bank-clerk.

All who could secure steed or vehicle rollicked off to witness the coursing-match. Abbott-buggies laden with ladies, dashing through timber, over fallen logs a foot high, across trackless creeks, galloping over open plains, threading in and out thick trees of the ranges, astonished the city men who had never before seen a "throw off" n the bush.

The "horse races" constituted the great event of the afternoon. Every "Cockie" for miles round had brought the pony that was "sure to win." The squatter sent his son with "the half-brother to 'Calyx,'" who won the Cup five years before.

"Races are right," decided the doctor, "bar three things—'betting,' 'beer,' and 'cruelty to beasts.' We shall wind up with a scamper or two for the fun of the thing—to prove our horse-flesh and our men. But he who bets, whoever he be, walks off the course."

Young "Cocksure," nephew of a neighbouring squatter, deemed this "all blow," as he publicly termed it, and offered "two to one on Travers' 'Temeraire.'"

True to his word, the host, approaching the young spruce, bid him "Good-bye," and putting arm in his escorted him off the course. None essayed "odds" after that.

"You spoil your sport, as you do your work, in town," explained the doctor to some friends. "We are going to have both pure and simple here. English folk take pleasures sadly, their labour moodily, owing partly to the greed that—in some form of gambling or exploiting—finds its way to every social sphere. I'll have none of it here. What say you, Brown?"

"That I am going to win the 'Wattle Blossom'—the prize of the day," was the reply. Arrayed in red flannelette and white pants, the village parson was leading his light-limbed steed by the rein, flung carelessly over his arm.

"Looks well, but not very dignified, in that get-up," objected the mining manager of the "Golden Stream," who held forth at the chapel on Sundays.

"Dash dignity!" retorted the doctor, energetically. 'Your churches are dying of it—or were doing so, until such as my friend Brown arose. Because he identifies himself with the lawful pursuits and pastimes of his people, in no namby-pamby, patronizing way; because he lives their life right down amongst them—and a higher one all the while, never forgetting it, though he does not always speak of it—he holds these people by the heart-strings. Brimful of life—animal spirits, intellectual force and spiritual life, as you call it—he is, literally, the father of his flock."

"I won't have this, Tom," Frank Brown was saying. "You know you couldn't sit your horse once round."

"I'm going to ride, and ride to win, nevertheless," persisted the little man, as he scraped some mud from the sides of a huge beast he was leading.

"Why, your mount's been rolling, and never even been groomed since," remonstrated Frank.

"You want me to scratch my .horse to give you a show," retorted Tom. "I won't do it! That's plain. I'm going to show you all how to win, hands down."

Unmercifully Tom had been chaffed concerning his horsemanship. He rather liked the joke, and loved to exaggerate his awkwardness just, as he termed it, "for the fun of the thing."

So cleverly did he mingle affectation of innocence with evidence of shrewdness, that it was difficult to discover where his knowledge ended and ignorance began.

"Let those laugh who win. I'll whip you all to-morrow," he had ominously declared.

Tom and O'Lochlan had put their heads together.

"I have a horse," said Larry, "that'll carry you first past the winning-post, if only you can stick to him."

"I'll do that, never fear," Tom assured him, "if they won't bump against me."

"That they'll do, right enough," replied Larry, laughing.

"I do not mind, O'Lochlan, if I get a good grip of the pummel. The man should be canonized who invented pummels. They are so convenient when you feel you're rolling off—*e. g.* when the brute stops suddenly—that's always awkward, isn't it?—and you lie on his neck ; or when he shies at a rustling leaf."

"Well, you hold on by your eyebrow, and you'll finish

right. The old stager knows his way about, and will jockey himself better than the 'Cockies' can their own horses."

Purposely Larry sent the old blood across with the marks of a roll in the half-dried dam still fresh upon him.

The appearance of Tom upon his mud-caked "Leviathan" was the signal for shouts of derisive laughter. One whispered that Lord, a moment before, had been bribing the stable-boy to "give him a leg up.".

"What shall I do," he was reported to have said, "if I come off in the race? I'll never get on again, myself, even if I'm whole lengths ahead, as I shall be. I supppose you couldn't follow us, sonny, just to be handy to pop me on again, in case I find myself on the ground?"

"Whiff!" went the pistol. Off the strange field started. Travers on "Temeraire," Brown on "the Rector," Tom astride "Leviathan," the village carrier on a mount borrowed from the local storekeeper, shearers on their Rosinantes—twenty, of all sizes, styles, and strides—jockeys high in stirrup, arching over neck, or leaning back to save their steed—all in a ruck. Now "Temeraire" draws out, Gumford storekeeper's nag presses him hard; "the Rector" creeps steadily to the fore.

Last time round; Storekeeper's nag well beat; "Temeraire" and "Rector" neck to neck.

"Two to one on 'Rector'!" incautiously cries one, of habit taught. All were too intent to heed.

"Well ridden, Parson! 'Rector''s got it!" was the cry. Turning towards "the straight," Frank Brown had clearly secured the inside running.

"Bravo, 'Rector'! 'Temeraire''s out of it."

Where all the while is " Leviathan," with his confident
jockey ? Forging along, with even steady pace. Others
may shoot forward, others drop behind, *his* level stride
neither quickens nor slackens. Nay, it is quickening
now ! Slowly from out the field he draws. The clay
brushed by living curry-combs from his shining sides,
the jockey clinging manfully with both hands to the
friendly pummel, the reins fluttering like ribbons in the
breeze.

Now the self-riding steed is riding past Storekeeper's
nag. Then drawing slowly ahead of brave " Temeraire,"
up to " the Rector," who is whipping hard ; head to
flank—to shoulder—they ride.

Neck to neck, they flash up " the straight," Frank
riding as a jockey bred ; Tom bundled up like a bicycle-
rider, all elbows and legs ! One second more ! Old
" Leviathan's" great eye glances round at his one
competitor. The huge beast puts forth, for one last
moment, his full powers. In a few strides Tom with his
pummel shoots past the post, ere " Rector's" nose has
come into line with it ! The cheers that greeted the
winner might have been heard at Gumford.

While other competitors were struggling to rein in
their steeds, still dashing onward, " Leviathan," a few
yards from the winning-post, duly comes to a standstill,
almost throwing Tom across his neck. Jauntily but
stiffly, the townsman dismounted, on the wrong side,
descending like a miner down a ladder, and dropping
from a little height on to the ground. Round the course
the prize-rider was carried, bowing and grimacing to the
applauding multitude.

" Didn't I tell you I'd beat the field ?" he called to
Travers and Frank, as they came to wring the victor's
hands.

"You stuck on gamely," they replied, "especially in that scramble round the far turn. I thought you'd come off."

"Couldn't if I'd tried," replied Tom, wagging his head. "There wasn't room to fall."

"It's a good job you didn't try," they answered.

"A hundred guineas for the veteran, Larry," said Travers, coming up to where O'Lochlan stood fondling the sagacious creature, of whose coat scarcely a hair was turned.

"Not a thousand," was the reply. "Not another horse in the country could ride itself like that to win."

"I beg your pardon," demurred Tom, "*I* rode the race. And won it too!"

CHAPTER XXIII.

AN OASIS IN THE DESERT.

"The little smiling cottage, warm embowered ;
The little smiling cottage, where at eve
He meets his rosy children at the door,
Prattling their welcomes, and his honest wife
With good brown cake and bacon slice, intent
To cheer his hunger after labour hard."—DYER.

"THE heavens were as brass, the earth as iron," desolation reigned beyond the confines of the little land of
Goshen, where everything flourished the more as the
air became drier and sun hotter. Elsewhere "the seven
lean kine," seven months' drought, ate up, as so often is
the case, the "seven fat kine" of prosperous years.
After every spell of excessive heat, the thunder-storm,
threatening all afternoon, broke with much noise and
glare, sweeping of dust, and rolling onward of majestic
cloud-cumuli, but, though every available tub and bath
about each homestead was set to catch them, only a few
drops of rain fell. Another day, wild stranger-clouds,
laden with precious water, rolled themselves upward from
the Southern Ocean, only to carry the watery store, for
which man and beast and land were thirsting, to deluge
oft-favoured zones with tropical rainfall.

Again the outlying "Cockie" must harness his emaciated beast to travel ten, fifteen, twenty miles for a barrel

M

of water, to last the sad, unwashed household for another week! In vain might the thirsty traveller crave one half-bucket of·that far-fetched fluid for his pinched-up beast! With grudging does the otherwise hospitable selector grant him a pannikin-full for himself. The wheat that had rejoiced in the spring sunshine has lost heart. It will make the best of a bad job, hastily form at the top of each stinted stalk a miserable apology for an ear, and await, bolt upright, the advent of the stripper.

Four bushels to the acre, the fair promise of spring yields to the sorrowing farmer, who must subsist on that starveling harvest for many a weary month. Burnt wheat his coffee, infused in water already the colour of the future decoction, his best beverage. Boiled wheat, baked wheat, fried wheat, his only food, and that of his children, for months to come, save for the occasional luxury of 'possum baked whole in clay, wallaby soup, or dainty snake pie!

What of his live stock and crops? The carcases of the few cows and sheep he possessed are lying beneath the shade of wire fences, bogged fast in the lignum swamp, or covering the gaping clay bottom of the long-exhausted "tank." Of other crops he has none. He is a man of one idea, and that is *wheat*. If that succeeds he settles his score with the storekeeper and bank; if that fails, he is lost. No tree has he planted, no shed built, no garden sought to form. Nor could he! Alone, unaided, the State has encouraged him to venture, void of capital or experience, "on to the land." Half the year through waters have flowed, not so far away, unused to the sea.

A few simple wood-and-earth works, and the frogs might be merrily croaking all the summer through, down that winding lignum-lined creek, and across the miles of caked lake-bed ; but that would have implied foresight and system with respect to settlement, not to be expected of a country where few look beyond their nose, or wider than the lobbies of Parliament House.

Nay, some water-works there may be near the thirsting selector. Of these, however, a few " boss-cockies " are the virtually self-appointed trustees. Their own wide wheat-fields they drown in ignorant endeavour to irrigate. Every care at least they take that no water passes them down the baked channels—run, by the way, beneath the surface instead of above it. The wheat-fed selector has the satisfaction of knowing that hundreds of thousands of pounds have been expended by an enterprising State on " colossal irrigation works." He may know that the overgrown farmer who represents him in Parliament has enough water and to spare. Strange to say, such reflections impart not extra relish to the baked-wheat coffee and 'possum puddings of his Sunday's repast. He is an unreasonable man.

Be it remembered, not every year, by a great many, brings a drought. Thousands of yeomen have overcome a score of the disabilities outlined in these pages, and by dint of sheer pluck have established themselves on the broad acres they own. Within the favoured Vale of Mimosa " the sound of many waters " was ever in the ear.

> " Clear and cool, clear and cool,
>   Lave in it, bathe in it,
>   Mother and child,"

the settler is singing. His wife is watching her rosy-cheeked two-year-old paddle amongst the sedges. Along the wide channels maidens are propelling their dingeys. The village hand is angling for " a bit of a fish to take home to the missus."

Along the valley for miles rolled the flowing sea of green—sorghum and maize, broom-corn and wheat. In the meadow, the well-watered lucern half hides the cattle that have strayed into it, while orangery, orchard, and vineyard streak with diagonals of green the red soil of the sloping hill-sides.

"I could not believe it was the same world," exclaimed a bronzed, unbarbered selector, as he leaned over the boundary-wire beside the topmost channel.

Twelve miles he had driven his jaded beast, to the music of the rattling, empty barrel and staggering, spoke-shrunken wheels. One who had never seen that plain of his before, could not imagine it as it had been in spring-time, knee-deep with prairie-growth of grass. Now, the very stalks of the last blade are blown away, the north wind finding but driven sand to sweep in its spiral sirocco-course; this, heaped high in the kangaroo grass—alone of all green things remaining—suggests the "desert" once supposed to spread from coast range to centre of continent. All, for hundreds and thousands of miles, fertile and smiling all the year round, if only water be conserved.

"Just you go and stand in that maize," suggests a settler, cutting watercress beneath the willows. "Creep in that there row and hold up your whip, and you ben't able to top the corn, I'll lay you."

No more he could. Burly Starveling with bushy beard disappears into the ocean of green, and only the rustling and laughing of the yellow beards far above his head indicate the position of the dusty man of the plains.

"Blowed if it ain't like a hot-house!" he exclaimed, as he emerged from the jungle. "It's clammy as cow's breath in th' mornin'. No wonder the stuff grows."

"It's all the water as does it," replied Smith, the

settler. "The Land of Canaan, what flowed 'milk and honey' pure,—leastways, which growed grass and flowers —was nigh all watered like this, Parson Brown, he says. That's why it reads so cool and fresh-like in th' Old Book. Now that the Turks, and the Rummuns afore 'em, has let all the water run off, Canaan's dry as a bone again, and dusty as your darned plain. It's all the water as does it. I reckon," continued Smith, eyeing the visitor critically, "you have not eaten a house down, exactly, this mornin'."

"Boiled wheat and 'possum," replied the selector, shortly.

"You come along of me. We're just in time for grub. See them herbs there," remarked Smith, as he conducted his guest along the winding path in front of his cottage. "I made nigh forty pound, few months back, from a bed no bigger nor that. The girls chops it up and puts it into old salt bottles. Here, Betsy Jane"—to a damsel busy, with her sister, chopping and bottling the dried herbs, "tell your mother a gen'leman from the plains is a-goin' to have tucker with us."

"What do you say to *that?*" as he led the bewildered "Cockie" to the garden at the rear. "You can have that melon to make jam on, if you can lift it—there now."

The stout selector essayed to grasp and raise the shining dappled monster, only succeeding in rolling it a few feet, so as to expose the white circle on which it rested.

"Never mind, covey, we'll get a couple of rails and roll it into the cart afore you go. You needn't bust yoursel' now."

"This be a cool place," remarked the visitor, as he stood in the porch, covered, as was half the roof of the

cottage, with clambering creepers. "There's not a green
leaf a mile of our hut," he continued. "Thistles is the
only thing thrives there, and they looks sick-like, and
stands far off one from t'other, as if they'd squabbled."

"Don't stint the butter, mister," urged the good wife,
as she observed her guest applying the slightest streak to
his bread. "There's a plenty where it comed from.
That brown bread's cooked this mornin'. Try them
scones Sar' Ann's just made."

"I've not seed butter nor milk sin' spring," exclaimed
the man. "No wonder your children looks fat. It's
two shillin's a poun' at Grogham's shanty."

"We sends tons away every week," replied Smith,
proudly. "Doctor says we gets top price, 'cause no
other coves has butter comin' in. 'It's an ill wind
blows no one any good,' says Mike Milligan, next door,
when the north wind's on. Leastways it makes a market
for we."

"Now, my good man," urges Mrs. Smith again, "try
this 'ere strawberry and cream."

"Bless you, I've not tasted the like," replies the guest,
"since I comed on these blessed plains."

"Well, eat your fill; there's miles of strawberries and
raspberries on Mimosa Vale. At same time, this comed
out of our own garding. We wants nothing from the
store now," she continued, "but a bit of groceries of
Saturday nights. You come over on Sunday, and we'll
give you a taste of somethin' good—sucking-pig."

"Yes," interjected Sar' Ann, "as Mr. Milligan says, we
knows what *appetite* means here. 'When I'm eatin', I'm
'appy; when I'm full, I'm tite.'"

"Sar' Ann," remonstrated the laughing mother, "don't
you repeat Mr. Milligan's rude sayin's."

"Bless you, he means no harm," she added, apologetically, "only he allers tries to be funny. And why shouldn't he? He's nothin' to trouble hisself about. No more's the rest on us, for that matter."

"I wish *I* hadn't," exclaimed the surfeited selector, as he stuck the haft of his knife and fork on the table—the signal that "he'd done," and "a child could play with him"—and he looked out of the open, paneless window, across the valley, and thought of the howling, poverty-stricken wilderness, not twelve miles away, with soil as good as this, but parched for lack of water; and his eyes filled with tears, at thought of the contrast suggested.

CHAPTER XXIV.

HELPING LAME DOGS OVER STILES.

"Amavimus, amamus, amabimus."—*Kingsley's Epitaph.*

"Blest be that spot, where cheerful guests retire
To pause from toil, and trim their evening fire;
Blest that abode where want and pain repair,
And every stranger finds a ready chair;
Blest be those feasts with simple plenty crown'd,
Where all the ruddy family around
Laugh at the jests or pranks that never fail,
Or sigh with pity at some mournful tale:
Or press the bashful stranger to his food,
And learn the luxury of doing good."—GOLDSMITH.

"Ploughmen, shepherds, have I found, and more than once and still could find,
Sons of God and kings of men in utter nobleness of mind."
TENNYSON.

ON the following Sunday, in accordance with the invitation of Mrs. Smith, Mr. Sandbach attended with his wife and children, and partook of the sucking-pig, together with luscious luxuries his children's mouths had seldom known. To save a trip he brought the water-barrel with him; three slender urchins standing up inside, to make room in the cart. In front of hospitable Mrs. Smith's garden the rattling wheels of the sun-baked dray staggered for a last time, and collapsing, rolled the barrel with its laughing occupants into the middle of the road.

"We'll get the wheelwright to do it up in the mornin'," said Smith.

"But I can't pay to have it mended," complained Mr. Sandbach, ruefully.

"Never you mind, put it down to me," said Smith, reassuringly; "it's paid for already. Last night's return at the store showed as I'd passed the red credit-line. They rules a line in red when a fellow gets into the right side of the books."

"Best thing you can do with your first credit, Sam," remarked his wife.

"You know that po'try Miss Maud painted in red and gold, and that Parson Brown framed and hanged up in the club-room," added the irrepressible Sar' Ann—

"'Do the work that's nearest,
Though it's hard at whiles,
Helping, when you meet them,
Lame dogs over stiles.'

"Mr. Brown says that po'try were made by the best parson ever lived these days—'Big-Gun Kingsley' they calls him, or some'ut o' that kind."

"'Canon,' you mean," says her father, "but it's all along the same. Parson Brown says it 'ud do *his* eyes good to see this place. He loved the poor, and the country, though they did leave him to die alone, and no notice taken on him, 'cause he spoke up for the people."

"Come on, Sandbach, bring the lady and the kiddies in," continued Mr. Smith. "You'll have to camp the night, I'm thinkin'. Come in and welcome."

Mr. Sandbach was overcome by the warmth of his reception. His wife, carrying a baby, that seemed to have drawn all the life from her hungered frame—the one of all the family that appeared to have thrived—at her expense—was speedily deposited in a be-cushioned and padded arm-chair constructed out of an empty barrel in Sam Smith's spare hours.

"There!" said the facetious host, happy to be able, for the first time in his life, to extend a helping hand to others; "your kiddies comed in a tub, now you rest y'rsel in one. Like old Dodgerknees they talks about," he continued, "what liked the sun, and told the Gov'nor when he called to get out of his daylight. Our valley wants nought of any one but sunshine, what God gives, and water."

"You're too good," protested Mrs. Sandbach, who had not for many a month sat still and watched other people bustling about.

"Duty's a pleasure, marm," remarked Smith, gallantly. "We should ne'er 'a been here if the good doctor hadn't a-helped us 'lame dogs over stiles,' and it's the least we can do to try shove along others, now we're in the swim."

"You should hear what Parson Brown says o' that," added Mrs. Smith. "You must come to-night. It'll do you as much good as water on the thirsty soil."

Mrs. Sandbach thought that if that were true, the village priest's discourse must indeed be refreshing.

No service had she attended, or parson seen, for years; save when one mild youth, with sickly face and white tie, rode to her door and asked half a bucket for his horse, and she had to refuse him, whereat he rode wearily away. Occasionally there was service at Mr. Fenceoff's, the squatter, but he and Mr. Sandbach "did not hit it," and Sunday, if they remembered the day, was a convenient one for water-carting and thistle-cutting.

On one occasion, indeed, Mr. Grogham had become seized with the necessity of Divine Service being held in his stable. The uncharitable did say that he had an eye to nobblers many and sundry, after service and before the tea-meeting. At any rate he charged the sickly young "Reader" more than the amount of the "collection," upon which, unfortunately, he had to subsist, for the privilege of tossing all night on a chaff mattress in which certain aggressive insects had made their abode.

Oats were given his horse. The "Reader" saw to that. But he did not observe Mr. Grogham scooping out the feed ere the jaded beast had well dived his eager nose to the bottom.

"Poor old Moses, you should feel better now!" said the sickly "Reader" when, twenty minutes later, he discovered the feed all gone. "You have eaten it quickly, my boy. Enjoyed it better than I the ham and half-hatched chicken, swimming in the fat of rancid bacon. The butter *was* strong, Moses, suggestive of cart-grease; the tea well boiled, and bread sour; but never mind, Moses, *you* have done well. *I* get my reward hereafter."

Mr. Grogham was devoted enough to ride round to urge the settlers to attend the little service that would " remind them of the old country." The good man wiped a tear from the corner of his eye. Mrs. Sandbach consented to attend. What was her surprise when, upon crossing the paddocks to the little beer-smelling shanty, she beheld Mr. Grogham ploughing his field!

"Well, you are a good 'un!" she remonstrated—"a-plaguing me to come to prayers, and you working this Sabbath just like any other."

Poor thing, she had rummaged up her grandmother's poke-bonnet, so suggestive of " church "; her father's massive Prayer-book was clasped under one arm, the youngest " hopeful " dragged wearily by the other, the duly " dressed " children following in straggling train behind.

She had mistaken the day! It was only Saturday!

Never after was she clear enough in her chronology to venture to Mr. Grogham's service again. She had misgivings, too, as to whether *that* was the way heavenward ; especially when she remembered the unfortunate condition in which her ordinarily sober husband returned from the ploughing-match ! For Mr. Grogham was a public-spirited man. Inaugurated races, too, merely " for the good of the district "—in his paddock. He is now member of Parliament for the county, having defeated old Fenceoff by twenty votes. He could have bought two hundred with his nobblers had it been necessary.

Many selectors, other than Silas Sandbach, were attracted by the flow of water and of the milk of human kindness towards the already famed valley. Weary of carting water, they secured from the doctor terms whereby they could settle below the lake opposite Hygeia.

By degrees a new settlement was formed. Five thousand acres were set apart for the fugitives from the plains, fifty acres each. The deeds of their own land, rescued by the doctor for a bagatelle from the store-keepers of Gumford and Cockietown, were placed *in Escrow* in the local bank as against advances made to the new-comers for provisions, materials, &c. A figure was agreed to as representing value per acre of the old land and the new.

The waters were carried on to the new land. Those who had failed to exist on their three hundred and twenty acres worked singly, prospered upon the fifty acres each, operated upon in common.

The new settlers elected their own trustees, with the doctor as chairman, binding themselves by means of an agreement as to discipline and mode of working. Kokiana, as the new settlement came to be called, benefited by the organization already existing. It was charged merely the cost to the old settlement of services rendered. The Mimosa Vale people derived advantages proportionately.

Though the lakes had held out during the severe strain

imposed upon them by the drought, the water level had been considerably reduced. Now, with the accession of a hundred additional labourers, it was determined to connect the Upper Lake with the Campaspe river. The storage power of both lakes was further augmented by raising the embankments. After the first winter rains, sufficient water was stored to meet the requirements of all the factories, and to maintain irrigation works for thousands more settlers. The finances and titles of the associated communities were kept entirely distinct. Failure or complication with respect to one, need not affect the position of the others.

Before many months had passed, the Kokiana folk had a common-land of five hundred acres under fodder crop. Upon the produce, duly siloed, of this alone, they maintained one thousand milch cows all the year round, about ten to each family, together with pigs and fowls, &c. in proportion. The dairying operations brought them in about £25,000 per year. They had a creamery and cheese-factory of their own. Stores were procured and produce dispatched in bulk for all the settlements. A branch store existed in each village, and a central emporium in the metropolis.

The refugees at Kokiana discovered that under the new system they could exist comfortably for half the expense it cost them to starve on the plains. Five to ten sheep fattened on one acre of irrigated lucern. Little fencing was needed. Their cottages were brought on skids from the scenes of desolation they had dismally dotted. Speedily the men paid for their fifty acres, and in many instances bought other fifty. The doctor took over the outlying selections, and credited their late owners with the value of them. By degrees other selectors, recognizing the advantages of association and the trans-forming effects of water, relinquished their distant holdings, and settled on the fringe of ever-increasing Kokiana.

The social growth was organic now ; like the polyp, ever throwing off new life from within, not to wander forth in sporadic adventure, but to cleave to the ever-widening fringe—like the associated action of animalcules, that have thrown up England out of the abyss of the Northern Ocean, and set her round with glowing walls of chalk—like the house-to-house, if not hand-to-hand, labour of coral insects, that have dotted the glassy waters of the Pacific with gem-like isles, encircled in rings of coral.

The young men and maidens of Kokiana, with their friends, attached here a fifty-acre block, and there another to the far-spreading sea of green, until the plains beyond the valley were brought under the influence of organized labour. Eventually extremes met, history repeated itself, the tides of the new system spread over the wastes left high and dry by the old. The deserted selections were absorbed, and where one family had starved, five flourished in peace and profusion.

Beyond Kokiana and Hygeia, towards the Silverbourne, Fabricia was later established, a settlement of men of various trades—boot-makers, clothiers, smiths of all sorts. In the centre were airy workshops ; in front, on either side, a row of cottages, each set in a " garden of cucumbers " and other growths that delight the eye and palate of man. Far away beyond, on either side, extended the garden-orchards, vineyards, and meadows of " The Jolly Smiths," as the farmers of Fabricia came to be called. Four hours a day each worked at his special occupation, earning enough to support his family. The remainder of the day the settler was free to cultivate his plot and to remember that he was no longer a machine, but a son of Nature and of God—a brother of his kind.

CHAPTER XXV.

CHANGES AND CHANCES.

"And the hot sun rose, and the hot sun set,
  And we rode all the day through a desert land,
  And we camped where the lake and the river met,
  On' sedge and shingle and shining sand."—A. L. GORDON.

IN due course Hilda and O'Lochlan were married. The magic of a woman's touch is seldom more graphically illustrated than upon the advent to the bachelor's homestead of the bride from the city. So, from the moment Larry lifted the wilful Hilda from her glowing chestnut across the threshold of their future home, was it at Bullaroo. Pipes, spurs, stockwhips disappeared from place of honour in the dining-room, relegated to a cosy quarter of the spruced-up barracks across the tidied yard. No longer from every sofa and easy-chair dogs greeted the visitor with snarl or whine. Cows were duly milked, and butter was made. No longer squatter and guest fared worse than "Cockie" who had a wife. Bread was not always sour and meat high. Hence Larry swore less oft. The Chinese cook despite his expostulations was relegated to the vegetable garden across the creek. A cook from town, housemaids with wondrous white caps and spotless aprons, flitted about the clean kitchen and renovated house. "Old Mary," the black gin, was not now permitted to ogle at all hours in the parlour window, nor her sable spouse and mates, with pickaninnies clad in seamless, some said unseemly, suit of black skin, to camp in the back-yard.

"Swept and garnished" was the homestead, and Larry and his visitors, clerical and otherwise, had reason to thank their stars that a lady had come to Bullaroo.

"The course of true love" does not necessarily "run smooth" after marriage, especially if it did not do so before.

> "In every life some rain must fall,
> In every year some days must be dark and dreary."

Scarce was the garden at the front, whence cabbage and melons had been removed, nicely laid-out, and the tennis-lawn, where the gallows had swung, was clothed with coat of velvety grass; scarce had the Vixen filly come well to her paces and she and Hilda fallen into harmony, than the first little home of the "happy pair" had to be broken up.

Did Larry, like many a married man, attend less to business now?

However it was, the terrible drought came upon him unawares. The "Cockie" he had "hammered" cut his best dam, just after the last rains; the new tank, not properly puddled, leaked. Heavily stocked, he tried, when too late, to lighten himself of his load. After the first draft to market, he would, he declared, rather "boil all down than accept such prices." The sun did the boiling for him, and the hot winds the drying of carcase and of fleece. Often did the newly-married couple return with buggy full of remnants, all of value that was left of the sheep whose wool was silvering the plains.

Larry welcomed an opportunity, after the first rain, of selling out. The "desert" of last week was a prairie of grass a foot high, when the Hon. Herbert Fitzhubert from the old country, with Messrs. Hyan's and Ramman's agent, came to inspect.

Despite the ominous carcases and still fleeting fleeces, a fine property was Bullaroo Plains. The new chum from England had capital; the old one from Ireland had lost his. It was well as it was.

The Hon. Herbert's sisters played the first game on Hilda's tennis-court, and "old Mary" was again permitted to flatten her nose—if flatter it could be—on the dining-room windows; for the Hon. Herbert was never caught kissing his sisters, and it was " such a good joke " to tell the folk about at home—this lubra looking in at lunch-time.

The very fact that the doctor was, as he termed it, "hard as nails," encouraged him to draw too heavily on his splendid reserves of physical and mental vigour.

Happy, in some senses, they who have occasional reminder that man cannot with impunity toil and think sixteen hours a day, who are compelled by physical admonitions to lie still awhile and taste of the bitter-sweet of repose.

The terrible strain to which the doctor had been subjected began to tell. For the first time he learnt that he had a liver and a heart. The medical adviser, whom his wife had by intrigue contrived that he should consult, insisted upon his absence for a while from the scene of his labours. A sea voyage would set him up.

Happily the advice harmonized with the indefatigable pioneer's plans.

The opening of an Emporium in London was in his mind, with a dozen expedients for placing products upon the best and largest markets. He would observe, too,

N

irrigation methods in the Western States, and the progress of co-operative enterprise in England.

" And you call that a holiday trip ? " exclaimed his wife, aghast, ere he had half enumerated the purposes to be served by his trip.

" A change of occupation, my dear," exclaimed the good man, "is the best restorative. You would not have me hang about the clubs and salons of London and Paris ? "

Travers had taken up his abode at the bungalow that he had built on the hill overlooking the lake. He was not himself. The mysterious barrier that had arisen between Gwyneth and himself preyed upon his mind. His duties, however, he discharged with unfaltering regularity.

Mrs. Courtenay and Maud could not be left alone in the great White House. Some one must take the doctor's place.

The O'Lochlans had come over for a few days to tell of their contemplated departure from Bullaroo.

"And what are you going to do next ? " asked the doctor.

"Lord knows," replies Larry. " I shall keep the few thousands I have left, until I see a good line. But I cannot be idle long. I'll be getting into mischief if I do. Run away with some other girl ! " he suggested, tickling on the neck with his riding-whip his wife, who sat embroidering his initials on a saddle-cloth.

" I have it," cried the doctor. " Men always come to my hand as I want them. You'll stay here, look after the old lady, with Maud and her curate, not to mention the few thousand folk scattered down the valley and across the plains."

" Not if I know it," demurred Larry. " It would be a

dog's life for me. No one but you could stand it. Besides I've too plaguy a temper."

"You're all right," said the doctor. "Though you must not go in for 'hammering' our boys! You get on well enough with people when you like, and for God's sake, do like, old man." And he went to the window and looked across the valley, and away into the middle of next month.

His wife placed a hand on his arm.

"Is not your heart outside rather than in?" she whispered, looking with a shade of sadness into his eyes.

He bent down and kissed her.

"My dear, I could not love my work as I do, if I did not love my God and you the more."

The wife's eyes filled with tears; she tried to understand, and could not.

The sacrifices we make are easier for ourselves than for those who love us. The woman, whose whole life it is to spend herself for others, rebels when she sees her husband expending half his energies so.

Meetings were held. Larry and Travers were appointed co-managers. Head men, who had for some time virtually held office, were duly appointed; nominated by the vote of the men and women, and approved by the doctor as president.

The announcement of the intended departure was received with regret and concern. The doctor's personality, to a greater extent than he realized, had conduced to the harmonious working of his plans.

His son-in-law was admired as a visitor. The villagers opened their eyes as he "cleared" their hedges and ditches, appearing and disappearing like a meteor of the plains.

The doctor had his misgivings. Earnest injunctions

he gave to his high-spirited son-in-law as to cultivation of temper and tact.   True as steel, open as the day, honest as the light, he knew Larry to be.   Unless unforeseen difficulties arose, all should go well.

" Now, my charmer," cried the Irishman a few weeks later at the door of the house he was leaving for ever, "give me your dainty foot.   There," as Hilda sprang, not quite as lightly as heretofore, into the saddle, " dry your eyes, my girl.   You'll want them undimmed. Chestnut's fresh, you know.   If fortunes are broken, our hearts are not.   And I don't mean my wife's neck to be either.

" Hang the gates, let's take the fences.   Across the country once more with the wind whistling in our ears to-blow out all the nonsense."

So saying he touched the chestnut on the shoulder with his whip, and "made believe" to press spurs to " Mooroo-bool's " sides.   Hilda caught one glance of the chickens she had reared running about motherless, of Mrs. Rails, the boundary rider's wife, crying, with a dirty apron to her face ; and away the two sped, over the fences, across the creek; she, as if flying from her destiny ; he, as if hastening to meet his ; and the blood rushed again to the girl-wife's white face, and the thought of past disappointment with sense of impending trouble passed away as they bounded in mad career across the hollow-sounding plains.   The wild Irishman shouted meanwhile—

> " Round goes the world,
>   Its troubles I defy,
>   Scampering along together, my boys,
>   My dear old wife and I."

" Larry, you must be steady now ; we are just turning into Kokiana.   You seem in good spirits at leaving our first home behind you."

"I never look behind, no sane rider does," was the reply. "I see a big fence in front, stiffer than I've cleared yet. I want all the nerve and spirit I've got, and I don't mean to waste any on useless repinings."

The wife understood. He was taking a smart run at his big fence.

"Hilda, old girl," he continued, "I'd never forgive myself if I got this affair knotted up. I would not touch it with a finger but for your sake and the old man's."

"There's a handsome pair," said Mrs. Sandbach, who sat at her door darning stockings, while her husband dug around some promising trees.

"Yes," said Sar' Ann, "they seems made for their horses, and their horses for they, as we're made for the broom, and the work for we."

"Handsome is as handsome does," remarked Mrs. Smith, who was visiting her friends. "He's a fine man, maybe, but 'a far cry' from th' good doctor. There's not the likes of *him* about in all the country-side. Good luck go with him, says I!"

CHAPTER XXVI.

GREEK MEETS GREEK.

" O what a tangled web we weave,
   When first we practise to deceive."—SCOTT.

" My friend, get money ; get a large estate
   By honest means ; but get at any rate."—HORACE.

" I hate ingratitude more in a man
Than lying vainness, babbling, drunkenness, or any taint
      of vice."   SHAKESPEARE.

" FIFTY thousand pounds that bit of paper's worth if only things take a right turn."

Elms sat at the table in his front parlour. Malduke bent over him scanning two documents, evidently objects of interest to both men.

" The boss will not rummage for them again, and won't miss them," continued Elms. " I was in luck ; he got me to help him overhaul the papers he's got registered in a book and stowed away in the safe. He was two minds to make away with this bit of a Will about the first affair. My heart was in my mouth. ' At any rate the land's there,' he says ; ' *it* hasn't run away, though the people have. If anything happened to me it might be worth something to you, Elms.' Then he adds a codicil, and sets two visitor chaps to witness it.

" ' This property I bequeath to my faithful co-worker, John Elms, for his sole use and benefit.'

"'The spot where we made our first modest venture,' he said, 'will be of interest, and perhaps of some little value to you. The scrub has got up again, I understand, but the land ought to be worth two or three pounds an acre.'

" He went on," continued the Sergeant, " to read this other will, settling Mimosa Vale and his other properties. He's certainly dealing handsome with the men," continued Elms, perusing the document. " The five thousand acres will virtually be theirs with all the improvements. Twenty thousand pounds if a penny ! And that's a low figure considering all the plant that's on the place.—Now let's see if this first bit of paper bears the construction you think it does," continued Elms.

Both read and re-read the few lines contained in the smaller document, whereby the property known as " Courtenay's Village " would devolve, in event of the doctor's death, to John Elms, as trustee in the interest of those concerned. The codicil made the disposition absolute.

This instrument had been drawn in town, before the larger venture was projected. Later the men were withdrawn to Mimosa Vale. Nothing had been generally known of the original tentative movement.

" By Jove ! you are right, lad," exclaimed Elms, after a long pause, when both were turning over in their minds a host of possible contingencies.

" If this other Will was out of the way, and if anything happened to the doctor, the Mimosa Vale Estate, the only place men know as ' Courtenay's Village,' would be mine."

" And mine," suggested Malduke, with a leer.

" Yes, and yours. You, of course, put me up to it. You'd have your share."

" First and foremost then," suggested Malduke, " make away with this stupid scrawl. I'll soon do it," and he seized the document spread before them.

" Not so fast," replied the elder man, laying his heavy hand on the crackling sheet. " He's been a good friend to me. This is a noble settlement of his property." The man hesitated. He looked out on to the bright, luxuriant garden, and then down to the dark floor, and seemed, as expressions of good and evil flitted across his face, to receive suggestion from the dark and from the light.

" Such a friend," growled Malduke, with vehemence, " as the conscience-stricken oppressor ever is to the poor who serve him. A friend remember, John Elms, who spurned your daughter from his son's side."

" That's true," muttered Elms, with an oath. " If they'd only let that come off, and not allowed their blessed pride to break the child's heart, as her mother's afore her, I'd have no need to think of this," holding up the slip of paper, " to get my girl her rights.—It is her rights," he continued, smiting the table with energy. " I have sworn she shall have the position her mother lost. She's a born lady, if ever there was one."

" It seems to me," Malduke could not resist slyly remarking, " that with all your levelling, old cove, you're always ready—specially you half-and-half chaps—to scramble up into the place you'd pull others down from.—At any rate," he continued, noting the fiery Irishman's darkening face, " your daughter's been badly done by; she's been scorned and shamed. You, too, shoved into a corner. No real leader as you're born to be —a mere farm-hand 'boss.' It wasn't for this you put the old man up to the business. See again," pointing contemptuously to the document, " he's not left you a thing in the whole blessed business. I call that downright robbery.

"Tear it up, man," continued the agitator, observing that he was working successfully upon the Irishman's pride.

"Where's your principles?" he added. "Sitting still and seeing a place like this handed over to a lot of scrambling individuals. Who's ever got right to give away the land that belongs to all? Where's your Communism here, I'd like to know? I say it's all base Individualism and bastard Socialism.

"Haven't you the right?" he continued, when the other still hesitated. "Who, I'd like to know, hit upon this idea and made this place but you? Haven't you every call to cast to the winds this one-sided scrawl that's written, like all their title-deeds, with the black blood of traitors and murderers, that leaves you, and your daughter, John Elms, out in the cold?" The wily persuader laid his hand impressively on his victim's arm.

"I have been treated scandalous, that's certain," growled Elms. "But tampering with another man's papers is mean." He hesitated. "Well, all's fair in love and war. I suppose I'd better. At any rate here goes!"

In a moment the so carefully prepared document of the man then visiting humble homes to say farewell, was torn across and across.

"Here, take it and burn it, you base leader, as your name implies," exclaimed the Sergeant, thrusting the handful of pieces into his companion's hands.

The latter went to the kitchen, caught up an empty tin that lay on the table, thrust the fragments into it, pressed down the lid till the jagged sides caught together, put the tin into his pocket, and, in less time than it takes

to relate, returned to Elms, who was staring at the remaining Will.

"One of them two inevitable things has happened,"
remarked Malduke, sententiously. "Number one, the
Will has disappeared. Now, as to number two, if anything should happen to the doctor, you must see to
that, Elms. You're to be his guardian angel."

"What do you mean, you devil of an anarchist?"
cried the elder, starting and turning a searching eye on
his companion. "You're a very fiend, Richard Malduke,
as all your cruel crew are. For all the estates in Christ-
endom I'll lay no hand on him."

"God may do that," replied the other, with mock
solemnity, feeling that he had been moving too fast.
"The man's done for. One foot in the grave already.
You are going with him to-morrow. A lot of things
may," he added, significantly, "happen between here
and the other side of the world and back."

"I'm not going to help them, at any rate," was the
dogged reply, as the tempted one thumped the table,
looking very savage and very virtuous.

"Well, consider at least these two things," said the
agitator, accustomed to marshal his crude thoughts
under artificial headings. "Think what you and I could
do with this here place, if it was ours—the kind of real
living commune we could set up. And consider again,
what's the good of a man when his work's done? Is it
not sometimes a mercy to remove him from trouble to
come—to put him out of his misery, poor chap?
What is the cause, I'd like to know, of the present de-
terioration of the race? Why, the insane way in which
useless people are patched up, in hospitals and asylums,
and set adrift to sow seeds of disease throughout the
community. One of our planks is, away with the useless!

A safe and speedy passage for them to the other world. If only your maudlin Christianity, with its mawkish sentiment, would not keep alive and maintain drivelling idiots, paralyzed paupers, sickly consumptives, and cancerous plagues of society, this world would be a fairly safe hunting-ground for a clever man. The poor wretches are happier in the other world, the parsons tell them. We're better in this, without them. It's for the benefit of all concerned that the sick drones as well as occasionally mischievous persons of importance should sometimes be got out of the way.

"Have you not a duty to Society?" he continued. "Are you always going to live for the individual? Don't be weak, John Elms. Rise to the level of the principles you profess. Now, to speak plainly and practically, would it not be well for all if your companion slipped by chance—though you happened to be near—say, out of the stern-lights of the *Mimosa* one dark night, or tumbled beneath a locomotive as you and he rushed across a line to catch a train? A hundred and one sad little accidents like that might happen anywhere between the Vale and New York. Eh presto! the thing's done in a moment. He'd go to heaven, and the property 'd come to you—and to me."

"We'll say nothing more about that," replied Elms, evidently torn by conflicting passions. "Maybe in the natural course the doctor will never return."

"He must not return. He shall not," said the other, with a diabolical expression on his cunning countenance.

"Look here, old man," he continued, with an ugly smile. "You're going to leave me sorrowing to-morrow. Just let's have a friendly understanding. You write down here what's to be my share."

" What do you want, disinterested mortal, Friend of the People ? "

" You know. Your daughter, and a third interest in the property."

After some demur, the Sergeant, who was turning over in his mind what he would do with the place, the palace in town he would build, &c., &c., if, by any chance, the coveted possession did fall to him, signed the agreement that Malduke dictated.

" A thing like that," Elms thought, " is not worth the paper it's written on. In any case the man must have a share, if fortune favours us."

" Now, give me your hand," said Malduke, rising, after depositing the agreement beside the tin in his jacket pocket. " Swear to me that, come what may, old Courtenay never returns to Mimosa Vale."

" I'll do nothing of the kind, you devil's son," doggedly replied the Sergeant with an oath, as he made the table creak again with a bang of his fist. " I'll not say what will happen, or what I'll do," and he turned to read the Will afresh, and to dream of the possibilities conceived for him in the womb of time.

" By God, you shall swear though ! " A hand clutched his shoulder. Malduke spoke in a tone he had not before adopted with his friend. " You'll not trifle with me ; I have a public duty to perform, John Elms. I have been trained to let no false sentiment come between me and such obligations. Listen to me ! Make no mistake. If Courtenay sets foot on that wharf, after to-morrow, I shall be compelled, mark you," the man spoke slowly, with emphasis ; drawing near he hissed in Elms's ear, " to denounce you, to expose the man, his trusted servant, who stole and tore up, in my presence, the Will, that I can produce "— tapping the tin—" who, moreover, sought to bribe me with a share of the spoil"—again laying his hand on the document in his pocket.

The Sergeant was trapped. Again, however, the firebrand had flared too fast. Springing forward, upsetting the table, the fiery Irishman seized his tormentor by the throat. They grappled and rolled on the floor. The younger man shook off his assailant and rushed into the kitchen, seeking to escape by the back-door. He stumbled in his haste. The Irishman sprang on his victim, and seizing a knife from the table, brandished it unpleasantly about the conspirator's throat. Elms was only hesitating for a moment, as he had done before. His animal passions, strong when aroused, were urging him to desperation.

"Murder! Help!" cried the horror-stricken wretch beneath.

At this juncture, fortunately perhaps for both men, the door was thrown open. Old Alec, with a huge pitchfork in his hand, appeared on the threshold, exclaiming—

"By the Hokey Pokey! Mr. Elms, what are you up to? I thought some one was being murdered."

"Only a bit of horseplay," replied the ready Sergeant, rising. "We've been having a farewell glass together, haven't we, Dicky? It's got into our heads a bit. Hope you're not hurt, Duke. And how's the world treating you, McDowl?"

Alec pretended to accept the explanation of the guilty pair, who appeared less at ease than their feigned merriment suggested. As the old man left, Elms was putting together some papers strewn about the parlour floor, while Malduke searched anxiously in another part for something he had lost.

"You don't see an old tin about, do you?" asked the

younger man, quietly, as if not to be heard by the other.

"Be you hungry, then?" queried Alec with surprise. "Miss Elms don't keep her lobster on the parlour floor, though for the matter of that, it's clean enough to eat 'em off."

"It's empty, man," replied Dick; adding to himself— "With paper worth fifty thousand pounds."

Passing out by way of the kitchen, Alec observed on the floor the very tin. He saw that it had been rudely closed and contained paper.

"The rogues have been fighting for this," muttered the old man, picking it up and putting it into his pocket. He said to himself as he departed—"I'll take care of it for them. I wish to God some other man than that dog Elms was a-going with the master to-morrow. The Lord preserve him!"

CHAPTER XXVII.

THE DOCTOR'S DEPARTURE.

"Work, love, and wrestle on,
   Loving God best ;
Then when thy work is done,
   Lie down and rest."

"Through sunless cities, and the weary haunts
   Of smoke-grimed labour, and foul revelry,
My flagging wing has swept."—*The Saint's Tragedy.*

PANTING, the *Mimosa* lay beside the wharf. The
villagers, who had a half-holiday to see the doctor off,
were congregated on the jetty to receive a last hand-
shake from their benefactor. Women were crying, men
lamenting, and discussing "how things would go without
him."

"He looks bad," said one, a calculating creature. " I
suppose it's all right with us, if anything happens him."

"God help us then ! " replied the other, fervently.

"The property's settled, ain't it ? " asked the first
speaker with concern.

"Property, property, property, that's what I hears 'em
say, rich and poor alike," replied his companion, with
feeling. "You heard him tell he was leavin' all to us.
What 'ud be the good of that," continued the good soul,
" if anything happened him ? I'd see no light lying

across Mimosa Vale, and the missus and the children 'ud break their hearts."

"Tut, man, no one can live for ever. He's a good sort, maybe. But he's only done his duty. What are the big 'uns for, but to look a'ter we? I don't feel under no obligation to no man. I works hard, I know, for all I gets."

"And when had you such a show of scooping the profits, Jack Tomkins?" replied honest Sam Smith. "It's coz the likes of you has no gratitude nor manly feelin', and allers thinks of your own belly and your own skin, that more doen't do like the doctor. 'T any rate most on the fellows feels that all their hearts is stowed away, with the butter and cheese, in the ship what carries our boss."

The children marched on deck holding up flowers which they deposited on the taffrail beside the doctor. In a short while the floral offerings almost touched the spanker-boom. Many a little one clung to the good man's knees till forcibly led away weeping by elder brother or sister. Mrs. Sandbach begged the doctor to "find out" her brother, who, when she saw him last, twenty years before, was working for a tinker somewhere off Cheapside.

"I dare say you'll see him thereabout, doctor dear," she added, "and if you'd give him this bottle of herbs, and say as how I growed and dried them, I'l be so much obleeged to ye." The good creature moaned as she essayed, with some risk, to "walk the plank" with apron to her streaming eyes.

Another would never forget the doctor's kindness, if he would, as he was passing, hunt up his father, who used to tend pigs in the Isle of Skye.

Innumerable were the commissions to "all sorts and

conditions of men," with which the doctor was en-
trusted.

" You've spoiled them," said his wife, clinging to his
arm. " They think you only live for them. Mr. Elms,"
said Mrs. Courtenay, turning to him, " I charge you to
bring my husband safe back. If anything befall him, I
hold you responsible."

Pale and worn the man shrank from her imploring
gaze. He was about to speak. By some chance his
eyes met Malduke's, and he was silent.

"Thank you very much, I am able to look after
myself," was the doctor's laughing reply. " I wish I
could feel as easy about you and these simple children
all."

" Larry, my boy," laying his hand affectionately on his
son-in-law's arm, "you will, I know, be patient and
long-suffering." The strong man's voice quivered.

" Governor, if necessary, I'll give my life for them—for
your sake," was the reply.

" Hush, Larry, do not say that," expostulated Hilda,
in whose breast, like that of her mother, a vague dread
lay.

" I'll hold the reins, bless you, with a hand of velvet,"
continued the Irishman, reassuringly, " I won't even
tickle them with the spur. I'll just tool them along,
without their knowing it, over every bit of fence we have
to take together. Never fear," he continued, "we'll all
be in at the death."

Again the young wife's hand twitched involuntarily on
that of her husband.

"'Tell my landlady in Loundes Street," called out Tom
Lord, "that I'll be back to pay her my little bill. And, if
you're passing, old man, pop in at Hill's, Bond Street, and
inform him that my last coat pinches abominably under

o

the arms.   And, I say, old fellow, don't be hob-nobbing
all your holiday with Tom Burns and Ben Tillett, or
stumping it beside the fountain in Trafalgar Square."

The bell rang for the decks to be cleared.   Father
and son stood hand-in-hand, while a dozen final directions
were given.

"Do not break your heart, my boy, over that girl,"
said the elder.   "If it is to be, it will be, and with my
blessing.   But duty first.   I look to you and Larry, you
know."

"We'll not fail you, sir," was the young man's reply,
as putting his arm in Maud's he hasted off the vessel.
Already a severe conflict was raging in Travers' breast
between love and duty.   He dared not, he felt, give
assurance that action might belie.

"Good-bye, Mr. Elms," said Maud, shaking the
Sergeant's hand.   "Take care of father.   I know he's
safe with you.   I will look after Gwyneth.   Come along,
child," and not thinking of the awkwardness of the
situation for her brother, on whose arm she leant, the
girl slipped her disengaged hand into Gwyneth's and
drew her weeping towards the ship's side.

"I'll do my best, miss," replied the Sergeant.

"Yes!   Your best, or never show face here again,"
hissed Malduke into his ear, as he leant forward from
the gangway.

The cheers, the sobs had died away.   The waving of
a thousand hats and handkerchiefs was merging into one
bright flutter on the receding shore.   The doctor sat on
the taffrail beside the mountain of flowers, symbols of
numberless silent prayers.

The streak of golden wattle, threading through the
vale, became engulfed in the ocean of green.   Far up
the valley the factories seemed, in the dazzling mirage,

as ships riding on a sea of emerald. On either side the vine-clad hills ascended to pine-dotted ranges amongst which white-fleeced sheep were moving. The smoke hanging in the clear atmosphere above lines of cottages told of good meals preparing, with which the housewife would cheer those regretting their loss.

On the vessel speeded, past Hygeia, where convalescents waved the spade with which they were playing; past Kokiana and Fabricia, where hundreds turned out to rend the air with acclamations. All the while, he who had clad the waste with gardens and peopled the lonely plain with rejoicing sons of labour, took up, now one, then another of the flowers he had made to grow in the wilderness, and cast them into the water, until from the quay, across the unrippled bosom of the lake, through the narrow winding of the canal, out on to the broad waters of the Silverbourne, extended a sinuous line of floating flowers, about which the birds dipped and fishes leaped, connecting the lonely man at the taffrail with the scenes of homely industry he was leaving behind.

When would his good ship plough that floral path again? Flowers would it be, or tangling weeds of sorrow and care that, returning, the boat would cast from her bow?

CHAPTER XXVIII.

BROKEN TRAPS AND BREAKING HEARTS.

> "Two paths lead upward from below,
>   And angels wait above,
> Who count each burning life-drop's flow,
>   Each falling tear of love.
> While Valour's haughty champions wait
>   Till all their scars are shown,
> Love walks unchallenged through the gate,
>   To sit beside the Throne!"—O. W. HOLMES.

> "The day drags through, though storms keep out the sun;
> And thus the heart will break, yet brokenly live on."
>   BYRON.

TOM LORD had taken up "a twenty acre block" beside the lake, and was "graduating," so he termed it, "as a co-operative 'Cockie.'"

He had purchased "a Snowden blood warranted" quiet in saddle and harness. Since his memorable victory at the village races, Tom disported himself in most correct "bush" garb. A pair of immaculate riding-pants and top-boots, Crimean shirt with fiery-coloured "cummerbund," neck-scarf to match, had been procured from town. The hugest of cabbage-tree hats, swathed in pugaree, completed the little Englishman's outfit. Nay, we must not omit the long spurs, whose frequent collision with each opposing foot had left scars on either shining toe.

By the village artist Mr. Lord had been photographed astride his " Snowden," mounting and dismounting. The instantaneous representations of the tyro cracking his stock-whip were not quite successful. Rejected by the ardent knight, the artist retained copies which attracted attention after Mr. Lord's departure for " a peep at the old country."

The tell-tale camera depicted hat sent spinning far afield by the unaccommodating whip ; which had, as Tom remarked, a remarkable affinity for his head, round which it coiled with boa-like affection.

Old " Snowden " was less patient, when the snake-like thong wound about the creature's ears, or inserted itself beneath his tail. He resented the indignity in a fashion that caused the Englishman anxiety as to " the tenure of his seat."

The gentleman-rider, as he liked to be styled, would, in true bush fashion, look after his own stable. True, his long-suffering steed raised objection to his currying its slender legs. The combing of its tail, when the flies were playful, caused anxious moments. Tom, nevertheless, had reason to be proud of the animal's glossy coat. Its food he administered in strict accordance with directions contained in a library of yellow-back works he collected on " The Horse," " The Pig," " The Cow," " My farm and four acres," with other such bucolic manuals.

Alas ! an evil day arrived. " Snowden " ate without a relish. Had he been licking salt too much ? That must be removed.

The hay might be sour, the oats musty ; Tom would complain at the granary.

Yet another day and " Snowden " refused food entirely, actually lay down in his stall, the picture of misery, and, later, seemed to be considering the advisability of departing this weary life altogether. His master was in despair.

Hastily the local vet., old settler Snooks, was summoned. Travers attended too, out of sympathy. Snooks suggested bleeding, and terrified Tom by thrusting his arm half-a-yard down the patient creature's throat to administer a ball.

" I was relieved," explained Tom afterwards, " when I saw his hand reappear."

The next day the sad animal was worse. Some cruel wretch actually advised "another ball "—*of lead* this time, to " put him out of his misery." The hay, the oats, the green stuff, the bedding had all been duly examined. None could surmise the cause of the mysterious indisposition.

"What water do you give him ? Let's have a look at that," said the leech in despair.

" *Water! By Jove, I never thought of that!* " exclaimed the amateur hostler. " *Blowed if I gave him any!* " speeding frantically for a bucket. " Poor brute, he's been nearly a week without a drop to drink ! You see there's so much to think about in a stable."

" Slowly does it," counselled Mr. Snooks. " Another bucket in an hour, and he'll be all right."

" If you're thinking of riding across the continent, Tom," remarked Travers, " he'll be in fine form now. As good as a camel to bear you over the waterless desert."

The little man's troubles were not yet ended. The next afternoon Gwyneth met him, disconsolate, descending the hill towards the settlement. He was leading the unfortunate "Snowden," about whom harness was loosely hanging. The remains of a shaft balanced in the belly-band. At every other step the creature trod upon its breeching and trappings.

"What *has* happened, Mr. Lord?" exclaimed Gwyn-eth, smiling despite her sad thoughts.

"What has *not* happened?" was the reply. "I never imagined before how stupid are the ways of horses. You must know I started off this morning in my buggy to see Mr. Bloakes the banker at Gumford. I 'hung up,' as they call it, my horse and trap to the post set for the purpose in front of the stuccoed building. It was literally a 'hang up.' I came out in a few moments to find my Rosinante actually strangling, tied up in the most awful way. The more it backed, the more it somehow pulled itself together, till down it fell, its head tied round its neck. Even now I don't know how it all happened. There's something very wrong about the ways of harness that acts like that."

"You left the reins *in* the rings on the saddle," suggested Gwyneth, laughing, "and then tied him up by them."

"Yes, I looked to see all was right."

Gwyneth explained, as best she could, that the Australian way, whatever gentlemen practised in England, was to draw the reins *out* of the rings under such circumstances.

"Oh, I see now," replied Tom; "why can't they give a fellow all these wrinkles, and not leave him to find them out by bitter experience?

"It's the way of the world," he continued, solemnly shaking his head. "No doubt it would take a long time to tell a man all he needs to know before he graduates as a bushman. Cambridge and 'the Little-go' are nothing to this 'big-go' in Australia.

"Well, that wasn't all," the rusticated undergraduate continued. "Some grinning urchins and a blacksmith, who, *I know*, was laughing in his greasy, upturned sleeve

all the while, extricated my lashed-up steed. The fat baker
was cruelly seated on poor 'Snowden's' head throughout the unravelling process.   Now *that* I am sure was
unnecessary.   I had had enough of the dusty streets and
smirched faces of Gumford for that day.   I drove slowly
homewards, a sadder but a wiser man.

"Across the bridge, you remember, is a rare patch of
grass. 'My poor old sat-upon beast, in more senses than
one,' I exclaimed, 'you shall browse the luscious herb
awhile.'   I was afraid to take the brute out of his terrible
trappings, lest I might be unable to incarcerate him again.
You know I never can remember the number of holes in
the 'belly-band' and 'turns' of the breeching round the
shaft; not to mention sundry needful adjustments of
traces and reins.   So I thought he should feed as he
was, while I enjoyed the more fragrant weed and cogi-
tated upon 'what may happen to an Englishman in
Australia.'

"How could he, I thought, see to eat and avoid the
wretched thistles with those horrid, hot winkers on?   In
tender regard for my long-suffering nag I managed, by
dint of standing on tip-toe (he would stick his ears in
the clouds, of course), to drag off, somehow, the head-
gear.

"I hardly know what happened next," continued
Tom, wiping the perspiration from his face.   "As one
possessed, hurling me into a bed of thistles, the creature
dashed off.   Trap and horse went bounding and crashing
over logs, through bushes, till, smash! they were caught
in a thicket.   I limped after them.   At sight of me the
creature started again.   By furious kickings, of which I
could not have thought my placid steed capable, he had
extricated himself from my precious 'Abbott.'   I caught
the beast at length, and here I am," concluded the

unfortunate Jehu, looking demurely upon his wrecked harness and dusty steed.

Gwyneth comforted the little man as best she could, and, inserting the straggling straps into buckles and rings, essayed to proceed on her way.

"Miss Elms," said Tom, placing his hand on the girl's arm. Her face had resumed the expression of settled melancholy that imparted to her clear-cut features a solemn beauty of their own.

"I have long wanted to impart some information to you," he began. "I can tell you something of your sorry young lover."

The girl started, imagining that he spoke of Travers. Malduke was in his mind, as he continued—

"He's not worthy of you. I can tell you of a little intrigue I witnessed at Heatherside."

The mention of Eva's home roused the girl.

"Thank you for your kindness, Mr. Lord," Gwyneth replied, "but really I do not care to discuss the matter."

"Do please sit for a moment on this bench," he replied. "I dare not hang up 'Snowden' again, but I can hold the reins. Let me tell you what I know."

Ah, why did she not stay and hear? A few words as to Malduke's movements would have cleared up everything. Days and nights of anguish would have been spared the lonely girl had she only listened to the little man's story. How often do the Fates, our own impatience, or readiness to believe the worst, cause us to miss the chance, when it comes, of forgiving and being forgiven!

"I must tell you," continued Tom, intent upon conveying his information, "I saw him in Eva's room, cutting out a beautiful representation of yourself from a silver case."

The girl would not hear more.

"Mr. Lord," she replied, with trepidation, "I know all about the wretched affair; please say no more."

Hurrying away, she left the little man scraping absently at his sorry steed's sides.

"There is some mystery here. I wonder where Travers comes in?" he muttered to himself as he turned toward his "homestead"—as he called his primitive habitation. "Confound it, if Travers were not in love with the girl," he said to himself, "I should fall head over ears myself. She looks 'so sweet,' as the girls say. But, hang it all, it's enough to drive a horse about, without seeking to chevy a wife. No, I'm game with cattle, and am getting on, but I'll not just yet undertake any further 'breakings in.'"

Gwyneth moved on, sad and desperate. She was absolutely alone in the world. Malduke had been tormenting her again, and hinting at the place being his, her father's, and hers, shortly. Some plot was brewing. Travers was not himself. A love-sick man has a short temper. The men were finding that out. O'Lochlan, with best intentions, was not succeeding. The men were unsettled since their day-star had disappeared.

Gwyneth seriously contemplated flight. In the city she could forget her troubles, and not ever be meeting the man she loved, who loved her not, and the man she hated, who loved her still.

She proceeded to the gooseberry field, where, with other maidens, her task was to pick the ripening fruit. Doggedly she settled herself to the "sad, mechanic exercise, like dull narcotics, numbing pain." Eva, passing by, happened to see her. In her impulsive, gleeful way, the child of the forest hurried forward, exclaiming—

"Gwyneth dear, you do look so charming! My dear," she continued, taking the elder girl's hand, " I must tell you. I have such news. I am so happy. I dare not inform any but you. Travers Courtenay," she added— Gwyneth's clear brow darkened ; all the world seemed conspiring to sound her ungracious lover's name in her ear—"has proposed virtually," continued Eva. " I think his way so much nicer than fine sentences lovers string together in novels. He's given me a beautiful silver case with—what do you think?—my own likeness and his side by side. He sent a message by my maid that he had taken the liberty of putting a keepsake on my shelf, and there I found it."

As a matter of fact, Malduke had given the message to the servant-girl, Ann, with whom he had ingratiated himself. Travers had, indeed, in an absent mood, plucked some flowers, as he strolled in the Heatherside garden, and, not knowing why, told Ann to give them to her mistress, with his compliments. Meeting the young man the next morning, Eva, in her simple way, had said, with the silver case in her mind, that she felt she ought not to keep his beautiful gift. He, thinking of the bouquet, begged her to accept his present as a souvenir of their pleasant drive. " I hope we may have a longer one together some day." The girl pondered the passing words. Her youthful imagination associated varied sentiments with the beautiful present so strangely conferred. She recalled the words with which Oliver Wendell Holmes' "Autocrat" proposed to the "little school-mistress." "Shall we take the long walk together?" This other "longer drive," what could it mean but life's pleasant wandering through Elysian Fields in company?

As to Travers, the girl's artless joy touched him.

Unconsciously it revealed to him the fact that he, whose few flowers, as he thought, had caused her such delight, was object of much interest to her. Love begets love. Travers, with pain and mortification, experienced the fact, in slight degree. Gwyneth was first and all to him in the universe—ever in his thoughts—but somehow, as he moved moodily about his lonely lodge on the hillside, the face of the bonny, brown-eyed maiden of Heatherside would obtrude itself unsummoned upon his imagination.

Gwyneth, as she returned at the close of the afternoon to her desolate home, said to herself—

"I need know no more. He discarded me for her There can be no mistake now."

Her father had arranged that Alec and his wife should live with his daughter and care for her. Throughout a sleepless night the heartbroken girl formed her plans.

Fortunately Mrs. McDowl was away, nursing a settler's wife. Alec's duties involved his absence. When the good couple returned at nightfall, they found on the parlour table a note from their ward stating that, feeling life in the old home intolerable without her father, she had resolved upon leaving for a while. Would they care for her domestic charges, and excuse her hurried departure? This episode, associated as it was with Travers' treatment of the village belle, did not improve the discipline of the settlement. The girl could not be traced beyond Gumford, where she had taken train for Melbourne. Travers, anxious for the fate that might befall the friendless maiden in the great city, after struggling long with the sense of duty that would keep him at his post, finally left the settlement to discover, if it were possible, traces of his lost love in the mazes of the metropolis.

CHAPTER XXIX.

BETWEEN DEVIL AND DEEP SEA.

"O well for him who has a friend,
　Or makes a friend where'er he comes,
And loves the world from end to end,
　And wanders on from home to home."
　　　　　　　　TENNYSON, *The Wanderer.*

"Open, candid, and generous, his heart was the constant companion
　of his hand, and his tongue the artless index of his mind."
　　　　　　　　CANNING.

THE doctor stepped ashore at Plymouth a restored man.
He spoke that same night to an immense audience
assembled in the matchless Guildhall, from whose pictured
windows the early settlers of England looked down.

Speeding by train through hedge-bound fields, beneath
ancestral oaks and elms, across the garden of England—
the fairy-land of Devon—winding beside gleaming sands,
beneath beetling cliffs, he paused at length as in a dream
—the joy of which only the exile knows—at his native
vale of Dawlish.

A lump was in the wanderer's throat, as, perfect
stranger, he mounted the sloping hill to right, and gazed
on the well-remembered lineaments of the vale that pours
its beauties on to the rock-sentinelled sands. He crossed
the valley and ascended the embowered hill opposite,
moving solemnly, as over the graves of ancestors and

relics of early youth, to the old church amongst the
trees, out by the lych-gate to the rectory, reposing, as
when first he awoke to consciousness of being, beneath
the giant trees in that fairy hollow.

He dare not move forward. His heart was too full
for speech with strangers, where parents' voices, long
since hushed, had so lovingly sounded. There hour
after hour he sat, envying the passing farmer and rustic
children, who, seeming not to realize that they dwelt in
a paradise upon earth, eyed him curiously.

When the warm beams of the July sun were beating
life into the decaying walls of old Exeter, he passed, one
Sunday morning, up the well-remembered winding hill
from the station to the Close in which stood the ancient
Norman pile. Under its time-scarred portal, from whose
countless niches the sculptured figures had departed—
as had the faces he once knew from the streets—alone
in the venerable nave he knelt as in another world. On
more than one great tablet of brass he read the names
of school-boy chums, fallen in battle, or distinguished in
State.

Slowly he moved in London, lost in its crowds; out to
the docks, where college-mates, who had promised to
impress the age, spent their lives in a desert of vice and
crime that gathers around the great store-houses of the
world.

Into the Black Country, seeking vanished faces, he
wandered, where strong men stalked the street craving
work that, half the year, never came. Thinking of
scenes afar, of thousands of unpeopled miles in his
adopted country, wasting for lack of people to till it, his
heart sank within him. Gaunt-looking men, vouched
for by clergy and employers, followed him, as he moved
from thronged halls in which he had been telling of the

resources of the lands across the sea.   Eager trembling voices begged—

"Oh, sir, for God's sake help us!   Take us to where is hope and work."

These faces haunted him.   Long he conferred with early friends, now in authority, but ever with the same result.

England would keep her battalions of abjects, that she might have a ragged army from which to select her underpaid hirelings.

"If you take the best, we must pay higher wages to the worst," they argued.

So, for the sake of gain, masters clung to their shivering, starving slaves, and cried—

"After us the Deluge.   Though the great arising come, please God it be not in our time."   Meanwhile they held to cheap labour and abundance to choose from, in the course of the infernal barter of flesh and blood for wage.

From Victoria Street, Westminster, came the echo of an equally coward cry across the sea—"If these men come to the Island Continent that a handful hold, then our monopoly fails, our wages fall."

So between the grasping ones who would keep and the greedy ones who would not have, our doctor beat his wings against the iron bars of a hideous custom in which he found himself enclosed.   None dared help him open up a highway between the landless people and the unpeopled lands of a world-embracing empire of lust and greed.

"One day," he remarked to some, whose appeals rang long in his ears as he afterwards moved in bright, distant scenes, "one day I may return, and thousands of you, carefully gathered, shall be borne away, in fleets bringing cheapened food, to rich unpeopled lands of yours across the sea."

In Europe and America plans were matured for disposal of produce, plant was procured, agents appointed, methods observed, and again the good ship turned her prow from American ports towards the lands across the Pacific, where the long roll of southern seas beat out their music on illimitable Austral shores.

The demon that accompanied Elms urged him more strenuously as the *Mimosa* glided each day two hundred miles nearer home. Would nothing happen?

Of the flight of his daughter from home, Malduke had given an account calculated to arouse resentment against the Courtenays and so against the doctor. Again and again, at a critical moment, the demon of passion and greed prompted him to stretch out a hand that would have consigned his master to eternity. A special Providence seemed to hedge him round.

While the good doctor was engaged reviewing business transactions, the Sergeant, to drown his care, betook himself to drink. Not until Elms was on the verge of delirium did Dr. Courtenay observe his condition.

One evening, when between fever and drink the Sergeant was wandering in mind, the doctor was surprised to find him, half-dressed in his cabin, poring over a document taken from his trunk. Standing unperceived at the door, the doctor heard him muttering: " If anything happens him the place is mine. Only I must destroy this Will, as we did that other. Dick Malduke's not here, the devil that he is, to clap it into a tin and hold it as a witness against me. There it goes," cried the lunatic, as, crushing the document, he flung it almost at the doctor's feet.

Something in the texture and colour of the paper

caused Dr. Courtenay to pick up the paper hurriedly. What was his surprise to discover one of the testamentary forms that he had left, as he thought, in his safe at Mimosa Vale! Meanwhile the Sergeant had rolled himself muttering into his bunk.

When the fever had abated and the stores of intoxicants that were discovered had been removed, the man rapidly recovered. The doctor, much perplexed by what he had heard, spoke to the Sergeant on the subject. His reply was evasive.

"That settles it," declared Elms with an oath. "God knows what I may not have said, how much he knows. He's such a cool customer you never can tell what information he possesses. Now at any rate *he shall not return.*"

The excessive heat that had contributed to unsettle the Sergeant's mind, culminated in a· thunderstorm and hurricane that, as in an instant, whipped the placid ocean into fury. The one possible course was to run before the wind. The ·tight little craft was, virtually, battened down, mountains of waters hurled themselves after her, as if seeking to overtake and overwhelm the scudding bark. Now and then a mighty wave would break on the quarter, causing the vessel to tremble like an affrighted steed, sweeping the deck fore and aft. The engine fires were extinguished, only the remnants of foresail and mainsail sufficed to keep her on her course. The howling of the winds and thud of the waves were broken only, all through a dreadful night, by the hoarse cries of the captain on the bridge, giving directions, or by the crash of rigging falling about the deluged deck.

Elms, not yet fully recovered from his fever, tormented by a guilty conscience, cowered in his bunk in an agony .of fear.

P

"Good God!" he cried, "save me from this death, and I will yet be an honest man."

The doctor, as the lurching of the ship and shifting of movable fittings permitted, proceeded calmly with the calculations with which he had proposed to pass the spare hours of the voyage.

His mind, however, would wander onward to scenes he had hoped he was nearing. Again he stood on the quay, felt the pressure of loving hands, those from whom he seemed so long to have been parted. Above the tumult of the elements he almost seemed to hear his daughter's voice singing, as so often before, 'Rocked in the cradle of the deep.' He hummed the familiar tune to the accompaniment of his hand on the empty saloon table. A smile settled on his countenance. "Soon," he mused, "we shall be there, if it is to be; if not, all is well."

He was awakened from his reverie, not an unpleasant one, by the shouting of officers, scrambling of slippery feet upon the treacherous deck, and, above all, by the cry ringing from end to end of the bounding vessel, "Breakers ahead."

"Ah," he murmured, "the end of the voyage may be near. It will have to come some day. I can do no good on deck." He looked at his watch. "Five o'clock; thank God we have daylight," he said.

"Make ready the boats," was shouted down the companion way. A wave of spent water followed and swept along the floor of the saloon. In a moment all hands were on deck. The dark outline of a cliff was looming out of the morning haze. To right and left, a mile or so away, the waves were hurling themselves scores of feet high, against two low headlands. These were the extremities of a small island towards which the vessel was running. The captain was evidently seeking to round the nearer of these points that lay to the starboard.

The dullest landsman's eye could recognize that there was but small chance of passing that cruel cliff.

Within an encircling ridge of rock lay comparatively calm water and a shelving beach. Hurled on that outer wall of coral, however, no man could hope for escape to the palm-clad slopes that seemed, tantalizingly, to offer an arbour of repose, "so near and yet so far." The doctor secured himself, as directed, upon the bridge beside the captain.

After a while it was evident that the agile craft, answering splendidly as she was to the helm, though almost broadside to the tempest, could never round the bluff or escape to the open sea.

"Let her run," shouted the captain, seeming to think that, dashed high on the outer rocks, some might be hurled over the bar into the calm beyond. As the doomed vessel flew, as if relieved to have the strain withdrawn and the matter settled, towards the cruel rocks, the breakers that were dashing scores of feet high above the bar revealed how slender was the hope of one man escaping to tell the tale of the last of the *Mimosa*. The line of breakers, stretching two miles in each direction, dead ahead, seemed but a hundred yards off. For one second the captain grasped the doctor's hand as he passed, with eyes still staring into the yeasty Maelstrom before them.

"We've done our best, doctor. This is the end of it."

"No good ends," replied the other calmly.

The next second the captain started, as if struck. "Hard aport!" he suddenly shouted. That moment a narrow opening through the bar, seemingly no broader than the vessel's width, presented itself. To the last, like British seamen, all had stood at their posts. Round whirled the wheel, about sprang the ship as though understanding what was being done. The hungry waves to the starboard dashed themselves on the rocks that the mainyard almost touched as it passed. A huge wave lifted the fragile *Mimosa* on its breast, and just in the nick of time, turning the vessel, as with unseen hands, fairly hurled her through the narrow opening.

A cheer, such as Englishmen alone can raise, even when death stares them in the face, rang out above the Titanic thudding of the breakers claiming their prey. The little vessel glided across calm waters within the bar.

"If the lagoon runs round clear to the lee, we need not even beach her," the captain exclaimed. In a few moments, as it seemed, the inner point was rounded, and, sheltered by the island-rock, in perfect calm the gear-strewn vessel lay.

Those who have battled a week on the Indian Ocean against the stiffest monsoon, spray painting white with salt the topmost ring of the leviathan's rolling funnel, to glide in an instant into still waters beneath the welcome cliffs of Socotra ; those who, after three months' voyage, having been hurled at last, by the storm with which Australian shores often welcome the wanderer, within the overlapping, precipice-gates of Sydney harbour, to find its bosom without a ripple, the flowers in the gardens of Watson's Bay scarce bending to the breeze ; those who have looked sudden death in the face, in a moment surveying all the voyage of life and conjuring up last fleeting pictures of blanched, praying ones at home— only they can estimate the feelings with which the small crew of the *Mimosa* dropped anchor in the calm lagoon, and lowered boats to reconnoitre the garden-isle that had threatened, so nearly, to mark the scene of their watery graves.

We may not stay to tell of pleasant rambles about the azalea groves and live-oak clumps of Walpole Island. It was quite uninhabited, being, as the captain explained, outside the beaten tracks of commerce, that follow one marked highway as closely as if buoys floated at every knot. It was removed, too, from the Polynesian groups, he showed, and was too small to maintain a population of its own.

"Woe betide," continued the skipper, "the trader marooned or sailor cast away on this lonely isle! A year he might wait the passing of some craft, swept, like ourselves, out of its course. A canoe driven to sea from the distant islands might land here for water and cocoa-nuts; but the visitors would, most likely, gobble up the marooner, if he were not too utterly starved to be tooth-some."

These remarks impressed the benevolent doctor. Ere they weighed anchor, after a few pleasant days' repose, a supply of stores was landed and stowed away in a cave that was duly walled up. Directions were inscribed on a board beside the beach.

When a last visit was made to the island by the doctor, accompanied by Elms, together with the first mate and apprentice, Doctor Courtenay further supplemented the provision made for any possible castaway by flinging into the cave a tomahawk, a few rough tools, a gun and ammunition, fishing-lines, and also a copy of Shakespeare and of the Bible. "The poor fellow would die," he remarked, "even if he had plenty to eat, with nothing to read. I am sure *I* should."

The party, having a few hours to spare, ascended the one cliff to which the backbone-like central ridge ascends, until, attaining an altitude of some hundred feet, it falls precipitously into the ocean.

The view was pleasing—a sweep of ocean on all sides, save for the little garden-isle of palms fenced in by a low wall of coral and foam.

The mate and the apprentice, his nephew, lay on the summit and smoked and dozed. Seeking, as he said, to photograph the scene on his mind, the doctor sat on the edge of the bluff. The opportunity he seized of conversing with Elms concerning his possession of the slip of paper supposed to be deposited in the safe.

As they conversed, almost angrily at times, the temptation came again and again upon the perplexed Sergeant to hurl the doctor from the cliff. His legs dangled over the edge. Once Elms started to his feet. One push from behind would effect his purpose! A bush hid them from the eyes of the mate. Elms gasped. He beat his breast as he stood behind his victim, fighting a terrible battle. The doctor, observing his excitement, which he attributed to his remarks, thought to leave the man a few moments to recover his composure. Perhaps he had pressed him unduly.

"Elms, lend me your hand; there's a good fellow. Here, take the end of my stick," he said, stepping down the face of the cliff to gather a rare rock-plant that had caught his eye.

"Hold firm, my man," he continued, as he stooped carefully on a slight track below which the precipice seemed to fall away, perpendicular, to the sea.

"Don't be frightened," cried he, as he felt the stick he grasped tremble in his hand. "I always had a cool head for this kind of work. Have often crept along wilder cliffs than this in dear old Devon."

"Come back, sir; for God's sake, come," suddenly cried the Sergeant. Somewhat startled, the doctor, raising his eyes carefully, beheld an ashen face peering over the cliffs upon him. The wretch was fighting the devil he had played with so long. Two men looked down on the doomed doctor—Elms as God created him, and Elms as the devil was making him. His mind was in a whirl. Here was his opportunity. The deed so long contemplated might be—must be—done. The arm of the better man, however, his very physical nature, refused to perform the treacherous act to which the devil-mind of the man prompted.

In the almost lunatic eyes of the wrestler the doctor read his own terrible peril. He must, however, retrace his steps, though few, with care. One sudden movement, and he was lost. Still he was cool. Fixing his eyes on the craven, on whose trembling hand his life hung, he steadied him with the spell of his powerful gaze. One step, now another, he felt his way back.

At the last critical point, when to round a boulder he must needs hang heavily on his friend for support, a wild, diabolical expression sprang into the face of the man he watched.

At times, so strained are man's nerves that they perceive, as by a flash of intuition, what no ordinary sense could reveal. Courtenay saw that he was doomed. His hour was come. With a hiss of hate or of madness, the wretch above, at the critical moment, deliberately released his hold on the cane on which hung the life of his benefactor. For one second the miserable man balanced himself, seeking to cling with one hand to the cliff, stretching out the stick with the other towards his companion, imploring with wide, despairing eyes and working features that he would snatch it again. Human Elms almost did so; the Satanic Elms restrained him. Again the human prevailed; the true man's heart beat. Relenting, Elms frantically reached forth the hand that had momentarily failed to seize the cane.

"Give it me again! Another inch further!" he almost shrieked, as he stretched forth himself over the yawning abyss. Alas! his victim's balance, almost miraculously maintained, was lost. With a last look the set face seemed to recognize the traitor's repentance. It was too late. Still outstretched, the stick described a circle in the air. The saviour of many human lives fell headlong down the cliff!

The wretched man above almost hurled himself after. Remorse, despair filled his breast. He was not by nature a bad man, as men term it. He was but a greedy, cunning one, that had played with his besetting sin till it mastered him. In a sense it was worse for him. From a higher height to a lower depth of torment he was falling.

On the face of the cliff the murderer grovelled. He tore the ground. "My God!" he cried, "slay me. Hurl me from this rock! I see it now; it is stamped with fire upon my brain. My friend! My benefactor! O God! his eye! That last look! He forgave me. Ah! he saw that I would save him. And I could not. My God, I could not!"

By wild cries the mate was awakened from a peaceful dream of return to home beside the inland sea. Starting to his feet, he was horrified to find the Sergeant alone, seemingly in a fit, on the edge of the cliff. No possible means of descending presented itself. The unfortunate chief, Elms stated half-coherently, had fallen by accident down the precipice. Dragging away the dazed, tottering man, who was calmer now, they descended to the beach,

Long they searched by boat beneath the bluff. The unfortunate man would have fallen into the water that ran deep under the beetling rock. His hat and cane they picked up. Two enormous sharks cruised round the boat as they searched. The doctor would be dead before he touched the water. They shuddered to think that doubtless his body had already been mangled and devoured by cruel fishes of prey. The stains of blood one thought he saw on the water. All the next day sorrowing investigation was made of cliff and shore, but no vestige or memento of the loss was discovered, save that hat and stick.

When the latter was brought to the ship, Elms at the sight of it shuddered, and talked all night in his sleep of a hat and cane, and a face that haunted him. None were surprised at the effect the terrible accident had on the doctor's fast friend and right-hand man.

As the vessel sped uneventfully westward, Elms slowly recovered. One part of him was dead, and the other part felt as though a burden was rolled away.

" I am sorry for the poor old man," he would mutter ; " but, as Malduke would say, it had to be. He had done his work, and now vaster prospects open out for Mimosa Vale—and plain John Elms."

For the twentieth time that day he folded up the precious Will he had recovered from the doctor's papers, and examined, with the interest of a proprietor, all the provisions the good man had made for extension of the new system he had inaugurated.

CHAPTER XXX.

FIGHTING THE FLAMES.

" As from one faint spark arise
    The flames, aspiring to the skies,
    And all the crackling wood consumes."—PINDAR.

"'Twas well ; he toiled till his task was done,
    Constant and calm in his latest throe,
    The storm was weathered, the battle was won,
    Then he went, my friends, where we all must go."
                        Australian Poets, A. L. GORDON.

"ARE not those flying squirrels peculiar little creatures?"
remarked Larry to Hilda as they walked by moonlight
in the garden of the White House. "See that fellow,
now, climbing by leaps to the topmost branch of that
great gum ; now he has sped out into space. How
gracefully he flies down to the foot of that box, now up
that red gum, to dart again down to another tree-trunk !
Always up and down—just like our life."

"Can they not fly up ? " asked Hilda.

" No," he replied, "nor even horizontally ; only down,
from one tree-top to another trunk-base. Just the way
we make our running, it seems to me. Painfully climbing up—no flying then. When, for a moment, we spread
our wings—such as they are—down we come with a
jerk, to the level we started from."

" You're in a philosophical mood to-night, Larry," said
his wife. " What has become of your wonted good
spirits ? "

" Well, this news from Queensland is not cheering. If I had gone in with my cousin, as he urged me to do, my fortune would be made at this minute. He writes— you have not read the letter yet—that the Artesian bore has struck water, and has converted the chain of dried-up holes into miles and miles of perpetually flowing streams."

" But did you not say it was costing •£1 a foot to sink the bore, and that they had got two thousand feet down in two places? Think of the risk and the expense," said the calculating wife.

" That's all over now. He's a made man! What's £5000 to pay for such a boon! Think of it—a river drawn from underground! Mitchell plains, with abundance of water, is the finest country on earth. The entire north of our continent will be fertilized in another few years by Artesian waters."

"Never mind, dear boy, you stayed here for my father's sake and for others——"

"Yes, and I'll see it through. But the pace is getting hot. I had a brush with some of the fellows this morning. They have no gratitude and no sense, and I, alas! little patience. See those flying-foxes sweeping down on the peaches—and those 'possums, too! 'Pon my word I must get my gun."

In a moment he returned with it. The foxes, like bats the size of bull-dogs, were darting about—ill-omened birds or beasts of night. Larry brought down two or three.

" Now why should God make such ugly, mischievous creatures?" he remarked, prodding an expiring fox with his gun. "Why link each pair of feet together so as to enable such uncanny flesh to fly and extend their depredations? So with some two-legged nuisances.

What are they made for? No sooner do you render some wilderness fruitful, than down sweep a few greedy creatures to spoil your labour. It will be like that in this valley, if the governor does not return quickly."

At that moment a figure, pushing its way through the sheltering pampas grass and bamboos, stood grimacing in the clear moonlight. Hilda, startled, clung to her husband's arm, then laughed aloud and exclaimed—

"Tom, where on earth have you been? You are a guy!"

"Useful rather than ornamental," the little man replied, surveying his costume. "We've been taking a bees' nest. Great fun! Despite all my precautions, however, I got terribly punished, till I took to my heels, with two or three swarms about my ears. They seemed to pick me out. None of the other fellows minded them a bit. Blood will tell," he continued; "mosquitoes, and now bees, prefer mine to any less blue. Now they're down my back, and up my legs! Hear them slyly buzzing before stinging," and the little man started off gyrating around the amused couple—now dashing his hat on the ground, now brushing the dazed creatures from his ears, now grabbing his legs as though he would tear away flesh and trousers rather than give the bee free play.

His was certainly a peculiar costume. A "viator" travelling-cap was pulled over head and ears, towel round the neck as though he were returning from a bathe, a great blouse, buckled by a saddle-girth about his waist, hung to the knees, his trousers were tucked into the top of woollen socks.

"I wanted to see the fun," he explained; "I would not touch the stuff for worlds. I'd rather spread my 'Row's Embrocation' over my home-made bread than eat that stuff. To see it hanging, sugar-bags full, in the sun, with all the flies in creation fighting for a footing— white comb, black comb, and breeding comb jammed into the same old sack! I'd as soon eat macaroni, after seeing it hang like hurdles in all the dirty narrow streets of Naples, as touch your bush-honey! But I thought my education would be incomplete if I did not just for once see them 'take the bees.'

"The way they found the hive struck my fancy. You know that little black boy, Barry, that's always cutting about. He watches, it appears, the bees going to the water-hole to drink, or get mud for their comb. He catches a bee, twines a bit of wool or silkworm fluff about its body. Off it starts for home, black boy after it. Over logs, round bushes ; he never takes his eyes from the sailing piece of wool. 'The Quest of the Golden Honey Fleece' you might call it. Miles away it may be, he observes the creature fly at length into the hollow of some lofty tree, through a crevice made by a broken bough. He 'blazes' that tree with his tommy— or billy, which is it?—and the next night 'lays the fellows on.' The biggest bit of comb they give him for his pains. They have three buckets full of the ambrosia-of-the-bush to-night. They are going to 'Italianize' the swarm, and set them up afresh on the bee-farm in the ranges.

"Bees, however," he continued, as he made a vigorous onslaught on his left arm, crunching an unfortunate captive, "are not the only creatures that carry honey in their mouths—or legs, is it?—and a sting on their tongue—or wherever they carry their arms.

"When the men had the tree down—didn't it topple with a crash!—I chased a 'juvenile 'possum perched on the back of its ma. She had experienced, painfully, the

truth of the lullaby she had been singing to the occupant
of her pouch—

> ' When the tree breaks the cradle will roll,
>   Down will come 'possum and mummy and all.'

"I missed my game, but barked my shins on one of
the boughs sprawling most awkwardly about. When I
returned I stood on a log, at a respectful distance from
the bees, who were buzzing ferociously inside the hollow
tree. The foolhardy men were cross-cutting close to
the hive. Ere long they chopped out the block of wood
between the cuts and laid bare the comb. They had
managed to perform the operation in the midst of the
dense smoke of a fire under the log. Some smouldering boughs they now put upon the aperture they had
made, and sat down to rest while the poor bees scrambled
away to the remotest ends of the hollow trunk.

"I could not avoid hearing snatches of the men's
conversation. They ought, they said, to be paid so
much a day for their labour, not merely to be credited
with a share of profits.

"'I've worked,' said Bill Bastion, as they call him,
'eight hundred days, I reckon. I'm a-goin' to have
£400 for that, in cash. They've got plenty—I'll not be
content with the miserable £50 they've given me, and
the rest in credit.'

"Others," continued Tom, "sought to explain that he
held the balance in land and improvements.

"'How 'm I to know as I'll ever get 'em?' replied Bill.
'Courtenay's run away—Boss O'Lochlan's mighty high-
handed. I'd not be surprised if some bright day one
jumped up and said, "Here, all you fellows, clear out !
This blooming place's mine !" He was determined to
have it out at the meeting to-morrow.' Bastion announced

that he intended to ask you to resign in favour of 'the Talkers,' as some call the committee. ' He's nowt but a squatter and a capitalist,' " he concluded.

" My thanks for renouncing a fortune," said Larry, bitterly. " Well, I've done the best I could, for the old man's sake, and if he finds chaos when he returns, I can't help it."

" The great bulk of them are loyal," replied Tom ; " but that Malduke is ever sowing dissension, and, as I always told you, these fellows are suspicious to a degree. Brown says it's not their fault—goodness knows ! That it's all owing to the system in which they have been brought up."

The next evening Larry had a bad hour with the men. Bastion especially, urged on by Malduke, was decidedly plain-spoken.

" What did O'Lochlan care for them, I'd like to know ? Who ever took up a job such as he had nobbled for any one's good but his own ? "

Save for the influence of Brown, who poured oil on the troubled waters, and of the better men, a painful scene would have been enacted.

Larry kept his temper admirably. All his old squatter instincts prompted him to go down and strike the man as he jeered amongst his comrades. The sense, however, that he was holding the position for another, restrained him. The task imposed of fighting a hard battle almost alone, had brought out all the better elements of his character. The rollicking, dare-devil young squatter had settled into a self-ruling, painstaking toiler for others.

Though touched to the quick, stung by the deadly bite of ingratitude, he that night smoked his pipe in seeming cheerfulness, and, owing to her delicate state of health, forbore to tell his wife of the indignities to which he had been subjected.

The settlers paid dearly for their three buckets of honey. Intent upon their rights, the men forgot to put out their fire. The next morning, before noon, an ominous column of dense smoke announced a bush-fire. The country was dry, and ere long the crackling of burning bushes startled the settlers.

Here again co-operation saved them. A thousand hands, all under discipline, moving like skirmishers in a long line on the edge of the fire, beat back the flames.

For the present the valley was safe.

Girls and children, like angels of comfort, brought the "squash," for which parched tongues were thirsting. Little ones wondered to see "how the water ran off daddy's face." For the moment there was breathing-space.

The fire, nevertheless, must be watched. It had a knack of creeping stealthily about, and leaping up where least expected.

Suddenly in the afternoon the wind changed with a wild gust. The slumbering fires leaped into furious life, tongues of flame sprang along dried trunks, and leaped from tree to tree overhead. Where only grass was burning before, the whole forest was ablaze now. A hundred feet high, clumps of scrub and undergrowth sent up a roaring column of fire, half-burnt leaves circling upward in a whirlwind, to be scattered far and wide. Scorched, the men fell back.

Human aid was powerless—save here, to sweep a road with bushes, or there, to burn back the grass on the side of the track that was threatened.

Suddenly Bill Bastion appeared. He was rushing

madly along the flaming hill-side, crying, "My child! My little Poll! My own wee Mary!"

Some of the children, it appeared, had been taking lunch to their parents on what was then the back of the fire. The sudden change and rise of the wind had converted this into the front. Up the valleys on each side of a hill the hungry flames swept.

With extreme difficulty the infant band had, by strong arms and swift feet, been rescued. Alas! one of their number, little Mary Bastion, was missing. She had been with the party on the ridge, and now "was not." Her parents were distracted. For a while none could pass that barrier of smoke and fire. When it rolled away, what would be left of wee Mary?

The hill on which she last was seen was partially protected by masses of bald rock, which had checked the advance of the fire in that direction. Ere long, however, it would creep through interstices, and, revelling in the thick undergrowth that crowned the summit of the knoll, envelop all in flame.

Larry, who had been galloping round all the morning, directing and encouraging the fire-fighters, appeared at this juncture on the scene.

In a moment he grasped the situation. At the wall of fire and down at his horse he glanced.

"I think we might manage it, 'Salamander,'" he cried. " I'm game to try if you are!" Patting the arched neck, his eye searched for some break in the mass of fire and smoke that was mounting to the skies.

Springing to his side Bastion laid a trembling hand on his rein.

"No, sir," he cried, "you shan't try it. No living man could ride through that forest now. When we can—it'll be—— But you couldn't fetch her out of it now."

Q

"Give me your hand, Bastion," cried Larry. "I'll bring your child back, if I find her, though, of course, to serve some selfish end!"

Remorsefully Bastion looked at the man he felt he had wronged, and was silent.

In a moment Larry, dashing spurs to his horse, was making straight for the roaring furnace. Women screamed.

"It's madness! It's certain death!" declared selectors standing by, who knew all that lay beyond that flaming cordon. "If he gets through that wall of fire, the smoke 'll smother him."

Yellow-haired Saxon and gleaming chestnut were in an instant lost to sight. One wild leap! and the impenetrable wall of smoke closed, as though a thick curtain had fallen behind them.

With lips compressed, eyes half-shut, peering through the resinous canopy, the daring rider dashed. The smell of fire was on him and his horse. On all sides trees crashed, boughs were falling from blazing tree-tops. Horribly, as here and there they found vent at the top, the fires roared through the hollow funnels of the trees.

Now reining horse on haunches, the rider escaped destruction from the six-foot trunk hurled across his path, then, dashing spur at critical moment, he leaped a tree-head ere the dust of its fall had arisen. Here to right to round the base of the gum that was falling to left, there to left to escape the forked tree-top descending upon him.

Blinded, gasping, smothering, he reels in the saddle. His legs mechanically hold him in his seat, as, when life is extinct, the ring-tailed 'possum clings by its tail to the bough.

> "Into the jaws of death,
> Into the mouth of hell,"

rode the O'Lochlan.

At length the knoll is gained. Across the bare rock limps the almost hairless 'Salamander.' "Co-ee!" shouts the singed and blackened rider emerging on the hill-top. The universe seems wrapped in smoke and flames.

Again and again—between the roar of the flames, the scream of the kangaroo enclosed in the fire, as snakes crawled away between the horse's feet to die, and the iguana hung to the blazing bark unable now to dodge the rider, as if playing "hide and seek" round the smoking trunk, as the hot rocks beneath his feet seemed to quake, and the hill reverberated with the crash of giant gums—the rider staggered round the little knoll, calling with thicker, choking voice—

"Mary! Coo-ee! Hullo—o!"

Ah! there, surely, is a response!

Only the death-cry of the opossum, awakened from dream of gum-leaves galore to find that for it "the end of the world" had come.

Hark! a moan of pain! Only the wombat that has dug, with bandicoot and rabbit, its own grave, and is being buried and cremated at the same time.

There, indeed, is a step behind! Only the emu singed, frightened no longer of aught save the fire, with native companion, blackened and graceful of gait no more.

The flames creep on. Soon the little oasis in the desert of fire will be swept by the devastating flames. Here already they have found entry. There is no beating them back. They have seized, with wild joy, the wattle-clump, and are leaping from its silver boughs to the pine-tree top above. Another moment and the bushy knoll will be wrapped in one sheet of roaring fire!

Ah! what is this, nestling in the heather?

"My God, I thank Thee! The child! The child!" cries the choking rider. He reels from his horse.

There, beside the prone trunk, whose head is already attacked by the flames, lies the rosy-cheeked, three-year-old, smiling in her sleep! She is clasping the flowers she had plucked—tapering, open-mouthed orchids, wild fuchsias with delicate maiden-hair.

Overcome by the enveloping smoke, stupefied but unhurt, the little one had cast her golden head across the dimpled arm that still clasped the flowers, and committed herself, unconsciously, to the guardian angels that keep special watch about children—and drunken men!

In a trice the daring Irishman is in the saddle; the child, half-stupefied, on his arm!

Down the hill he dashes, as the dried bracken, on which the little one had lain, catches fire, sending a lurid column to heaven, to mingle with the firmament of smoke above.

Again, over blazing logs, round crackling, tottering trees, through walls of smoke and flame—for the cruel wind keeps high—the limping steed and reeling rider stagger—

> " Back from the jaws of death,
> Back from the mouth of hell."

Hours seem to pass! A hundred deaths impend!

At length, ah! can it be? The light of the outside world penetrates the canopy of smoke. They must be near the edge of the ring of fire. They may yet escape from their Inferno!

"A few strides more, 'Salamander,'" Larry hoarsely cries. "Ah, another branch! Leap, lad, leap!"

The spent horse is slow. ·

He responds to the warning spur. Half a second too late! The cruel bough strikes the fated rider on the neck. The broken fork-ends of the dead branch penetrated the ground on either side. Stooping low the horse walks free from beneath the yoke. With wild eye the terror-stricken beast seems about to fly. It pauses; utters a plaintive whinny. It paws the ground as though in pain; sniffs the cheek of the motionless form stretched beneath the upright fork, but still grasping the unconscious child.

The bough that struck the blow shielded the pair from branches that fell about. The hot breath of the faithful steed recalled the fallen man to life.

He moved his head. It was agony! He sought to raise his body. The weight of the world seemed resting upon him, though the fork was six feet off!

"My God, my back is broken!" exclaimed the wounded man.

Still his steed pawed the ground, and turned himself about as though to say, "Mount on me, and I will bear you out of this hell."

"Go, 'Salamander': go! You must not perish here: go, and tell them where we are."

The creature never stirred. With a painful effort the wounded man sought to throw a stick at the faithful animal. It only shook its head, while the silken mane fell over its bowed neck. It absolutely refused to leave.

The maimed man dragged himself, after a while, along a track, beside which he had fallen. Here the gravelly soil had afforded little for the fire, that raged overhead, to feed upon. Clinging to the child with one arm, writhing along with the other, the horse following with nostril sniffing the ground, and burnt hoof casting up the heated ashes, as in grief, the procession neared the opening on the hill-side.

Now, from very pain, the indomitable Irishman faints. He recovers again.

" I must save the child," he gasps, "whatever comes."
Again, along the pathway of pain he drags himself.

When night had fallen, he found himself—he knew
not how—on the track outside the timber, where the
party had swept and burned.

The tide of fire had rolled away westward. The
searchers, some of whom left the spot almost as he
emerged upon it, were hoping now to get from behind
upon the hill, where traces of Mary and her rescuer
were expected to be found.

The shifting breeze from the south had swept the
valley clear of smoke. In all its beauty it lay untouched
below.

Supporting himself on one elbow, while the other arm
clasped the child he had saved, the dying man looked
out across the valley he was to scamper over no more.
His eyes rested on the White House, where, at that
sunset hour, his wife clasped in her arms a new-born
child that was never to know the light of a father's smile,
or the inspiration of his voice.

As he clung to the child of his enemy of yesterday,
the father seemed to think it his—the little stranger he
was leaving in a world of woe. Ineffectually he tried to
brush a tear from his eyes.

"Happy little vale!" he murmured, as he looked
down on the smoke-crowned chimneys, beside which old
folk were discussing, "Where they'd find Mister Larry
and poor little Mary's corpses."

"I've done what I could! For the old man, for duty,
and for God!" he gasped.

Up the stretch of glittering water the last rays of the
setting sun were dyeing red and gold, he looked for
the returning vessel so long expected. He thought he
saw it approaching. "In at the death! Relieved at

last!" he cried. "Hilda, to horse! Governor! My child." Convulsively he clung to the little one sleeping on his arm, and in death still fancied it his.

When the darkness of night was lighted only by the lurid glare of some expiring flame, that flickered here and there about a blackened tree-bole, little Mary awoke.

"Daddy," she cried, springing to her feet, and bending over her preserver. "No, it's not! Why, it's dear Mr. Lochlan, fast asleep! Mr. Larry, do look at me," she piped, toddling about him. "Talk to me, please. Vill you take me home? I's so frightened!"

She tried to turn his head. It was stiff and cold.

"You'se not asleep," the child half-laughed and half-cried; "you'se eyes open. But you's so cold."

Poor little Mary! Happy little Mary!

Never before had she looked upon death; knew it not when she saw it! Partially stupefied still by the smoke, the wee one crept again into the encircling arm, stiff in death, and slept beside the smouldering fires as if in Paradise, with the brave man's spirit that had passed.

In the morning they found them.

The horse that had been feeding about during the night stood whinnying by. The golden wavy hair of the dead man was blown by the morning breeze back from his smooth icy brow. A smile was fixed on the clear-cut face! The hand still supported the firm, resolute chin. The eyes were widely open—looking out across the valley, and, seemingly, on into another world. Scarce could they believe him dead.

Bastion, as he clasped to his bosom the crowing, chattering child, knelt down with bowed head, shaking like an aspen leaf. Strong, rough man as he was, scalding tears of bitter remorse fell drop by drop upon the cold brow of the wronged man, who had died for his child.

CHAPTER XXXI.

THE FLAG HALF-MAST HIGH.

"Thou bringest the sailor to his wife,
  And travelled men from foreign lands ;
  And letters unto trembling hands ;
And, thy dark freight, a vanished life."
In Memoriam.

By his self-sacrifice and death, Larry achieved more than by wisdom and firmness in life. In their sympathy for the young widow, the people forgot imagined wrongs, and contended to assuage her grief and to second the efforts of the sorrow-stricken women upon whom, for a while, control virtually devolved.

Hilda was softened by her great grief. She reproached herself for the self-seeking, and contempt of those beneath her, that hitherto characterized her life. Her first visits were to the cottagers, who had sent loving messages with other tokens of their sympathy. So it came to pass that, as often is the case, strength came by suffering, and a new love arose out of the ashes of the old.

About a month after Larry's death the telephone announced the *Mimosa* in the lower canal. Ere long the entire community had assembled at the lake to greet the wanderers. A chill struck to the hearts of all as the word passed from lip to lip—"The flag !—it is half-mast high !" The mother whose son, the wife whose husband had sailed a year ago, felt a sickening dread steal over them.

"I sees my Johnnie at any rate!" "There's my old man!" cried one and another, as the vessel drew nearer, and returning ones waved to those they recognized on the shore.

"Where is the doctor?" cried or thought every on-looker. On the bridge beside the captain stood Elms, seemingly in some authority.

"Perhaps he is not quite well," suggested old Dowling to Mrs. Courtenay, who, with face of a ghost, was leaning heavily on his arm.

None on shore dared ask, no one on board dared tell the dreadful news. Upon the hushed multitude a spell lay as though a terrible woe were impending. Slowly, almost solemnly, the ropes were flung, seized and made fast; the very captain giving his orders as though some dread ceremonial were being enacted.

When the blow fell and the truth was told, one long wail of anguish arose from the bereaved community. Women and children wept, while strong men trembled. Mrs. Courtenay's face became like marble. She tottered, then, with sheer force of will recovering herself, strode like a stricken lioness to the deck and confronted Elms. His blood-shot eyes fell before her searching gaze.

"Man," she cried, hardly knowing in the first rush of despair what she said, "where is my husband? Did I not charge you to bring him back? Where is he? I say. What! you do not answer? Before his bereaved people I denounce you as his murderer."

Accused so unexpectedly, the man caught at a rope to steady himself. Could she know his terrible secret? The vessel seemed to swim round. He sat on a seat and gasped. The captain in a few words explained the nature of the catastrophe that had befallen the doctor. Mr. Dowling seizing Mrs. Courtenay, as she seemed about to fall, led her away, calm, majestic, and broken-hearted.

"I know not why," she exclaimed, as the good man supported her through the throng, "but I had presentiment of evil. That man, strange to say, was always connected in my mind with it. I never trusted him. When first I saw, I shuddered. Did you mark how he cowed? how the brand of Cain seemed written on his craven countenance? I feel sure there was foul play."

The shadow of death brooded over the once smiling valley. With muffled voice men and women spake of the wise and good—seemingly greater in death—mysteriously snatched. By degrees a terrible rumour, that touched them more acutely still, went abroad. The entire property, upon which for years they had laboured, had devolved unconditionally, it was whispered, upon Elms.

"That could not be!" all exclaimed. Again and again had the doctor assured them that every provision had been made for protection of their interests. Could he, all the while, have intended to hand them over to the tender mercies of this man all instinctively distrusted? Alas! the deed was drawn three years before—was actually in existence when the doctor gave his specious assurances.

More powerfully does loss of property affect many than the death of their dearest friend. Witness so often tears of sorrow suddenly drying on the face, that glows with rage when it is discovered, after the funeral obsequies, that in the will the mourner has been forgotten. Considerations respecting property and gain rule, alas! under a devastating system of competition, the world of grief, as that of action and of joy.

"My friend is gone," may be a sad thought. "How does that affect me?" is, inevitably, the first question asked. Oh, self, self! prominent in our prayers and pains, cherished in the "business and bosoms" of all, underlying our charities, affecting our friendships, raising its horrid head in the very hour of sorrow and of death.

Wonder not, that in the breasts of these simple ones, whose homes were about to be snatched from them, and the hopes of years blasted, a terrible revulsion of feeling took place. There was no escape from the inevitable conclusion that the doctor had deliberately sacrificed them.

"Did we not say," some, wise after the event, would urge, "never trust a capitalist? They cannot help theirselves. Seem they good, and mean they well, they cannot escape from the traditions and customs of their class."

A further explanation Malduke took pains to offer and enlarge upon. When this will was drawn, the doctor's son was engaged to Elms's daughter. He dared not devise the property direct to his son. He had so left it that, in the ordinary course, it would pass to him and his. So the cruel, silly tattle passed along. The name of him who had devoted fortune and life to their cause was, as is so often the case, execrated and defamed.

Some there were—Alec and the Smiths, Sandbach and Bastion—unreasoning enough to believe in the doctor still, to cling to the hope that all would be cleared up yet. There was some dreadful mistake.

"How do you make that out? Facts is stubborn things," urged those who laughed them to scorn. "There's not one blessed thing you can rake up that looks like fair dealing."

"If all the world riz up and told me as Jinnie was bad," argued honest Alec, with animation, "would I believe them? If every darned thing seemed suddent agen her, would I 'spect th' old woman? When the Lord seemed to 'a forgotten me, as when He took our only child—God rest his soul!—would I hold from believin' on Him? All can stick when all is spic and spankin'. Love wants no larnin' and logic. It sticks to its man, and its God, coz, in its in'ard heart, it knows Him and trusts Him. To my dying day," continued Alec, with energy, "I'll believe in the doctor, whatever fair-weather friends may say. And look ye here, Dick Malduke, don't you be tellin' none on your wicked lies in my hearin', or, sure's my name's McDowl, I'll see if there ben't enow strength ieft in this 'ere arm of mine to ram the lie down your wicked throat."

The law took another view. Probate was granted, and Elms assumed entire control. Kokiana and the allied estates, together with the remainder of the Station, were adjudged not to be included in the property assigned to Elms under the name of "Courtenay's Village."

The Sergeant called a meeting, and delivered what he considered a rallying speech. He was a friend of theirs, he said; had suggested the undertaking to the doctor.

"Curses on you for it!" interjected one of the company. "Were there no workhouses in town, that you must bring us out here to be starved and robbed in the wilderness?"

"Hitherto," continued the Sergeant, "you have pursued a wrong course. You have merely modified Individualism. I propose to sweep it all away, to set up a pure Communism. But I shall act fairly by all if they are worthy."

"Who's to decide that?" asked one.

"I shall," replied Elms, his blood rising. "I'm a soldier. I believe in discipline, I can tell you. So no nonsense, or, mind, you walk ! That's plain."

Poor creatures. The iron was entering into their soul. Inwardly they cursed the dead man for devoting them to such a tyrant.

"We are agin private property," continued Elms. "No playing at individual allotments and 'private accounts' with us. We're all equal in the sight of God, and mean to remain so."

"I hope you will," growled one, stooping behind a friendly back.

"Three cheers for Pure Democracy and Socialism Undefiled !" called out Malduke.

No one responded.

Forthwith committees and boards were abolished. The books that contained records of each man's standing were ordered to be burnt. Happily Frank Brown managed to secure and to hide them.

"Individualism, Familism, must be killed," decreed the dictator.

At every cross-road, great kitchens and eating-rooms were run up in weather-board. All were compelled to eat in common.

"It means a great saving in time and food," claimed Elms, "instead of every busy-body of a woman pottering about with her own provisioning."

None were permitted to claim ownership in cattle, poultry, or other stock. All was to be regulated. And so it was. Men and women worked as little and as ineffectively as they could. Cows were dried off; vegetables ran to seed; crops were spoiled; machinery was smashed; bad work performed. None felt interest in the duty he was called upon mechanically to discharge.

Elms and his lieutenant were hated. The doctor's good memory was defamed.

"It seems to me," remarked Mike Milligan to Joe Smith, over the fence that now parted them, "we had one extreme in town, now we've got the other here, and atween the two, the frying and the fire, we seems pretty like to be cooked."

"At Kokiana," replied Joe Smith, "Sandbach says things goes smooth enough. They've just had another five shillings a share dividend, and half-a-crown carried for'ard in the books."

"Ah, they've got the right thing," replied Mike; "what the doctor intended here, if that scheming lunatic Elms hadn't got hold on him. At Kokiana each helps t'other, and all gets the bringin'-ins of his own labour."

The Dowlings and Frank Brown often dropped in during the long summer evenings, to cheer the desolate party at the White House. Mrs. Courtenay would have left the place for ever, but that her daughters were now more than ever wrapped up in the interests of the suffering people. They tried to comfort them; submitted to many a door being slammed in their face, and many a vicious word uttered as they passed.

"Poor folk!" they said apologetically, "they have been terribly disappointed. Of course we know that dear father never intended this—but how can they know that? All appearances are against him in their eyes."

It was strange to hear Hilda taking the people's part as against Tom Lord's denunciations.

"Did I not always say," he would remark with more feeling than he ordinarily exhibited, "that these folk who raised their 'Hosannas' so high, would cry 'Crucify Him'? 'Not this man, but Barabbas'—the robber. The same old story over again."

" But, Tom, they have much seeming provocation."

"See again," he would say, "the tender love of democracy ; the tyranny of the precious pair, and the handful that self-interest has already gathered about them. Any one would sell the other and their whole cause for a song. The possession of money or power transforms your most exemplary democrat into a demon of oppression, the moment he gets his chance."

" That is only another way of saying," replied Hilda, " that human nature is a monopoly of no one class. To improve the social state it is not sufficient to shift the balance of power. You must elevate the moral nature and touch the heart."

On the evening in question, Mrs. Courtenay asked Mr. Dowling to accept, in memory of her late husband, the walking-stick, almost sole memento of him who was gone. Dowling showed it to his wife, who was putting the finishing touches on her patchwork quilt. As moonlight flooded the room, Maud sang softly Blockley's setting of 'Enoch Arden's Dream.' Hilda and Tom continued their conversation beside the open window. Mrs. Courtenay lay on the sofa lost in thought, listening to the words her husband had loved—

> " It was my dream in lonely beauteous land,
>   To tread once more each old familiar scene.
>   And she was there ! Oh, could each dream remain !
>   But when I woke, my heart was yearning still,
>   If I might look upon her face again."

" Richard," whispered Mrs. Dowling, in a strange, soft voice, as if her thoughts were far away, while nervously, as one blind, she returned the walking-stick to her husband, " I suppose it is the music, or the moonlight, or all the sad memories influencing me ; but I see so clearly the doctor clinging to his cane for life, and a savage-looking man, like Elms, but different, looking down on the poor soul. Ah, the creature has treacherously let go the stick. He's lost." So saying, the doting dame raised her hand to her brow as if in pain.

The song proceeded, and Mrs. Dowling continued—

"It is so strange! He is walking on the beach, up and down, alone—long-bearded and grey. He's looking out across the sea, like poor Larry from Hillside. He's shading his eyes. Now sitting down with elbows on his knees and face buried in his hands."

"Thank you," murmured the company, as Maud finished the song, that seemed to come from the depth of an aching heart.

"Thanks, Rachel, you may light the lamps," said Mrs. Courtenay to the maid who entered. Under their unwelcome glare the elder ladies appeared pale—the one who had heard and pondered the strange words of her friend, the other whose fancies had been set roving by touch of the dead man's cane.

CHAPTER XXXII.

AMAZONA—THE FLIGHT OF THE MAIDENS.

"Be good, sweet maid, and let who will be clever !
Do noble things, not dream them all day long :
And so make life, death, and that vast for-ever
One grand, sweet song."—C. KINGSLEY.

"Yet no cold votress of the cloister she,
Warm her devotion, warm her charity ;
The face the index of a feeling mind,
And her whole conduct rational and kind."—CRABBE.

ON the morning of her flight, Gwyneth sallied forth
with merely a small bag, which waxed heavier as she
proceeded. Looking down upon the Vale, as she topped
the hill, she thought with aching heart of all that had
happened since the cavalcade of fugitives had joyfully
descended that way. She avoided now the dusty track
that meandered about the wide, fenced road. She shrank
behind a gum-tree as a cloud of dust hurled itself, with
ominous rattling accompaniment, along the road, and by
degrees there emerged from the thick canopy two horses,
a tray-wagonette, a silk-coated selector, and wife with
faded finery that had done duty in Bourke Street. The
man was smoking, the woman suckling a child. From
the pillar of dust they emerged for one moment, into the
cloud they disappeared, and Gwyneth pursued her way.

Now, past the old township of Hampstead, left
out in the cold by the railway, the distant roar of

R

whose infrequent traffic resounds through the world of gums, three miles away. New Hampstead—now styled Gumford—scorning the older, whose very name it cast off, seeking a lustre of its own, revels in all the luxury of two trains a day, and all the township turned out to interview them !

No "Cobb and Co." rattles now along the "straight-run" into the deserted township of Hampstead, with its one length of "macadamized" swept clean by rain and wind. No bushranger, or strange suspected character, flings now, as of old, from his horse at the shanty—once famed hostelry—and, casting down "a fiver," demands "drinks all round." No camp of blacks obtrudes itself amongst the wattle-boughs beside the sinuous, high-banked stream. The Australian "Auburn" lives alone on the memories of halycon bygone days, of which, in the long summer evening, a handful of fossilized fogies tell, beneath the once-animated verandah.

Across the long bridge at Gumford Gwyneth passed. A timorous glance she cast at the camp of nomad non-entities that ever sprawls and holds high conclave beside the friendly piers. That sacred fire, around which grizzled beards of the bush, smooth chins from the city are gathered, is never suffered to die out. Ere one weary tramp, or party of aimless wanderers, leaves the rendezvous, another old sinner from the stations, or youngster from town, not yet carrying swag as though part of him, takes up the vacated position and piles high the never-failing logs.

> "Hungry, and thirsty, and footsore, and old,
> Oh ! sad are the years that his grey hairs have told ;
> All trackless the desert lies stretching before
> The eyes of 'Old Archie' grown blighted and sore ;
> He drags his tired feet through the hot burning sand,
> With a swag on his back and a stick in his hand.
> The bottle he carries is drainless and dry,
> And all he can do is to lie down and die."

For records of rascality and crime, for tales of youth's fair promise blighted, for sights and sounds suggestive of the white man turned savage, and the free man slave, for a glimpse, from the " Bridge of Sighs," at a stream of weird, wasted life, flowing perennial from station to homestead, forest to plain, from north to south of the vast continent—streams of humanity uncared for, unthought of—men of promise of yore, who work and drink and trudge again, to beg at last and to die, with crow to caw the funeral obsequies, and ant to compete for the last legacy of flesh—for a peep into this world unique, stand for one moment, as Gwyneth did, upon the bridge that spans the sapling-shrouded stream, ere you cross the tarred timbers and find yourself in Great Gumford.

Gwyneth made for the railway-station, as the benighted traveller on the illimitable plains for the light in the window, the scrambler in the dark forest for the barking of the dog.

The straight, level line of rail that connects Gumford with the outer world, divides the township and countryside into two hemispheres. On that side, plain for hundreds of miles ; on this, forest : there, they drink squash and shandygaff; here, whisky and strong beer : there, they wear silk dust-coats, affect tray-buggies, and shave ; here, the bullock-team holds its own, German wagon and lumbering dray, the beard is thick and tangled : here English Churchman, who swears by his own, Scotch Kirkman, sinewy ".Holy Roman "; there, smooth " Bible-Christian " Primitive Methodist, with light dash of mild " Salvation Army." Speedily climate and physical conformation of country affect the habits and character of the population.

The plan of Gumford is simple. Facing the all-important railway-line run two rows of opposing public houses and stores. Here, at the conservative corner, where squatters imbibe, Thomas Coke holds sway. Mark him as he stands, with legs well set beneath a portly frame, head of a Bismarck, on broad, unrounded shoulders, descendant of generations of Irish gentlemen. Blood and breeding tell. A lay-rector, brought up to sniff Popery, sip port, and bag game, ruined by the O'Connell Reforms of which, with clenched fists and flashing eye, he still speaks. Wife and daughters he left in Ireland, so that he might seek fresh fortune and a new home in Australia.

First the paid manager, then the proprietor of rural hostelries, the disendowed rector, with the dignity and grace that never forsook him, played the host for profit, as erstwhile for love. Tom Parnell and "the Radical crew," as he termed it, of this new land he roundly denounced, turning away thereby clients more liberal to Will Short's 'Farmers' Arms' opposite. "He went on Sunday to the church," not to "sit among the boys," but to occupy front seat and to hand round the plate, looking the squire of the parish he was born to be. He wrote each week ¡to the daughters in Dublin, and sent them means to maintain the position the family had ever filled. For thirty years father and daughters never wavered in their ardent, Hibernian affection. Here, they never saw each other more. To the last, in dusty, sordid, brawling Gumford, Tom Coke held his head high, ever sober, solid, dignified—a gentleman and Christian, untainted by all the grossness of the bar. God rest thee, Tom Coke, and keep thy memory green !

As Gwyneth passed, Coke's quick eye observed her, as did that of the young bank-clerk spending his spare hours in the only way that suggested itself, lounging and refreshing oft, beneath the hospitable verandah.

L'homme qui rit of the township, who stands talking to the bank-clerk, checks for one moment his hilarity as the maiden passes; the half-stupefied tramp, sitting on his swag and leaning against the verandah-post, looks up with admiration, as he grinds his tobacco in revolving palms. The bank-manager is crossing the road with the twentieth client to commemorate at Tom Coke's bar, account-squaring results of a fruitful harvest.

"Deuced fine girl!" he exclaims, as the frightened. thing hurries past. The bank-clerk—with handsome face and open heart, who might be a man of worth to-day, if the wealthy institution he served had bestowed one thought on the pitiable lot of such as he—follows the girl·to the platform. The appearance of such a girl in Gumford was an unwonted experience. With the absence of ceremony acquired in the country, the youth, curious and admiring, asks can he "do anything for her?" The round man who ever laughs is rolling, with hands in pocket, across the desert of dust to see "this pretty piece of goods."

"No train for two hours," the lounging station-master reports.

Here, to be gazed at and questioned by half-intoxicated natives, Gwyneth cannot stay. She remembers the St. Clouds at the store opposite, whose pretty daughters had been delighted with her retreat at Mimosa Vale, and had repeatedly asked her to spend a few days at Gumford.

Smiling, good-natured St. Cloud almost leaps the heaped up counter, when he sees the anxious-looking maiden threading her way amongst bags and tins and cases that range about the floor.

The wanderer is taken by storm; begged to remain in the cosy, domestic addendum to the busy store. The girls play and read and paint. Gwyneth could be happier resting there, where the freedom and freshness of the country are associated with tastes and accomplishments of city life ; but she dare not ; she will, as soon as possible, hide herself in the metropolis.

The three clear-eyed, round-cheeked specimens of rustic beauty " see her off " from the platform upon which, including storekeeper King of the township, with tall hat on side of head, all Gumford, from bank-manager and mad doctor to tramp and tinker, stand ; and, in the "second-class ladies' compartment," midst bottles and babies, Gwyneth pursues her weary journey towards the distant seaboard.

Past deserted "flats " and "rushes " and "gullies," where maddened thousands once dug, where the crash of " cradles " exceeded the present roar of the train as it speeds through miles of half-filled graves of golden hopes ; past the gardens into which, here and there, enterprising holders of "miners' rights " have transformed the ocean of mingling mullock heaps ; through now civilized Quartzopolis, where oak and elm mingle strangely with gum and curragong,—casting pleasant shade and bright streaks of green across the city, greed-for-gold left so bare ; past the roaring "stampers " treading out the yellow specks embedded in milk-white quartz ; past "Poppet heads," where the ringing signal-stroke of metal on metal gives the word for earth's treasures to be hauled from two thousand feet below the roaring city ; now rushing through the lonely "stations," whose sheep spread over pastures where millions of human beings might prosper ; through the garden of the land, across Dividing Range where rain falls oft, and the black soil yields a richer harvest than all the gold-spangled rock left behind ; on, ever on, screeching past sleepy platforms and nameless "sidings," towards the glow in the southern sky, where myriad lights of the never-sleeping city cast their Aurora Australis on clouds rolling up from the Southern Pole.

More terrified, and with reason, than in forest and on plain, the lonely girl extricated herself from the mass of human freight which the express disgorged on the seething platform ; hurried through the throng of boisterous, beckoning "cabbies," of friends welcoming travellers and monopolizing half the platform in the process, of porters looking carefully after those having no luggage or needs.

Stepping into a tram, Gwyneth in half-an-hour found herself at Bridge Road, Richmond. A few steps brought her to the shop of Mrs. Strivens, a whilom neighbour of hers.

The good lady was counting the takings of the day. Hers was a small green-grocer's shop. In the window was a card, that Gwyneth was relieved to recognize still in place, "Apartments to Let." A warm welcome Mrs. Strivens accorded the wanderer.

"Yes, there was a bed to spare, though not a room. Pennie Scribblings and Millie Cole were still with her, and a new boarder whom Gwyneth would not know."

The two old friends, who happened to come in a few moments after, received Gwyneth with delight not unmixed with surprise.

"There, I'm not going to kiss you any more !" exclaimed demonstrative Pennie, panting. "Now, sit down. Take off your bonnet. Mrs. Strivens, kindly oblige us with 'coffee for four' without the pistols ! Now, Evangeline—you know that was always my name for you—I'm going to keep to it—tell us what good luck brings you to town. We thought you had renounced the city for ever."

"Gwyneth, darling, you are more beautiful than ever," said Millie, the Academy student, as she took her friend's hands and looked lovingly into her face. "You shall sit for me to-morrow, dear. But, stay, your countenance is more pensive. There are fresh lines of thought and care; you have a story to tell, darling. Now we will hear it."

Gwyneth did not tell the story; at least not the more important part. She explained that her father had been called away, and that she, finding the life dull, had resolved to see her former friends again. To Pennie that night the poor girl confided more.

Pennie was correspondent for two papers, reported for two more, was sub-editor of another.

"But I'm heartily sick of the Society trash!" she exclaimed; "of taking notes of nothing, and writing up everything not worthy a thought."

"What of your book?" asked Gwyneth. "Has that been a success?"

"Just where it was, half-finished. I get no time for real writing; scribbling for a living is my one occupation."

Millie's report was little better. Sometimes the girl had a little picture sold. She had a few pupils. But there was no incentive. Life for her, too, was a dull struggle for existence.

The third boarder was a widow of nineteen, without a penny and without a friend, Mrs. Gussey Gore, whose husband had run through his money and lost his health in twelve months, leaving her after a short year of wild expenditure, which the young couple mistook for happiness, alone in the world. Twelve hours a day Gussey Gore plied her needle to the order of the "Ladies' Work Association," and of Buckland and Joshua's in Bourke Street. She managed to pay for her board. The future she dared not anticipate.

The evening hour was the bright spot of their existence, when the friends returned and books were read
and talked about, and pictures discussed.   Then the
lonely three lifted themselves above their depressing
surroundings, and revelled in a world open to all
who possess the *entrée* to spheres of art, literature, and
science.

Each of the trio contributed from their respective
connections, small commissions that enabled Gwyneth
to pay for her board.   Pennie dispatched her to a
garden-party to report for her paper, *The Solar System*.
Millie managed to dispose of one or two of the studies
with which Gwyneth occupied her spare hours; while
thin delicate Gussey Gore was glad, when orders came
in apace, to share her labour and slender reward with the
new arrival.

Gwyneth discovered, however, that she had been
incapacitated, by sojourn in the country under such
different surroundings, for the hard life of the city.

. She pined for the freedom and pure air of the Valley.
The close foul atmosphere of the narrow streets sickened
her.   The ruthless competition, in which all about her
were involved, seemed like the scramble of wild beasts,
half-starved, compared with the Arcadian simplicity she
had discarded.

Poor Mrs. Strivens poured the tale of her woe into
the girl's ear.   She had been making a bare livelihood.
Forthwith a large shop, with much wealth of paint and
window-gilding, had opened across the way.   Having
some little means, the new-comers were able to undersell
their rival, although Mrs. Strivens' margin of profits was
already a vanishing factor, despite the fact that she
purchased goods at the earliest market, and little Johnnie
wheeled them home.   Her husband, a printer, since his

second son apprenticed to the firm could do his father's work for nothing, had lost the situation held for twenty years.   The old man, who felt his life-work slipping from his hands, bitterly upbraided poor Charlie for "taking the bread out of his sisters' mouths" and "cutting his own father out."   What could the youth do but weep when sore pressed?   Was he not "bound" for years to come yet?   Had he not to do what he was bid?   The eldest son was a saddler just "out of his time," but gentlefolk were "putting down" their horses, and after five years' application there was no demand for the saddles William had studied to make.

"If I'd only learnt to plough with the horses, instead of to harness them," the young man complained, "I could go on the land to-morrow—that's always there—and make something grow, if it was only 'Turks' heads' for mother's window."

Their straitened circumstances and Gwyneth's account of the new system that was establishing itself beside the lake, set the four girls thinking and talking. Why should they not transfer the scene of their labours to such a favoured locality?   Might not a party of homeless girls win a living there, and spend spare hours in writing, sewing, and painting, with other delights, as their tastes and acquirements suggested?

"One fact alone is significant," remarked Gwyneth. "Here it costs us one pound a week to live, or starve, whichever you care to call it; there, a number of us could exist, in comparative affluence, for two shillings a week each.   Though far from town, we ought to be able to earn with our hands and our brains as much as that, and a great deal more."

The girls revelled in the idea.   At the Work Association, Academy, and Salon, they canvassed and expanded it.

The proposal was enthusiastically entertained by scores of girls struggling disconsolately for a living. The idea of homes and gardens, cows and fowls of their own, with Art as a pastime, presented itself to their youthful imagination as a possibility almost too good to be realized.

Travers had sought out Gwyneth, and endeavoured by all means to converse with her. She steadily avoided him. Her heart, however, was breaking; the freshness was departing from her spirit. She was restless; felt she must have change and fuller occupation.

Her father wrote begging her to return. She replied that she could not settle down again to the old life; but would he, she asked, let her know whether she and some of her friends could establish themselves on the southern end of the lake? Eventually a scheme was formulated whereby five hundred acres should be ploughed and prepared, fifty cottages built, and a site laid out for the proposed novel colony.

Ill at ease himself, fearful of his daughter's dissatisfaction with the part he had lately played, Elms was glad to facilitate Gwyneth's return to the neighbourhood, though not to his home.

As to the domestic arrangements other designs were in his mind. The White House, the natural centre, must be his. It ought not to be a difficult matter for a man of his parts to win the widow of the deceased doctor. Meanwhile Gwyneth was just as well out of the way at the other end of the lake. If she must go into retirement, better there than to a convent.

The perfected scheme was laid by Gwyneth before a special meeting of "the Salon of the South," and Artistic and Literary Club for Ladies, that Pennie Scribblings had done much to promote.

With a beating heart Gwyneth ascended the lift and

laid aside her shawl and hat in the ante-room. The
spacious L-shaped Salon was filled with ladies of all and
every class and attainment.

Many were young and prepossessing, personally
attractive still to the eye of the outer world—some few
plain but powerful—many long since escaped from the
tender simplicity of "sweet seventeen." From every eye,
however, intelligence gleamed; on many a face genius was
stamped; on each high brow force was written.

Here and there a few much-overshadowed men were
bestowed on corners of couches and edges of chairs.
Sub-editors, not yet quite "case"-hardened to the
charms of fair women, young doctors who had been
prevailed upon to "read a paper," with art critics whose
wives thought them safe ensconced at the Club!

Gwyneth's paper created, even in this august company,
quite a sensation. The proposal was welcomed with
acclaim. Why should not daughters of Eve return to the
Garden of Eden, the Graces be ensconced beside the
streams, and nymphs explore the woods again?

So it was that Amazona was founded.

Fifty of the fair, whose duties were of such a character
that they could be performed at a distance, set forth for
the home beside the lake. For each five a cottage had
been erected.

A light breakfast and lunch each household prepared
as best they could, but dinner, which was veritably "a
feast of reason and flow of soul," was partaken of in
common in the large weatherboard mess-room, that
served also as concert-hall, reading-room, and theatre.

Four cows, a crate of fowls, five acres of land for
garden purposes, already ploughed, were apportioned to
each party; seeds were supplied, directions given, technical papers read. From the common store each party

received their weekly provisions.   The product of farm-yard and field was disposed of in connection with agencies already in existence at Mimosa Vale.

Millie's pictures, painted under brighter auspices, fetched double the price she used to command. Pennie's paper had to exist without her, while she gave herself in spare hours to completing the volume that ere long, with others, brought her fame and fortune.

None but those who know from experience, could con-jecture the reason why a freshness and pungency, lacking in earlier efforts, pervaded her subsequent works.   Many of Millie's students followed her.   Once a month Gussey Gore dispatched to the Work Association a small parcel that now readily commanded purchasers.   One or two hours' work with her needle per day sufficed to keep her in credit on the books.   As time wore on it was discovered that the cows and the poultry of each fair settler yielded them return at the rate of fifty pounds a year. The garden of cut-flowers for the market, the perfume-farm and apiary, silk-worm grove later, with a dozen other natural indus-tries for which feminine hands were adapted, yielded profits that brought wealth to the promoters, and prompted daily applications for admission to the ever-extending garden-community of Amazona.

On the lake, after work on the soil, the maidens developed their muscles and cleared their brains after study or sedentary occupation.   At the annual regatta their yacht distanced all male-manned competitors !   A score strong, the Amazons would ride forth, after cows had been milked, and gardens cared for, to hunt the kan-garoo in outlying portions of the station.   The maidens became sure of eye, as fleet of foot, and came to handle rifle and revolver with a readiness calculated to deter any —had there been such—who would invade their retreat.

One of the most successful of all the associated settlements was the fair and famed Amazona. For a month, or a longer term, those who could not entirely tear themselves from the city were permitted to sojourn at the settlement. Largely it helped to solve the question, "What shall we do with our girls?"

When, shortly, a direct line of rail connected the settlement with the metropolis, many nurses and seamstresses, writers and others, worked about their garden homes, when no special duty called them away, while at other times they spent a few hours, or days, profitably in the city

By degrees, not, it must be supposed, because of their comparative wealth, but by reason of their womanliness and aptitude, the maidens of Amazona were largely sought after, and shortly the synonym for a good house-wife and worthy woman of mind was "a Daughter of the Lake." All were free to wed or wander as they willed. But only those approved at the monthly parliament could join the sisterhood and settle at Amazona.

Any ceasing to reside could retain their garden farm—cultivated at their expense—and share in the quarterly dividends.

For Mrs. Strivens and her family a corner at Kokiana was found where, with none to compete, but all to help as they were helped, she flourished.

Only, as is often the case, the promoter of the fairyland was unhappy.

Gwyneth could not but grieve over the change that had come over her father, and ponder in her mind by what dreadful devices Malduke and he had gained control at Mimosa Vale. For Travers, too, she pined, always, despite her anger, haunted by the thought that some terrible mistake had parted them, and made him appear in such despicable light.

And so, with the burden of responsibility pressing upon her, the young creature worked and worried on, fading and failing, as her friends feared, from day to day, finding chief consolation in visiting the pale consumptives at Hygeia, taking them out in her yacht on the lake, and striving to impart to others' lives a brightness and joy that had vanished from her own.

CHAPTER XXXIII.

THE WHITE MAN OF THE WOODS.

" Like a rock that breasts the sea,
   Firm he stood in front of foes ;
To his friend a sheltering tree,
   That in changeless beauty grows.

Firm alike to friend and foe,
   Firm in gentleness and faith,
Firm in ' yes,' and firm in ' no,'
   Firm through life, and firm in death."
                              SIR HENRY PARKES.

" The flying rumours gathered as they roll'd,
   Scarce any tale was sooner heard than told ;
And all who told it added something new,
And all who told it made enlargements too ;
In every ear it spread, on every tongue it grew."—PRIOR.

BESIDE the lonely beach the doctor sat, with elbows on knees, his eyes sweeping, for a thousandth time, the unbroken horizon, that never revealed speck or sail. As the soft breeze whispered amongst the palm-leaves, and the waters gently lapped the coral shore, the desolate man often dreamed that he heard his daughter's voice singing in the distant vale.

" If I might look upon her face, and know that she was happy ! "

Starting to his feet he paced the gleaming sand, stretched forth trembling hands across the deep as though he would draw to him the loved forms he sometimes fancied he saw before him.

" Too hard, too hard to bear ! " he groaned, pressing

with his hands his throbbing temples, and, all unnerved, sitting down again to weep.

Some twelve feet below the top of the cliff from which he had fallen was a ledge, invisible from above, that protruded from the face of the rock. Catching on a projecting bush, he fell on the ledge, and rolled inward against the cliff.

Stiff and stunned, he lay all day on the horizontal fissure. Now he opened his eyes and half realized his position; now closing them, dreamed of distant scenes he had hoped so soon to visit. Again he awoke. It was night. He dared not move. Hour after hour he watched for the dawn. Daylight fully revealed his terrible position. A few feet from where he lay, the wall of cliff descended precipitously to the water. Not a goat could clamber to or from that dizzy shelf. Above him arose the cliff, sloping outwards to the sea.

There was no escape. He lay down to die. Possibly a rope might be lowered, but how could the searchers imagine that he had found lodgment on that cliff face? The action of Elms and the expression on his face convinced him that the search would not be protracted longer than he could contrive.

As he thought of the treachery of the man he had befriended, of the Will of which Elms had been mumbling in his fevered ravings, of the incoherent remarks about Malduke, and the document that had been destroyed, the doctor recognized the whole truth. The provision that, with a few lines, he had made for the disposition of the first venture, might be read as applying to the later estate.

The thought of his people and his life's work in the hands of these treacherous intriguers caused him, seeking means of escape, to tear again with his hands the smooth

s

walls of his prison-house, and to scan with a practised eye the face of the cliff.

The coral rock, up-thrown by volcanic action, and exposed to the climatic influences of ages, was crisp and yielding. A slight foothold would suffice him. He could balance wherever chamois or its hunter could stand.

Out on the face, yard by yard, he cut footsteps, a narrow siding, in a slanting, upward direction. A sharp, flat stone served as chisel. A few yards along the dizzy precipice face he had levelled when night fell. From sheer hunger and exhaustion he slept. The next day, the third, he continued his labours, while the wild-fowl circled about him, and the white foam, restless to receive him, laved the rocks hundreds of feet below. Before the sun sank his task was accomplished. Out upon the cliff top the captive tottered, blood streaming from the hands that had torn a pathway from a living grave, suspended, like Mahomet's, between heaven and earth. He staggered to the knoll where the mate had slept. A blood-stained handkerchief he waved, shouting till the sea-birds, sweeping in wonder around, drowned his cries with their screeches. Away, towards the horizon, was a dark spot on the water, and a lingering line of smoke, that seemed unwilling to leave him to his fate.

"Lost and cast away!" he cried, as he grovelled on the hill-top, and wondered why the cruel ledge should have intercepted his descent to oblivion. "For the first time and last," he bitterly thought as he dragged himself down to the cave he had stocked, "has the provision I have made for others brought benefit to myself."

Water, fresh and tasteless, was procured, by sinking in the sands a few feet above high-water mark. Fish and mutton-birds with their eggs, cocoa-nuts and roots, served to eke out the store he had made.   A hut he built him-self; later he planted a garden, and, to pass the time, sowed seeds he discovered in his store.   The wild-fowl he sought to tame.

A catamaran he constructed, and set forth on one occasion to cross the Pacific on a raft of logs !   A merci-ful gale hurled him the next day on to the beach.   Months passed, much as they have done for thousands shut up with themselves on desolate rocks of the ocean.

The " Two Greatest Books in the world," as he called them, helped him to preserve the reason, which some-times seemed to be failing.   Hour after hour he would read aloud dialogues and description, and live and con-verse with those whom genius and inspiration have rendered immortal.   On margin and cover of each volume he wrote, with his one pencil, annotations and comments, that served to occupy his mind.   With the indomitable resolution that had ever marked him, he refused to lie down and die, or to relinquish the priceless spiritual and intellectual powers that were left him.

Of the very irony of fate it seemed that he—who had decried so persistently the evils of individualism— should be taught, on that desert island, what complete isolation involves; that he who had devoted himself to social enterprise should be reduced to communing with the fancied and the dead—should realize how helpless the most gifted, cut off from his kind, deprived of the power of co-operation and communion with his fellows.

Again the stars, that had looked down on the ledge on which he had lain and first realized his desolation, returned.   Almost a year, he knew, had elapsed.

A hurricane, that swept away his hut in the night, hurled a " dug-out " canoe, empty, on the shore.   His blankets he converted into a sail.   A store of fresh fowl and eggs, with kerosene-tin of water, he stowed in the hollow trunk of his out-rigged craft.

For days the lone man sailed over placid waters, out of sight of land. At night he directed his course by the stars, trusting to good fortune to do the same for him by day.

On an evil morn he awoke to find that his tin had sprung a leak, and given out its last drop of water. Days passed, when the sun beat down upon him, still sailing on, he knew not where; nights, when deadly dews descended upon his aching limbs and fevered head. At times he raised himself from the coffin-cabin in which he lay, and, in a moment of returning consciousness, wondered when it would end, how long he would be sailing over placid seas to some impossible "nowhere."

Now he was in his coffin, wild birds his mourners, stars his funeral tapers, dews of night his shroud. It is daylight, a steaming white craft is bearing down upon him. The blue flag he recognizes, of the "Royal Thames Yacht-club," of which years ago he was a member. He is dreaming, surely. Youthful days are returning to him. White jackets, however, and friendly bronzed faces are bending over the bulwarks of "the white ship." Bare, brown arms are lifting him out of his floating coffin !

"Ah, ah !" he laughs, "that is not kind, to disturb a man in his grave."

Kindly they laid the fevered, emaciated form on good Captain Bongard's own bunk.

The *Southern Cross*, returning from a six months' cruise amongst the palm-clad isles of the coral sea, drew next day in sight of the tapering pines of Norfolk Island. Wives and children and black scholars, two hundred strong, all clad in white, descended to the quay, waving and shouting and weeping for joy, to welcome the bronzed men whom duty had called half a year from their home.

Between two of the Christian pioneers of civilization the gaunt and haggard stranger staggered up the hill-side, casting wild eyes around, seeking for some face, he ever saw, to welcome him ; weeping when he learned that he had not yet come to the home beside the lake. The good Bishop, himself crippled by the deadly dews of the treacherous seas, welcomed the social missionary to his bungalow.

The man revived, and feasted with the three hundred of all ages and grades, who, in the great mess-room, suggestive of an Australian wool-shed, partook of their meal in common.

Pitcairn Islanders welcomed the victim of a modern mutiny, showing him their clean-swept, macadamized roads and leafy avenues, and receiving him to their massive stone residences, relics of the labours of long-defunct convicts. In the stone chapel, beautiful as the Isles in which it gathers the music of the coral seas, memorial of the bishop-martyr who fell, fearless, at Santa Cruz, the doctor, with dark-skinned Christians in white robes, worshipped.

Later the *Mary Ogilvey* brought letters three months old to the isolated community hungering for news. The restored wanderer accepted the invitation of Captain Gartle to voyage in his trim schooner to Sydney. A brief stay at Lord Howe's Island, pleasant basking under the unrivalled palms that fringe the bright seaboard, and on to Sydney.

The doctor was afraid to telegraph, knowing that he must be accounted dead. He took steamer to Adelaide. Still unnerved, though daily gaining strength, he dared not make himself known. He clung to the vessel, and

so thought of returning quietly by water as he had
departed.   At Echuca, as he voyaged, he experienced
a shock that stunned him.

Strolling into an hotel, he took up, to while away the
time, one of those society papers that—

> " Like the flies of later spring,
> Lay their eggs and sting and sing,
> And weave their petty cells and die."

His eye fell on a column headed in large characters—

"A VILLAGE ROMANCE."

The writer recalled the fact of a Dr. Courtenay having
sought to establish a Village Community on a tributary of
the Silverbourne.   How a year ago the founder had lost
his life, leaving the estate in question to his manager and
friend—one John Elms, Esq.   This gentleman was now
candidate for a seat in the Upper House.

His   friends   accused   him   of   exchanging   Radical
principles for Conservative.   A man with property and
position such as his, was wise to modify his opinions.
He had experienced difficulty, however, with respect to
the people so strangely left at his mercy.   Matters had
come to a crisis.   There was prospect of the entire
community being summarily evicted unless they could
see their way to sinking their individuality and falling in
with their despotic master's peculiar ideas.

Love, of a romantic character, had, however, as is
often the case, promised to cut the Gordian knot.   The
disconsolate widow was, so rumour had it, likely to
yield to the blandishments of the lucky man who had
stepped into her husband's shoes.   Mr. Elms, it appeared,
was willing to concede favourable terms to the distressed
settlers if their advocate, the fair widow, would accept

the late manager's suit, and agree to an alliance that
would unite the two properties. The projected union
was likely to be happily consummated at an early date,
when the villagers would be assured of their title to their
lands, and their master to the rich widow, &c.

The wretched print the doctor laid on his knee, and
gazed blankly, for an hour, at the picture of Millais'
' Huguenot' that happened to hang on the wall opposite.
His whole life passed in review before him ; since a
lovely woman first nestled to his breast and confessed
that she loved him. The parting beside the lake, the
eager longing for return, the face that haunted him as he
paced the sand of his exile, all flashed in turn before
him.

And it was for this he had persevered and lived !
To find his wife the accepted bride, nay, perhaps already
the wife, of his would-be murderer ! He would return
to the island retreat and spend his remaining years in
companionship with the sea-fowl. He walked forth
beside the wide river. Might he not fling himself on its
turbid bosom, be lost, and remain forgotten ? Nay, he
was cowed, but not coward yet ! He would go on to
the bitter end !

Apparently his unhappy wife was, at worst, but sacri-
ficing herself to purchase terms for the oppressed people.
She was their champion in his absence.

He would see her again, though she should not know
him. He must avoid that man lest murder should soil
his name. Nay, he might yet, if it were not too late,
unravel the mystery and save his wife. But not if, even
for others' sake, she had yielded to this man's impor-
tunities. She would never again be his !

His canoe the traveller had lowered from the deck
into the river and made fast to the stern, professedly to

ascertain that it was taut and sound.   In the early
morning he dressed himself again in the tattered island
garb, brought as a relic to amuse his friends.   He
looked in his cabin glass.   He had grown older and
whiter in the night.   He thought, with a sickly smile,
there would be little likelihood of his being recognized.
Clean-shaven, round-figured, well-dressed and upright, he
had gone forth, nearly two years ago—he returned
with grey, flowing locks and beard, stooping and worn.

With first streak of daylight the mariner stepped into
his canoe, paddled unobserved, softly, from the wharf,
spread his blanket-sail to the morning breeze, and sped
past startled sheep, and wondering punt-people, up the
Silverbourne.   The red-gum splitter flung down his axe
and called to his mate, cooking the morning meal, to see
the wondrous sight.

In a few hours the white-haired voyager entered the
canal.   Wattle-blossom, blown from myriad branches by
last night's wind, floated like a streak of gold on a silver
stream, past him to the sea.   The mimosa-scent brought
him thoughts of home and the treasured past.   He
recalled to his mind the bright pathway of flowers that
had marked his departure amidst the prayers and bless-
ings of those who now cursed or had forgotten him.
No loving hands had plucked this wattle-bloom ; it was
hurled by the wild wind to its watery grave, as he was
cast away on the stream of life, to disappear in the ocean
of oblivion.

A flush returned to the wan cheek, as the founder
observed the downs of Fabricia dotted with close-lying
gardens, and pleasant booths of industry; as the children
of Kokiana ran to meet the singing house-father returning to his vine-clad cottage.   Away, over the plains, the
orchards now . spread.   Even the palsied hands of

Hygeia had covered the hillside with corn and lowing kine. And here, beside the lake, a new settlement had arisen, where only women moved, vieing with the magpie and canaries in song. Girls sit in the sun and sew, others with writing-pad on lap hold the pen, while maidens descend laughing, with brimming pails of milk in either hand, from the farmyard on the hill.

Beneath a golden wattle, about which paroquets are shrieking as they flit amongst the white waxy gum-blossom, a girl is painting.

"Will he pause a moment," Millie Cole timidly requests, "while she sketches his gliding coracle?"

Seizing a bough, the white man acceded. In a few moments Millie had caught the outlines of a picture that brought her fame when the grey man was famous.

Across the rippleless lake, towards the quay, where the band is playing, and knots of men, women, and children are lounging, the venerable voyager proceeds. All crowd to the pier-end to observe him. Speculations are rife as to who he may be.

"Some 'wild man of the woods' from the sources of the Silverbourne," suggested one.

"An old 'hatter' been in hiding most like," hazards another.

"A log hollowed out into a boat," screech some children with glee; "and got a little log aside it. I'd like to ride on it."

"Why don't he have one on t'other side?" laughs Sar' Ann Smith, "to match it?"

"Blowed if the old cove hasn't his 'bluey' for a sail!" exclaims Mike Milligan.

"He's not wore no new suit, nor seen no barber, for many a day, I reckon," cries Sar' Ann.

Oblivious, seemingly, of the curious eyes fixed upon

him, and of the animated comment he was exciting, the
mysterious stranger made fast his canoe, ascended the
steps of the pier, and slowly and deliberately made his
way through the gaping crowd. As though wearied, he
seated himself on a bench beside a woman with one
child in her arms and others about her. The children
shrank away startled.

"You seem tolerably happy here," remarked the
visitor, in an absent sort of way, looking languidly
around upon the settlement that warm suns and genial
waters had so rapidly developed.

"Speaks English 't any rate," remarked some of the
company aside; "though, like the deaf coves at Hygeia,
he talks like as he'd half-forgotten how."

"Happy!" exclaimed the mother, after a pause, while
she considered whether she should reply; "you're better
off, wherever you've been, all by yoursel', than us here.
Sold, is what we calls it," she added, after further
observation of the stranger. "A flash fellow of a
doctor brought us all here. Swore as we'd be all right.
Then went away; died, tumbled over a precipix or
som'ut, and left us to a wild beast of a man."

"How do you know that no provision was made for
you?" inquired the stranger.

"Know? Haven't we all seed the bit of a Will he
did leave? Look here," continued the woman, with
animation, "that child there were called a'ter him,
'Charles Courtenay.' When he goes away he says a lot
of soft things, and puts his hand on his head, and the
child gived him flowers. Now, they hates him. I've
scratched his name out of the big Bible and wrote the
child 'Beelzebub' i'stead—though Billy's the short we
gives him. When the childer wakes up of nights and
thinks they see a bogie, they calls out, 'the doctor's

comin'!' That skeers 'em more nor Bunyip hi'self.
'Doctor's' same as devil hereabouts."

"Was he not kind to you when he was here?"

"Maybe, good enough, but he's spoilt it all. Curses
on him!"

"Then you've forgotten all the good he did," said the
stranger, rising and causing the company who were
ogling around to fall back from his wild, withering
glances. "Just the way of the world!" he exclaimed,
with indignation. "The first lie heard you have accepted. Have taught your very children to curse their
benefactor."

"Benefactor!" cry they all; "beast we calls him!
Deceiver! Murderer!"

"There's one blessed thing," exclaimed a woman with
crooked nose and a cross eye, "his missus is goin' to
marry the man what has the place. I pity her, but,
anyhow, we'll get our rights."

"Better not get them at all than in that way," rejoined
a stalwart man, who pushed himself forward. "Sure's
my name's Bob Bastion," he continued, "the matter'll
be cleared up yet. I distrusted one, in the cowardly
way we all do, his son-in-law, and he died for my child.
I'll never suspect another friend again until I die. With
men like Elms and Malduke about, any fool might
reckon there's more to be said yet."

"Hear, hear!" cried some.

"What about the son-in-law?" inquired the stranger,
grasping Bastion's arm with a trembling hand. "You at
least are an honest man and true," and he looked him
hard in the face; "I'll believe you." Then very slowly
—"What was that you said"—his voice faltered—"about
the man—that died—for your child?" Involuntarily
the stranger put his hand to his brow and shuddered.

"It's up there, cut in stone," Bastion, in a hoarse voice, replied. "We all subscribed to have it. None can forget it now. See and read for yourself, old man. I don't like to talk 'bout it."

The stranger moved through the crowd, past the pleasant homes, up the steep hill-side, amongst the vines, saying to himself as he beat his breast, "A Beast, a Murderer! My poor wife! My boy Larry!"

The sun set. Darkness was swiftly descending on the valley. The wanderer read the chiselled lines that told how his son had died. Flinging himself beside the stone figure, all the world became dark as that valley, and cold as the recumbent figure staring for ever across the ungrateful land. One at least had done his duty, and died for it. Alas! no achievement without sacrifice, no life without death!

CHAPTER XXXIV.

THE LIVING DEAD.

" She is not dead, and she is not wed !
  But she loves me now, and she loved me then !
  And the very first words that her sweet lips said,
  My heart grew youthful again.
　　*　　*　　*　　*　　*　　*
  And I think, in the lives of most women and men,
  There's a moment when all would go smooth and even,
  If only the dead could find out when
  To come back and be forgiven."—LYTTON.

" Ah, God, for a man with heart, head, hand,
  Like some of the simple great ones gone
  For ever and ever by,
  One still strong man in a blatant land,
  Whatever they call him, what care I,
  Aristocrat, democrat, autocrat—one
  Who can rule and dare not lie."—TENNYSON.

NEVER had Mrs. Courtenay been quite in sympathy
with her husband's enterprise. Now that he was gone,
however, her one aim was to conserve the interests of
his people.

The advances of Elms she regarded with detestation.
Never could she unite herself with him. The hallucin-
ations of her friend, Mrs. Dowling, haunted her. Nightly
she dreamed of his return, and awoke to know it impossible. She could not marry another; least of all this
man she loathed.

But the poor women and children who clung to her,
while the men implored her intervention ! They knew,

and hinted at, the terms upon which she might purchase their emancipation. Should she not sacrifice herself for them? It could not be for long. Under stress of sorrow and anxiety, her heart had troubled her again of late. At any time the end might come. Would she not sleep well, at last, with the consciousness of having sacrificed herself for others?

At one time, the distracted woman went so far as to permit Elms to have a deed of settlement prepared, whereby the rights of the villagers would be secured to them. This document was in her possession. That very evening Elms was coming to learn finally whether she would accept him and his terms.

The man was intoxicated with success. Always vain and covetous, he had set before him, as the height of his ambition, occupancy of the White House, alliance with the family of his deceased master, and an assured position in society.

His daughter should yet have the rights to which, by birth on her mother's side, and by talents on his, as he liked to think, she was entitled.

Mrs. Courtenay was sitting in the garden as the day closed, that was to decide the fate of those whose destinies hung on her work. It was a terrible thought! a gruesome position! She started as the straight, slim form of the Sergeant appeared. He wore a close-buttoned frock-coat, and tall hat. A cane was in his hand.

"Good-evening, madam," he said, as he approached, touching his hat stiffly, as to a superior officer. His was the demeanour of one who had power, and intended to use it. "May I ask," he continued, leaning lightly on his cane, "whether you have perused the document I submitted to you, and approve it?"

"The settlement is satisfactory," replied the lady, looking him steadily in the face, "so far as the people are concerned. Can you not, I implore you to consider, give effect to it without the conditions imposed?"

"Why should I yield all without receiving anything?"

"Because, by your showing, all was given to you on such terms."

"Was it, by Jove!" exclaimed the man, lashing, without moving from his position, at a poppy-head. "Who, I should like to know, devised this scheme for the social redemption of the people, and made this place all it is?"

"My husband," responded the lady, shortly and significantly.

"One who may be your husband, madam," was the reply, "if you are wise, and care for the people as much as you profess."

"That can never be. It is out of the question," was the prompt reply. Then, more persuasively—"Let me, Mr. Elms, as a friend, beg you, as one in whom my husband reposed much confidence, to give these people their rights. Think of the opportunity of doing good that presents itself. Be magnanimous; sign this document to-night, and for ever I will be indebted to you. I will bless your name; and," she urged, "your daughter might come and stay with us in town. We could take her about as the child of a good man who, when he had the power of doing otherwise to his own profit, secured his friends in their lawful possession. John Elms," she continued, with emotion, "think what this threatened eviction means to those poor women and children, to the men who have toiled here so hard and so long! You cannot, you will not, I am sure, cast them out."

She might as well have appealed to the gnarled gum-tree beside her.

"What of myself, madam?" was the almost insolent reply. "A man must think of that sometimes. What should I have? Nothing. I give away all my property to a useless set of folk who would, to-morrow, laugh at me for my pains. No, madam. If assured of the position, in every respect, your late husband occupied, I should be willing to yield all you ask; but, be sure, Mrs. Courtenay, on no other conditions. Dear madam, good lady," he continued, in more softened tones, "there is a soft side to my nature. I am devotedly attached to yourself. I sorrow deeply, I assure you, for your bereaved condition. Let me try to fill, humbly, the good doctor's place. I can manage; I can command. This vast property so richly improved would be the envy of all beholders. You could live mostly in town, where I should be only when the House sits. You can enjoy yourself, and grace society," he added, with a grim smile, "with the sense of having made this little world of ours and, may I add, plain John Elms himself, for ever happy."

The Sergeant bent on his knee in the moonlight, and sought to take the lady's hand. Mrs. Courtenay withdrew it hurriedly. She rose from her seat, and turned towards the house.

"Mr. Elms," she said, with decision, "that, I say, can never be. You must not humiliate yourself and me. I could never, for any consideration, marry again."

The man sprang to his feet. He, the dictator of Mimosa Vale, had humbled himself in vain! had been spurned! Seizing the document that lay on the bench, he passionately tore it into a dozen pieces and cast them to the winds.

"Madam," he almost shouted, "you will rue this

decision. This night your precious crew get their notice to quit on the morrow. I'll set people here that I can depend upon. As for you, proud woman"—he scowled upon her and shook his fist—"when you hear the children cry and see the women weep, when you think of men cursing your husband for lending them wild impossible hopes, you can remember that you did it; that you sacrificed them to a morbid sentiment; that one word from you would have saved them. And you would not say it. Now, good-night, madam, and thank you for nothing." The Sergeant strode off, cursing the misguided woman who could refuse John Elms.

Mrs. Courtenay, trembling, seated herself again on the bench. A pang shot to her heart. A cold moisture suffused her brow.

"My God!" she exclaimed, with panting breath, "my hour surely has come. What have I said? What should I do? Oh, my husband! His poor people! The children that clung about his knees! Ought I—God, tell me—to sacrifice myself for them?"

And so, while her heart beat tumultuously with an ominous thud, and then almost seemed to stop, the distracted woman sat, in the cold, unsympathetic moonlight, and wondered and wished herself dead—"Save for them," she gasped, "for his work!"

Passing from Larry's grave on the hill-side, the white-haired visitor moved unobserved along the line of cottages. Opposite the church, he was almost startled by the sudden leaping and gambolling of a dog about his feet and knees. It was his own "Collie"—the one thing that recognized and greeted him in all the valley. Stooping down, he caressed with trembling hand the faithful creature, while it licked furtive kisses on his cheek.

T

"Dear old Collie!" exclaimed the visitor, fairly hugging the animal that whined with delight.

"Good God, what's this?" exclaimed Alec, shuffling up. "The dog's never noticed a soul for nigh two years. Maybe you knowed his master, sir, the good doctor that went away and died. Collie thinks you're some'ut to do wi' he. He's as 'cute as a Christian."

At that moment the dog, seeking to lick the face of the visitor, knocked the slouched hat off. The head and brow on which the moonlight streamed, revealed to the old man what love had told the dog.

"My God! it's the doctor himself, or his ghost," exclaimed Alec, clasping one of the visitor's hands in both of his, and gazing into his face. "Ah, it is you, master. I can see you now, spite of the white beard. Them eyes! And that look! There's no mistaking the voice."

The doctor stood hesitating. He had desired that none should recognize him as yet. The strong moonlight shed an unearthly glamour upon the tattered garments and thin bare arms of the wanderer as he still embraced the dog, while a wealth of grey hair fell, like a cloud, about the nestling companion of former days.

Alec, wiping his moist brow, drew back. There was something uncanny about the ghostly apparition that uttered no voice.

"Alec, good soul," exclaimed the doctor, putting down the dog and placing both hands tenderly on the old man's shoulders, "I did not mean any should know me, but the dog and you, cleverer than all the crowd, have found me out."

Voices of men approaching recalled the excited pair.

"Quick, others are coming," whispered the doctor; "let us out of the way."

They crept into a back room of the dark school beside them. In a few words the doctor explained how he had survived. A meeting, he learned, was to be held that night, when the question of the eviction was to be finally settled.

"That man, he is not married again?" inquired the doctor, as though he could not trust himself to ask.

"Not exactly, sir. But he hopes to be," replied the old man, significantly; "all depends on to-night."

His companion understood and shuddered.

"Thank God! thank God!" he murmured.

In the course of their hurried conversation, Alec alluded to the tin box containing torn paper that he had secured. Requested to do so, he speedily brought it from his house. The doctor, recognizing the pieces, procured some gum and a sheet of foolscap in the school-room, and proceeded, as the two conversed, to gum the severed pieces side by side. In a short time the Will was restored.

Elms entered the great hall and pushed his way through the assembled company, rage and mortification in his heart, and a black scowl on his face.

"It's all up," whispered some, "she'll have nowt to say to him. You see. Plague on her!"

Elms explained that from the first he had done what he could for them. They, however, had been ungrateful and indolent. He had resolved to fill their places with persons better calculated to carry a communal experiment to a successful issue. He had hoped that another turn might have been given to events. Mrs. Courtenay had it in her power to arrange an amicable settlement, if she cared to do so. At a last interview, however, she had finally refused to intervene in any way. "She leaves you to your fate."

"'Thank God!" cried a deep voice from behind.

"You wouldn't say that, gov'nor," called one standing near the grey-haired visitor, "if you knowed what hangs on 't. She's as unnateral as her husband afore her. What's we to the likes of them? Dirt! Drat 'em all!"

From under his slouched hat the stranger's eyes flashed, but he said nothing. With arms akimbo, he seemed to be holding himself together, restraining himself.

"Now I've done with you all," continued Elms. "To-morrow at noon you all clear out. A posse of police will render any assistance needed," he added, significantly; "indeed," jerking his thumb over his shoulder, "they're now enjoying themselves at euchre in the room hard by."

The poor men argued and implored, threatened and raved in turns. Elms was imperturbable, gratuitously insolent—that was all. The women and children who were gathered about the doors, hearing the dreaded edict, sobbed aloud.

At this juncture Frank Brown leaped on the platform.

"Elms," he cried indignantly, "I have sought by all means to appeal to your sense of justice, to your better feelings. But all in vain! Now, I tell you that you shall not be permitted to alienate these people from their lawful and hard won possessions. Cast them out to-morrow," he cried with energy, "and I will raise such a tempest of righteous indignation from end to end of the country as shall render it impossible for you to persevere in your policy of spoliation. These people shall have their rights, and you your deserts, if I speak and labour to my dying day to secure them."

Stolidly, with something between a smile and a scowl on his darkening features, the dictator stepped towards the clergyman.

"We want none of your meddling, young man," he said. "What has parsons to do with social questions? Go and pray with the women. That's what the likes of you's fit for." And he rudely jostled the young man with his shoulder, as though he would push him from the platform.

In another moment the Sergeant was high in the air. The cleric seized him round the waist, and, lifting him like a kitten, stalked with his struggling tormentor across the platform, depositing him with a thud in the chair, that groaned again with the impact.

"Don't you dare lay hands on me," cried the clergyman, in his excitement shaking his fist in the bully's face. "You are one of those I have met with before," he continued, "who think they can insult a clergyman or a woman with impunity, imagining that the one will not and the other cannot resist the indignity. You made a mistake this time, however. We may have dealings with one another yet, John Elms. For you are not going to do as you would with these people. Don't you, as you value your skin, have resort to physical methods. I do not want to thrash you. I ought not to do it, but when I think of the insults heaped on the wife of my dead friend, and these brave fellows here, I feel I should welcome an opportunity of thrashing you within an inch of your life."

At a sign from Elms the constable at the door had summoned his comrades from the building adjoining. A score or two of white helmets were now visible amongst the shock heads of the company.

"Sergeant," cried the dictator, "remove this disturber of the meeting. He has just assaulted me."

As the police approached the chair the settlers gathered in threatening attitude about their champion, daring the constable to lay hands on their parson.

"We're three hundred to thirty, old man," cried one of the residents to the sergeant in charge. "Don't you make no manner of mistake. We're not a-going to see he touched or walked off."

Speedily all became confusion. Elms tried in vain to make himself heard. At more than one point the police were in conflict with the settlers. After a while, Frank Brown managed by signs of deprecation to secure silence.

"You have not the right," he cried to the constables, "to remove me. Nor have you," he continued, glancing round at his supporters, "the power. Men, sit down," he urged, "let us finish this wretched business. Only beware, Elms, how you act. I have another shot in my locker." And he said very deliberately, gazing scrutinizingly at his adversary, "God alone knows what happened on that desert isle, but I can surmise."

It was but a desperate, haphazard suggestion, intended, if possible, as a last resort to deter the man.

The shaft, however, struck home. Elms winced and drew back in his chair. Then, as if resolving to set at rest for ever the doubts that had been more than once hinted at—suggestions that the doctor might not have had fair play—the man, coming to the edge of the platform, said, with some trepidation—

"I know what you mean to imply, that I am in some way responsible for my predecessor's sad fate. That is a lie! If the dead arose from his watery grave to-day he would exonerate me. He would acknowledge frantic efforts to save him at the risk of my own life. I call the dead, whom I served, to acquit me of your foul slander." The man spoke impassionedly. A solemn silence followed.

"The dead, John Elms," exclaimed a voice, almost sepulchral, from the back of the assemblage; "the dead do rise and denounce you as traitor and murderer."

All turned and looked in the direction whence the sound proceeded. Elms became ashen pale. Then, seeing only the white-haired visitor, of whom he had heard, pushing his way determinedly through the crowd, he heaved a sigh of relief, and, recovering himself, called out, waving the man back with his hand—

"Strangers are not permitted to take part in these proceedings. You, old man, have no voice here."

"*Only the voice of the dead,*" exclaimed the doctor, gaining the platform and removing his hat. Simultaneously all recognized the old ring of the well-known voice and the outlines of the lofty, massive brow. Seized by a strange superstitious dread, the rough men, whose nerves were already highly strung by excitement, fell aside in fear and awe. Elms staggered back towards the chair, clutching it with one hand and passing his hand over his brow with the other, as though he were in a dream and would remove a terrible apparition from his sight. Had high Heaven indeed heard his blasphemous words? Had the dead indeed come back to accuse him? The room reeled round him. Those eyes he knew so well! Dumbly they had implored him, when he hurled his friend to destruction. Those eyes, that voice, had found him out! Quailing before the terrible gaze of the injured man, the culprit sank into the chair he had lately occupied with such nonchalance, covered his ashen face with his hands, and cowered before the silent condemnation of that worn, wrinkled countenance.

" He who was dead has come back at your summons, John Elms," exclaimed the stranger slowly. " He whom you cast to destruction has returned to convict you."

The would-be murderer neither spoke nor moved. A deadly silence lay upon all. Women outside fled away screaming—" The doctor's riz from the grave and come back." Children scampered down the avenue crying, " A ghost !—a real, live ghost ! "

Police pushed their way into the assemblage, their faces almost as white as their helmets.

" Take that man," cried the doctor in unmistakable accents. " I am a magistrate, as you know ; I will sign the charge-sheet later. Arrest him on my information for attempt to commit murder. You came here to witness the eviction of honest owners of the soil. You can take with you the spoiler and wrongful possessor."

The doctor's manner was commanding. The guardians of the peace made their way through the bewildered company, mounted the platform, and laid hands on the abject creature almost slipping from the chair.

" Come on, Mr Elms," they said. The wretched man, still hiding his face in his hands, writhed in the chair and groaned. They raised him, supported him across the platform, down the room, his face still covered in his trembling hands. He verily believed he had looked upon the dead. All night in the log-house he moaned to himself—" The face from the grave ! The voice of the dead ! "

Not a word was spoken as the self-convicted culprit was removed. Then Brown seized and wrung the doctor's hands. One by one the men plucked up courage, and with some shame-facedness approached him they had cursed so hard and so long. He received them quietly.

He was the same, there was no mistaking him now—but changed.

The anathemas he had heard had eaten into his soul. He could never, he felt, be the same man again. Instinctively the audience apprehended the fact. The men on their part were self-convicted, self-condemned. The mere presence, without one word of extenuation, of those we have misjudged often tacitly acquits the wronged, and condemns the hasty accuser. Some sought to explain and excuse. Not unkindly, but firmly, the doctor waived them off. He explained in a few words his almost miraculous preservation.

"Now," he said, "I have come to establish you, to finish the work, and to depart for ever. You will have the land; that is all you want," he added, with some bitterness. "When my death seemed to come between it and you, you cursed me, as you thought, in my grave. I ought never to have expected more. I told you at the outset that lack of confidence between man and man, selfishness of purpose, readiness to believe the first lie concerning those who would befriend you, is your failing —the failing of the race. That is not your fault personally. The conditions in which you have been reared are responsible for it. See, at least, that your children, whose lot, please God, shall be a happier one, believe in man, stand close together, and learn to be true till death. I forgive you. You knew not what you did. But my heart can never forget."

At this juncture a voice sounded from the body of the hall—"It's all bunkum; I happen to know that he never made no Will but the one what old Elms had. He never left the place to us as he promised. Where's the Will he blows about? Let him produce it if he can."

The doctor recognized the voice.

"That is your last shot, Malduke, is it, you arch-scoundrel?" he replied. "You and Elms, I happen to know, made away with that Will, as you thought you had done with me. Here it is, however, preserved to confound you—as by the providence of God I have been."

The doctor handed the restored document to one who stood near.

As they read its provisions and discovered them more favourable and liberal than ever the doctor had indicated of old, the sense of their ingratitude unmanned them. They felt as the citizens of Rome when Anthony read the depositions of "Great Cæsar." They were filled with remorse. They tried to express contrition.

The doctor seemed as though he heard not.

"It is easy to trust me now," he said calmly. "Would to God you had done so when appearances were against me!"

Some of the company in their rage sought Malduke. He had disappeared.

The doctor, whose thoughts were of another, slipped away, leaving the excited company to pore over the recovered Will, and discuss the unexpected turn events had taken.

"It is she," the doctor murmured, as moving towards the White House he drew near the bench upon which his wife was seated.

"I could not do it—even for their sakes," she was saying. "I dare not dishonour the dead, even to serve those for whom he died."

She pressed her hand to her heart as though to stay its wild, tumultuous beating.

She heard a step approaching.

"That man again!" she exclaimed, springing up. She

trembled from head to foot, pressed her hand to her side. "My husband, thank God, my husband!" she exclaimed.

She would have fallen. The strong arms embraced her and set her on the bench again.

The long waiting was over. She opened her eyes, and beamed on the face of him who was dead. "I did what was right!" she murmured; her arm clasped his neck. "God has rewarded me!" The wearied head fell on his breast.

The shock, the revulsion of feeling was too great!

The smile the moonlight illuminated settled into a fixed expression of peace and rest.

The doctor's wife was Dead!

CHAPTER XXXV.

THE LILY-MAID OF ASTOLAT.

"One pain is lessened by another's anguish,
    One desperate grief cures with another's languish."
                                    Romeo and Juliet.

"And when I learnt it at last, I shrieked, I sprang from my seat,
I wept and I kissed her hands, I flung myself down at her feet."
                                    TENNYSON, *Charity.*

"And I knew why we love and suffer,
    I saw through what white lakes of fire
The souls of some mortals must tremble,
    Before they are fit for the higher.

And the secret of living was loving,
    And loving must ever be pain
Till He, by whose word came our being,
    Shall summon that being again."
                        Australian Poets, AGNES NEALE.

SOME months had elapsed. The doctor, sad but steadfast, was occupied, happily for him, with plans for putting the affairs of his settlements on a permanent and self-governing basis. Hilda, subdued now, took special interest in the development of the Amazona community. Gwyneth directed her. Half her time the girl spent about the beautiful hill whence the consumptives looked out on all the land of promise that was ripening, but not for them. Her work was done, Gwyneth felt. The perfecting of it she left to Hilda and the friends who had assisted to establish the girls' colony. The strain imposed by concern for her father's absence, his

mysterious return, and subsequently his arrest and disgrace ; the cruel treatment to which, as she felt, she had
been subjected by the man she still loved deeply—all
told upon a not robust constitution.

Brightness and joy she still brought to many a desolate
occupant of the Mount, but the seeds of disease, as a
result of her untiring devotion, were implanted in her
slender frame.

Daily she grew more ethereal and lovely, as the con-
sumptive often do. The sweet spirit that was hers
shone from the delicate frame that was languishing.
She almost welcomed the prospect of soon being laid to
rest beside the fresh-made flower-beds that crowned the
hill where those she had comforted were sleeping. Sad
she was, but not morbid. To the last, life afforded her
opportunity of engaging in work she loved. Calmly
about the lake her yacht glided, as she sought to cheer
those who like herself were passing to another shore.

"You have not escaped me this morning," said Hilda,
gently laying her hand on the girl's arm, as the latter
was about to step into her boat. Gwyneth, with a
wearied expression, sank on to the seat on the pier and
gazed pensively at the waters rippling against the peaceful prow of her yacht. "I have been wanting for a long
time to see you, dear," said the young widow, softly.
Seating herself by the sick girl she took her hand in hers,
and stroking it lovingly, added—"I want to ask your
pardon for a great wrong I did you."

"I do not quite understand you, Mrs. O'Lochlan,"
replied Gwyneth, with a shade of reserve.

"Do not speak like that, Gwyneth. Look at me, dear."

The girl turned her head and gazed, almost vacantly,
into Hilda's face. Her thoughts were far away.

"I, too, have suffered," pleaded Hilda, "for my pride and selfishness, I suppose. Let me relieve my mind by confessing my sin and securing forgiveness."

The thought of all that the gay young bride of a year before had endured touched Gwyneth's heart. Schooled to forget her own grief in that of others, she tried to say something sympathetic. Words, however, failed her. She merely bent her graceful neck and kissed the young widow's anxious brow, while the gentle breeze blew the unconfined tresses of golden hair about the other's pale face.

"Gwyneth, I shall always hate myself for having written that horrid letter; for having despised you—you, who were so vastly my superior in every way — for having striven to separate you from my brother. Can you forgive me?"

The dying girl placed an emaciated arm round the other's neck, bent her head, as if tired, on Hilda's breast, and said—

"Forgive you? I *thank* you, now. It had to be."

Through her closed eyes tears found their way, and moistened the long lashes upon which they glistened as dew.

Hilda kissed the frail girl, and stroked the transparent cheek. Bending over her she whispered—

"It had not to be, Gwyneth. He loved you dearly. Never for one moment has he wavered in his attachment. I know it."

The sick girl opened her eyes that seemed to have expanded and gathered lustre as her frame decayed. Fixing a searching gaze on her companion's face she exclaimed—

"It cannot be. I have imagined every possible explanation of his conduct. Only one remains."

Hilda produced the silver case. The girl's eyes glistened. Her hand shook very distressingly. With trembling fingers, as once before, she opened the little casket. Her mother's and her own likeness were there, as when with girlish pleasure she had presented it to her lover.

"Can it be all a dream?" she exclaimed, as she bent over the love-token, and the hectic glow suffused her delicate cheeks. "Those other faces I saw there! Could they be the creation of a diseased imagination?"

She kissed the little casket, bathed it with tears, while the breeze wiped it again with her hair. Quickly and quietly Hilda told her all. What Tom Lord had seen; the part that Malduke had played.

Gwyneth opened her eyes, clasped the silver thing amongst tresses that lay upon her breast, looked up to the soft, cloudless sky, and her eyes sang her *Te Deum* and *Nunc Dimittis* in one breath.

"You must see him, dear, and be reconciled," said Hilda, cheerfully. "You will soon get better now."

"Too late—for that," replied the girl, smiling through her tears. "If it could have been, I should have loved this world too much. But tell him, please, I loved him dearly to the last. Ask his forgiveness for my having doubted him. Everything was so against him. I was so alone. Now, if you do not mind," she added after a long pause, "leave me, dear Hilda, to accustom my mind in solitude to this last new joy."

Weeping and embracing they parted. Gwyneth loosened her little boat, whose sail was already set, and as it skimmed over the rippling surface of the waters, the dying girl, who knew at last that she was loved, lay on the white pallet she had placed in the stern for her sick passengers. The little cargo of flowers she had shipped

for others lay about her slender white-robed figure, as
she reclined beneath the snowy sail.

"Now I may trust my eyes to rest upon the scene of
our happiness once more," she murmured. "I will
approach within a mile and return."

She made fast the stern-sheet, and, still resting amongst
her floral offerings, almost lost in a reverie of happy
thoughts, glided unconsciously onward with tiller against
her back and a lily in her hand, towards the village pier
at the other end of the lake.

The birds skimmed curiously about the barque,
whose lovely occupant was still—sleeping or in a faint—
as the flower-laden barge drew towards the wattle shores.

    *   *   *   *   *

Travers had returned, moody, despondent, and heartily
ashamed of himself. He confessed to his father that he
had betrayed the trust reposed in him. He had felt, he
said, that under the circumstances his presence in the
valley was rather a hindrance than otherwise to his
brother-in-law. From colony to colony he had wandered.
News of his mother's death had aroused him from his
selfish inaction. He had "come to himself," and
resolved to stand by his father's side and to atone by
single-handed devotion for failure in the past.

It was the doctor's birthday. A quiet family picnic
had been arranged, with the view of withdrawing him from
labours to which, as a solace for pain, he was devoting
every waking hour. The party drove to the spot where
the creek debouched into the lake. The wattles were
untouched, although on either side, beyond their fringe
of gold, the gardens and homesteads ranged.

The Dowlings were talking to the doctor of Travers
and his troubles. Mrs. Dowling was speaking of Gwyneth,
and how unwittingly she had caused her pain, of how

feelingly the girl had read to her the tragic story of Elaine.

"I cannot help it," the fanciful old lady continued, "but, now that I know all, I am ever, in my dreams, associating Gwyneth with Elaine, and seeing the child herself reclining in the barge in which the Lily-maid voyaged to Camelot."

On a bank below the old people, the young folk, Eva and Maud, Travers, Frank, and Tom, were sitting, close to the rivulet brink. The girls were plaiting wreaths of wattle and clematis. Travers was bravely battling with his despondency. Seizing the garland Maud had woven, he had bent forward and laughingly placed it on Eva's brow, exclaiming—

"So I crown you Queen of the Vale."

Instinctively he thought of the one who was still the queen of his heart. He raised his eyes to look across the lake to the vine-clad hill beyond, where, it was said, its guardian angel spent her days.

He started to his feet.

Mrs. Dowling, above, who had just concluded her remark about the Lily-maid, uttered a startled cry. All stood as if spell-bound.

Upon the lake, a few hundred yards away, a boat with white sail was bearing down upon the very spot where they stood. The tiny vessel seemed filled with flowers. Amongst them lay a frail form, clad in white, a lily in her hand. Her eyes were closed, a smile played upon the wasted, ethereal face, about which lay a profusion of golden hair.

No one moved. Not a sound was uttered. Like a fairy vision, the little vessel glided onward towards the picnickers. It brushed along the bank on which the fresh-crowned Queen of the Lake was sitting. The sail,

U

catching in the overhanging wattle-boughs, moored the bark within a yard of the lately animated group.

Travers, not knowing what he did, sprang forward, bent over the motionless figure, took one of the transparent hands in his. The silver case was clasped on the still heaving breast.

"Gwyneth, my darling, speak to me!" cried the young man with quick, eager breath. "Gwyneth, you are not dead! You shall not die! You have come to me at last, my child!" Slowly the maiden, recovering from her swoon, opened her eyes. Only that one distracted face she saw bending over hers.

"You forgive me," she murmured, after a long pause, during which she gazed, wonderingly, into his face. She tried to say more, but voice failed her. She put her slender arm about his neck and drew her lover towards her. He kissed the cold brow, on which the dews of death were gathering. "I came—I do not know how— nor where I am," she whispered, slowly, with difficulty. "I came to tell you—that—I love you still. That I know, now, that you loved me always. Now let me fall to sleep again. I am so tired! so tired!" she repeated, as if to herself. "Ah! but so glad!"—and the old smile set on her delicate features. She pressed his hand, though she seemed to sleep.

"Gwyneth," cried the young man wildly, "you shall not die. This is only a swoon. Speedily you will recover now. We will be happy together yet," and he chafed her hands as though she were in a faint, and showered kisses on the cold forehead.

"Hush!" at length, opening her eyes again, she murmured, as the flame of life flickered. "That may not be. I am bride of Another now, who gave His life for me. We are one in Him!"

"Eva!" she murmured after a pause, as the girl, with the mimosa wreath still about her chestnut locks, stole near and bent a terrified face over the floating death-bed of flowers.

"I know you loved me," said the dying maiden, slowly, to her lover. "Now you shall love her. She is yours, and you shall be hers. Often I shall look upon you. Your joy will be mine."

Still clasping the lily sceptre, the dying girl sought the hand of each, clasped them together upon the casket on her breast, the smile, as of an angel breathing benediction, as of the wearied going home, settled on her lovely features, the tresses on her breast ceased to heave. "The Lily-maid of Astolat" had passed to "where, beyond these voices, there is peace."

That day Travers learned all the intrigues of Malduke. How he had sought to compass the doctor's death and frustrate his plans. Willie's father had recognized him, and related how, evidently, he had sought to drown his love and his rival in the canal works. At his door lay the guilt of the tragic death of the Lily-maid beneath the mimosa boughs. Travers was maddened by grief and rage. He paced the bush distracted. The evil-doer, he learned, lay in hiding beyond the ranges.

"JUSTICE! REVENGE!" cried the frenzied man, as he beat his breast. Seizing his horse he disappeared along a mountain track. Fearing his friend's passion and despair, Frank Brown, with a boundary rider who knew the country, started in pursuit.

Along the side of steep mountains, across slippery out-cropping rocks, upon the edge of precipitous "sidings," Travers, as one demented, rode. That face in the boat haunted him. "My murdered child! My wronged

Gwyneth!" he cried between his teeth, urging his reeking steed, mad in sympathy with himself, to leap ravines and dash through blinding scrub; now rattling down the fern-tree gully, now swimming the swollen mountain torrent, again dashing up the almost vertical pile of slippery boulder.

The sun had set. Beside a dismal lagoon, in which the frogs were croaking as though all that world were theirs, stood, in a low gorge beneath the hills, a lonely splitter's hut. Travers sprang from his steed, white with the sweat of a twenty miles ride. With a trembling hand the young man opened the rude shutter that served for a window.

Stretched on a bunk, clad in crimson shirt and mole-skin trousers, the outcast lay asleep—a revolver on the table beside him, a gun in the corner at his head. Travers stole into the bark-hut across the earthen floor, and took the revolver from the table. As he reached over to seize the gun Malduke sprang up. Travers leaped towards the door. The trapper, trapped at last, stood at bay. He was ashen pale. His eyes glared with fear and rage as he stood facing his foe. He saw that for the moment his assailant was mad.

"At last I have you," cried Travers. "Powder and shot are too good for you. One of us will never leave this hut alive. Coward! You need not tremble so. There, my own hands shall settle you, not your miserable tools." He threw the arms far into the bush. Then, keeping his eye on the object of his frenzied hate, he barred the door with its great cross-piece of wood.

"Now, craven, defend yourself!" In the middle of the hut, illuminated only by the ghastly moonlight, the two met. Wildly for each other's throats they struggled. Malduke was the heavier; Travers more agile and

skilful. Now the rude tenement trembled as though a
branch had been whirled against it by the storm, while
the two hurled each other against the slab sides. At
length Travers secured the grip his practised hand sought ;
over one shoulder, beneath the other he passed his arms,
back across the table he hurled his foe. With knee on
chest he grasped the other's throat as in a vice of iron.

Another moment and the miscreant's course would
have been run. Crash! The tressel gave way beneath
the strain. Travers, half-hurled by his antagonist, fell
heavily, his head striking on the log that served for a
bench.

A deadly silence reigned in the rude cabin, save for the
laboured breathing of the half-choked wretch who stood
trembling in the midst of the earthen floor. He opened
the door and drew a deep breath. A beam of moonlight
streamed across the hut on to the white face of the
unconscious man.

"I'll settle him now," muttered the other, as he sought
with trembling fingers the revolver among the branches
that surrounded the deserted hut. "Ah, here it is.
This'll finish him!" hissed Malduke, as with a more
assured tread he re-entered the shanty.

Travers had come to himself. As the other entered
he sprang again upon him. Again they wrestled for life.
Two desperate men beating out each other's life, the
hatred of their panting breasts, in the silence and
darkness of the lonely ravine.

Whiz! at length went a shot through Travers' hair,
grazing his ear. Again he seized his foe, hurled him
beneath him.

Two figures appeared at the door.

Another shot. A death-cry!

An awful stillness, broken only by the plaintive wail

of the curlew and dismal howl of the dingo on the hills. "More blood, more blood!" the cuckoo seemed to cry.

"Quick, Bob!" cried Frank to his companion. "Strike a match. I fear we are too late."

The two lay as dead. Smoke was issuing from the deadly weapon Malduke still grasped in his hand. A stream of blood was oozing from his temple. The shot intended for his enemy had, in the death-struggle, entered his own brain. Malduke had gone to his account. Travers, who, owing to loss of blood, had swooned again, was stretched across the corpse.

For two days he was dazed. Gwyneth he followed to her grave on the hill-top, as in a dream. By degrees the sense of duty and obligation returned. He recalled how she, whom he had loved and lost, brought life and hope to thousands for whom, while her own heart was bleeding, she "made a way in the wilderness."

In the long evenings at Heatherside, new plans were evolved, old sores sought to be healed, but not one word of love was spoken.

CHAPTER XXXVI.

THE FAIRY ISLAND.

"As on the smooth expanse of crystal lakes,
The sinking stone at first a circle makes ;
The trembling surface by the motion stirred,
Spreads in a second circle, then a third :
Wide and more wide, the floating rings advance,
Fill all the wat'ry plain, and to the margin dance."—POPE.

"Earth at last a warless world, a single race, a single tongue—
I have seen her so far away—for is not Earth as yet so young ?—

Every tiger-madness muzzled, every serpent passion kill'd,
Every grim ravine a garden, every blazing desert till'd,

Robed in universal harvest up to either pole she smiles,
Universal ocean softly washing all her warless Isles."
                        TENNYSON, *Sixty Years After*.

"The English Wholesale Society possesses six steamships, choco-
late, woollen cloths, biscuit, sweets, soap, boot and shoe-works,
and a corn-mill. It has fifty-eight officers of departments, and
3758 persons in its employ. It issues a handsome volume
yearly, the *Wholesale Annual*, with illustrations of its many
works and depôts, with statistical facts of its remarkable progress, and essays of great value on economic and public questions."—HOLYOAKE.

THE doctor, with Travers, when fully recovered from
the shock he had received, proceeded to perfect and
complete the organization that had been for so long in
course of development.

All were agreed that communism, pure and simple,
such as Malduke and Elms had sought to establish, was
distasteful and impracticable. The principle of representation and management that the doctor had inaugurated
was definitely formulated.

Each settlement was divided into four wards, or "quarterns." These elected, each, by ballot of men and women, three representatives on the Village Council. In the same way all associated industries and factories were represented. The council elected annually its own president, and officers of the crafts. The council transacted all business connected with the domestic affairs of its own settlement. The presidents and chief officers, together with a special delegate from each quartern, represented the village. This supreme body controlled all the associated settlements. Five of its number, elected every three years, acted as a supreme court of appeal and arbitration, to which all questions, undecided by the local board, were finally referred.

The financial committee of each village and separate industry published a statement, each quarter, showing the position of every member of its community.

Three classes of labour were recognized—skilled, unskilled, and a third class. This last consisted of youths, old people, and the less effective workers. The second class of farm, dairy, and labouring hands. Those convicted, before the Bands of Labour, of not working satisfactorily, or of malingering, were subject to degradation from their class, and finally to expulsion from the settlement. The agreement each had signed was proof in any court of law that they had rendered themselves amenable to the decisions of the community. The knowledge, however, that due discipline could and would be maintained, and prompt effect given to the decision of each community, restrained the indolent and unruly, or caused them quietly to withdraw. That subtle force, public opinion, was against them. If offending, or contending, they had not only one employer to deal with, but an entire community. It was to the interest of all that every man should contribute his fair share of labour, and receive only his due proportion of profit. The complete system of representation rendered it impossible that any despotism could be established.

Ten per cent. more of dividends the second class received than the first, and the third than the second.

Those whose accounts were in credit might draw half their share of dividends in cash, or all in coupons.

These latter had ten per cent. larger purchasing power at any of the stores or settlements, than cash. So men were encouraged to leave their capital invested in the vast co-operative enterprise that was beginning to attract world-wide attention.

For the first time the principle of co-operation on a large scale was being applied, by the same persons, to both production and distribution.

Two sheep-farming communities, associated with the earlier ones, took over the remainder of the doctor's station, together with the Selectors' Plains from which Kokiana folk had fled. The Hon. Herbert Fitzhubert was glad to sell out to the " Co-ops.," as they were called, who speedily secured the intervening country.

No fires devasted the country, no dams were cut. Hands were not called out, or eyes of the country " selected " by would-be black-mailers. All, from manager to "tar-boy," had regard to their own interests, since all had their due place in one of the three classes of industry.

In the ranges were mines that, owing to the demand for high wages enforced by frequent strikes, had long been worked at a loss; these lines of mines the " Co-ops." by degrees purchased. The labour difficulty vanished. The ore was won for half the cost its mining entailed before. Those who laboured received the necessaries of life, and were afforded an opportunity of purchasing an interest in the enterprise, and a holding on the agricultural settlements.

The accounts of the special industries were kept distinct. If, owing to no fault of the workers, any enterprise happened to continue unprofitable, it might, if deemed worth preserving, be subsidized by the central Parliament, until it should become self-supporting. On this principle costly machinery was, when necessary, erected and paid for by the workers in course of years.

Conspicuous among the ever-multiplying factories were the flour-mills. The "Co-ops." had bought out the large wheat-growers that lay between Mimosa Vale and Gumford. Fruit- and meat-preserving, cheese and butter factories, together with saw-mills, ship-building yards, iron-works, brick-yards, woollen and leather factories—on the cottage-and-garden principle—tanneries and workshops of almost all kinds, were established.

In the metropolis, and later in Sydney, Adelaide, London, and New York, colossal Emporiums were located. Direct from the spot where the produce was grown or wrought, it went to the vast stores without intervention on the part of any cream-skimming middleman. Each vessel and store, as factory or settlement, was credited with its own work done or money earned. This was apportioned in dividends to the three classes that manned every vessel and ran every store.

In the case of the five-storied Melbourne store, that eventually covered two acres of ground, all hands were allotted rooms in the Labour Palace adjoining, or cottages in the suburban "village" at Blackburn. All received the necessaries of life as their friends in the country did, membership of their clubs, etc., and wanted for little else. They were virtually catered for wholesale, and cost the community in cash little more than half the amount that must otherwise have been paid away in wage. The dividends that they received in coupons, representing the equitable distribution of the entire earnings of their own store, constituted comparative wealth laid up for them in course of years.

As head became silvered, or children grew up, the store employee of the city might purchase, by merely a transference of accounts in the books, without a penny passing, one of the garden-retreats at Lilydale, or a home on one of the ever-extending settlements beyond Mimosa Vale and on the Silverbourne.

By degrees factories at Brunswick and West Melbourne fell into the hands of the settlement folk. A share of the inter-colonial and ocean steam-ship trade was secured. In South Australia a vast tract was acquired. The Southerners were shown how to farm the plains, well watered now, at a profit.

Later on, powers were taken from the Government, and a trunk line of railway run to Port Darwin. The day of railway commissioners and octopus bills passed away. The three classes, duly represented, managed and worked their own lines for their own benefit, in conjunction with fleets and factories, settlements and cities of labourers associated with them. All along the line, Co-operation triumphed over Competition.

" What is to hinder," asked Tom Lord of Travers, as, in the early days, they discussed the marvellous developments of their enterprises, " the inevitable disintegration and falling apart of the allied industries? Your several stores and banks and insurance offices in town are bound to become independent."

" If it suit them to go alone, they are welcome to do

so," was the reply. "All are free with us. The fact is,
however, it is to their interest to remain loosely associated
as they are now. Our settlements charge the Stores only
the fair cost of production, the Stores again only an
equitable charge for distribution to members. If a factory
or allied institution essays to stand alone, it at once
becomes subject to the action of competition. It relin-
quishes its favoured position. Middle-men come in, and
profits are materially diminished. If it suit two hundred
to co-operate, it stands to reason the benefit is proportionately increased when two thousand join hands."

"But will not this prodigious organization," objected
Tom, "fall to pieces of its own weight? Will it not
become too cumbersome to be managed from one
centre?"

"Not necessarily. Our constitution provides for local
self-government. Each enterprise is really self-contained,
save that it is associated with other organizations worked
on the same principle. Only in case of dispute and
difficulty need reference be made to the central authority.
All who benefit, however, are compelled to abide by the
articles of association. That is the condition on which
they receive the world-wide benefits of our organization."

"In so large a concern, what protection have you
against exploitation and corruption?"

"Universal representation and supervision on the part
of the various boards."

"But will not the individual interest be lost sight of in
this vast organization?"

"Not in the least. Each department keeps, as we see,
its own accounts, makes, on an approved scale, its own
division of profits. Every man feels that he may, by
application and economy, benefit himself directly.

"There is no doubt," concluded Travers, "that we

have contributed something towards solving a vexed social problem, and towards reconciling, by combining them, the interests of capital and labour. Life need no longer be a hopeless drudgery for any of our people, while the thrifty secure the due reward of their self-denial."

Dr. Courtenay did not witness the fuller developments of his "New Order."

"It shall increase, I must decrease," he was wont to say. "My life is spent. My work is done." Ere twelve months had elapsed, he prepared to bid farewell to the scenes of his disinterested labours.

The distrust of him, when he was on his trial, the domestic bereavement he had suffered, the conviction that his communities should now learn to govern themselves, rendered him impervious to all requests that he should remain.

"I have forgiven them," he would gently but firmly say, "but those curses poured ignorantly on my head ring in my ears, and will do so to my dying day. I do not blame you. I accept the inevitable. No man ever yet served the people without dying, or being prepared to do so, for them—perhaps by them. I shall return to the palm groves that sheltered me when man had cast me off, and was hurling anathemas on my head. I want you to know that you cannot distrust a friend and retain him; that to foster love is of more worth than to win wealth. Ah! escape as you can from the spirit of selfishness, greed, and distrust that has marked and doomed the 'Old System.' Go forth to welcome the spirit of trust and love that must characterize the new."

Elms served the ten years to which he was sentenced, then disappeared.

Frank and Maud toiled radiantly on, at times tempted to renounce the vows that contempt for the selfishness of others had imposed, and to seek their own happiness in wedded life. On such occasions they redoubled their energies, threw themselves more resolutely into labours for others. They survived the ordeal, to laugh at the prevalent opinion that man and maid may not love all their life, as brother and sister, and nothing more !

Only once they kissed and embraced—when, long years after, the aged Bishop-of-all-the-Settlements bent his snowy head of flowing hair over the angelic but aged face of a smiling woman, who was passing away. In momentary despair he cried—

" Maud, I cannot live without you."

"Then you have loved me?" she murmured, taking his hand.

" All the while, from the first till now," he answered, as the great, unwrinkled brow fell on the breast of the angel whose spirit had fled !

Hilda became Mrs. Tom Lord, and schooled her husband, volatile to the last, into some sense of the dignity that became a landed proprietor and member for his district. Eventually Sir Thomas became one of the most popular members of a powerful Ministry.

For a year or more, Travers, the president of the " New Order," sought in the " sweet vale " of Mimosa, at Heatherside, to " heal him of his grievous wound."

No love was overtly made. Men and women do that but once. But on the anniversary of the coming of the Lily-maid, Travers took Eva, ripened now into graceful womanhood, to the wattle grove beside the lake. Sitting on the grassy bank, beside which the mysterious barque had glided, he took the maiden's hand in his, and quietly said—

"Here, Eva, were we betrothed, here let us renew our vow." For the first time he kissed the ruddy cheek, and felt the fountain of hope and joy unlocking again in his breast.

None could be much with Eva, much less love her, and be unhappy.

All the old vigour and joy returned to Travers' sunny face. His laugh rang high again. He went forth to charm by his very presence the simple folk, who would trust him now to the death.

Mrs. Travers was the light of the valley as of her old home. Her mother had her wish; though, sometimes, she would remove her spectacles and wipe her scarce-dimmed eye, as she thought of her son-in-law's first love, who slept amongst the flowers on the oft-visited hill-top.

On his distant coral isle the brave doctor was not unhappy. All the charm that taste and art could lend to nature, was imparted to his island retreat. Seeds and plants from all the coral isles, frequent visitors brought him. His bungalow of books and bamboo house of curios and paintings were the admiration of Royal Navy captains, who ever contrived to have some business to transact at the "Fairy Island," as they re-named the desert rock he had converted into a garden of paradise.

The doctor's yachts and steam-launch lay safe within the coral-bound lagoon. Often he voyaged forth to meet the passing vessel of the "New Order" bringing him messages of love, and tokens from grateful hearts across the sea.

A bent, close-shaven, care-worn man on one occasion stepped on the beach from the boat of a passing vessel.

The doctor was mending his yacht-sail, and whistling a song of the sea.

The man sprang towards him, kneeled on the sands, and grasped the grey old yachtsman's knees, took his disengaged hand, and kissed it.

"I have come," said a deep, almost sepulchral voice, "to crave your forgiveness. I could not die till I had done so."

"Elms, my man!" gasped the doctor, "God bless you for that word! I have often grieved for you, knowing you were tempted and misled. Now my cup of joy is full."

The "right-hand man," in his right mind now, restored by suffering, took his place beside his patron, and served him with devotion and veneration until he died.

Only old Alec, who had secured permission to join the doctor after Jinnie's death, demurred. He was jealous, but only for a moment.

So, midst books and notes, palm-groves and coral walks, the "good grey" hair of the three "old salts" long floated in the breeze that gently fanned the shores of their beauteous Fairy Isle.

THE END.